Relentless Pursuit

A Lou Gault Thriller

by

Dave McKeon

Copyright

Relentless Pursuit Copyright ©2022 by Dave McKeon

All rights reserved.

No part of this publication may be reproduced, distributed, or transmitted in any form or by any means, including photocopying, recording, or other electronic or mechanical methods, without the prior written permission of the author except in the case of brief quotations embodied in critical articles and reviews. For information, email to contact@ahowardactivity.com

This is a work of fiction. Names, characters, places, and incidents either are the products of the author's imagination or are used fictitiously. Any resemblance to actual persons, living or dead, businesses, companies, events, or locales is entirely coincidental.

Edited by Paula F. Howard, A Howard Activity, LLC

Interior design by Paula F. Howard

Cover design by Bob Hurley. ImpressionsBookDesignServices.com

Published by Aha! Press, an imprint of A Howard Activity, LLC

PRINTED IN THE UNITED STATES OF AMERICA

ISBN: 979-8-9872226-4-5

Available for purchase on Amazon.com and at TheWritersMall.com

To Sandy

Thank you for all the joy

you have brought into my life.

Part 1

The Territory

Chapter

1

Lou Gault sat on the edge of his cot, drenched in sweat; nightmares had woken him again. The pill usually allowed him to sleep, but it wasn't working tonight. His dreams were haunted by the constant collateral damage, faces of noncombatants who had been in the wrong place at the wrong time and were now dead. He fell back on his bunk, frustrated. He was fighting in a war that wasn't his fight.

How long had he slept? He didn't know, nor had any idea what time it was. But it didn't matter, he was up when reveille sounded.

Like every other day, the patrol headed out well before dawn. Their mission never changed . . . drive the Taliban from the Wakhan Corridor.

The Canadians had been in-country for over two months now, but they still struggled with the sweltering heat and ever-present dust of the Afghan landscape.

By late morning, the Canadian JTF2 Commandos had already engaged a band of insurgents in one village and watched a small group of fighters flee into the barren hills as they approached another.

By midday, they reached a third village, one from which they had already driven the Taliban weeks earlier.

Gault and two members of Bravo Squad were sent in on-point; the rest of the patrol stood down. It was common for Gault to be the lead, he seemed to see signs that others missed.

The road leading into the village was narrow, twisting and turning like a serpent slithering toward its prey. It was no surprise that every window was shuttered and every door was closed. It was a common practice to help keep the brutal midday heat out. Dwellings lining both sides of the street were all two-storied which meant this village was a little more prosperous than most. That said, they were all made from the same reddish-brown desert soil that every village used.

As they advanced Gault thought: *It's odd there's no laundry hanging from the lines that stretch between buildings. Hell, even the pungent smells of spices from the cookpots are absent.* Except for a stray dog, the street was empty, too. They had traveled far enough into the village that they should have been able to hear noises coming from the marketplace just ahead.

"Quiet, eh, Lou?"

"It's gotta be the heat."

After another hundred yards further in, Gault radioed back to his patrol: "Clear." The full patrol moved into the village. When the men on-point were well forward, the trap was sprung.

Bursts of automatic weapon fire came from every window, every doorway, and every rooftop, pinning the patrol down. Both squad leaders frantically yelled: "Fall back! Take cover!"

But there was no cover.

The Taliban's attack had been well-planned. Bravo and Echo squads were caught out in the open and the Canadians began taking casualties.

As soon as Gault heard the automatic weapons, he signaled to circle back. Rounding the last bend, he saw the chaos, and the warrior spirit within him erupted with fury.

"This way!"

Using his shoulder, he broke down the nearest door, and all three men raced to the roof, two steps at a time. Within minutes, the shooters on the rooftops were picked off as easily as if they had been rubber ducks in a traveling carnival's shooting gallery.

Once rooftops were cleared, Lou brought the fight to the insurgents inside the buildings.

"You two take the opposite side. I'll work this side."

There was no discussion; these were men of action. When Lou reached the second-floor landing, he kicked in the door with his foot, opened fire, and sprayed the interior, eliminating three shooters in seconds. Changing clips, he chambered a round and hugged the wall as he came back downstairs.

The first-floor room was empty, and they exited the structure.

In the next building, insurgents were all positioned on the second floor. Lou crept up the stairs and lobbed a grenade into a room. The force of the explosion blew two shooters clear out the window, a third became a mangled mess of blood on the floor. He didn't see the fourth fighter until the man lunged at him. With a step forward, Lou parried the assailant's knife with the barrel of his rifle, then brought the butt of his gun swiftly up, shattering his attacker's lower jaw. Lou ended the man's life with a second blow to the head, crushing his skull.

One building over, the insurgents sensed that someone was behind them and posted a rear guard.
As Lou exited his building, a shot splintered the wooden door frame near his head, missing him by mere inches. Now, out in the open, he was completely exposed.

An assailant stood one doorway over, smiling as he brought his weapon up. Suddenly a burst of fire came from behind Lou and the threat was eliminated.

Across the street, Fletcher Martin stood in an alleyway changing clips.

Lou hugged the front of the next forward building and lobbed a grenade into its doorway. The explosion took out two Taliban who had been crouched, waiting for him.

As soon as he entered the next building, a gunman appeared at the top of the stairs. The Afghan sneered as he opened fire. Lou narrowly escaped into a first-floor room, only to come face to face with a bloodied knife wielding insurgent who lept at him full-force.

This assailant's body was slick from the blood already covering him. Lou struggled to gain a firm grasp on the hand that held the knife. A stench from the man's breath was nauseating. His knife repeatedly struck Lou's protective Kevlar vest. Finally, Lou was able to overpower his attacker. Twisting him around, he snapped the man's neck. Breathing hard, he lobbed a second grenade up the stairs to the next landing and waited for its explosion before racing upstairs to make sure the upper floor was clear.

Building by building, Lou and his two comrades continued to work their way back up the street, fighting on stairways, in hallways, room to room in hand-to-hand combat. The carnage was horrific; the fight to reach their comrades was like nothing they had ever encountered. Finally, covered in blood, and exhausted, they persevered and routed the enemy.

When they reached what was left of their patrol, they collapsed among the wounded, briefly scattering the blowflies that somehow materialized from thin air when there was death.

That day, the heroic action of the three men on-point saved the lives of numerous comrades. Lou Gault, Fletcher Martin, and William McDuffie-Ferguson each received Canada's prestigious Award for Bravery.

Gault never saw himself as a hero and refused to wear the ribbon. He felt he should have recognized the warning signs of the quiet street and known they were walking into a trap. He blamed himself and swore an oath it would never happen again, not on his watch.

Fifteen months later, Gault's JTF2 enlistment was up. He'd had his belly full of war and fighting someone else's fight; he longed for the peaceful life he'd left behind.

Returning to New Brunswick, he and Grey Elk, his Abenaki grandfather, built a sweat lodge, then spent the better part of a day purifying their spirits together. Even in the dim light of the bark-covered lodge, Lou could tell that his grandfather had aged in the two years he had been away. The older man was not the same man that had lifted Lou up with a sweep of his hand holding him aloft like a feather.

When it was time to leave the lodge, they began their rituals. Grey Elk lit the ceremonial pipe that had been handed down to him. After honoring each of the four directions, he drew a long inhale from the pipe, then offered it to his grandson.

In turn, Lou honored the four directions, drew from the pipe and held it out for Grey Elk. But instead of taking the pipe, Grey Elk placed the ancient beaded deerskin wrap, which had protected the pipe for many generations, onto

Lou's forearm. Lou nodded and understood Grey Elk's intent. With that simple gesture, responsibility for the safekeeping of the ceremonial pipe, and all of his grandfather's lands, had just passed to him.

Chapter 2

It was early morning and the lake was placid. Loons had just begun their haunting morning calls. Lou smiled and inhaled the crisp, clean air. *This is the life I choose to live,* he thought.

He now operated the sportsman's resort known as *Havre de Poisson* in a remote area of central New Brunswick. Six miles north there was an Abenaki village, other than that, the nearest settlement in any direction was nearly thirty miles away, "as the crow flies."

At one time, all the land in central New Brunswick had belonged to an eastern band of the Abenaki people, Grey Elk's people . . . Lou's people. In the early twentieth century, the band's tribal council had acted to protect what was left of their homeland, and legally claimed it under Canada's Indigenous People's Act. When their claim was approved, Grey Elk had gathered his people and said: "Rejoice! What has been our land from the time *Gluskape* fired his arrow into an ash tree, and humans sprung from that tree onto the earth, will no longer be questioned. Even the others agree."

Lou had inherited the fifteen square mile tract of land surrounding the lake when his grandfather, Grey Elk, had passed a year ago.

Operating a business this far from civilization was demanding and attractive to only those who were truly self-reliant. Gault had overcome more than a few challenges in life by drawing on his natural instincts and resourcefulness inherent in his mixed French and Abenaki bloodlines. The life he now led energized him and kept him physically fit.

The epitome of a quintessential outdoorsman, Gault had an enviable independence about himself, obvious to even the most casual observer. Standing at the water's edge, his rugged six-foot-two stature cast a long shadow. He was totally in his element now with a calm, self-confident demeanor that masked a warrior's spirit hidden deep within him. He lived a quiet, peaceful life now – which was about to be tested.

Havre de Poisson was situated on the shores of an obscure glacial lake in north central New Brunswick. Like many, Gault's remote lake was identified on maps by only a number. His lake was number 980. Four miles long, the lake was slightly over a mile across at its widest point. Heavily populated with rainbow and lake trout, it sustained a natural population. The trout constantly gorged themselves on smelt which bred in streams that flowed into the lake. As a result, many of the trout grew to trophy size.

Approaching Havre de Poisson by air, the only signs even remotely suggesting the presence of civilization was a wooden dock jutting out from the shoreline with small boats tethered alongside. A few thin wisps of smoke slowly rose through the trees from the cast iron stoves inside twelve cottages, all of which were part of the wilderness sportsman's camp.

The cottages were rustic, but basic essentials were provided. Gas lanterns prevailed and the outhouses were a shared luxury. There was no WiFi, and cell phone reception in the valley was spotty; electricity was limited to a small generator which was seldom used, as it competed with the outboard motors for a precious supply of gasoline kept on hand. Communication with the outside world was mainly achieved by snail mail, which came and went once a week – by float plane.

Havre de Poisson was also accessible by an abandoned logging road, although the road was only used by Gault a few times a year when he brought in supplies at the beginning and end of a season.

The adventurous sportsmen who chose this destination all arrived by float plane. The cost of an all-inclusive, fly-in trophy fishing adventure on an isolated lake with very little fishing pressure didn't come cheap. But when the week was over, the majority of guests immediately booked for the following year.

During prime season, life was busy at the lodge, and everything revolved around the comings and goings of clientele. Lou's primary objective was for every guest to enjoy their week and book a return stay. If a visitor complained that the fish weren't biting, Lou took them out to one of his hotspots and showed them how to catch fish. If a hunter complained he wasn't seeing any deer, the next morning Lou accompanied him, placed him on a stand, and drove the deer toward him.

Early each morning, the lake was as smooth as a millpond, but once the sun peaked over the mountain, the wind would come up fast causing a good chop out on the lake. Once that happened the boats that hadn't already gone out would gently bump up against the dock in rhythm on the windward side and a few waves might splash onto the dock. Over the years, Lou has become masterful in helping guests safely step down from a float plane rocking in one direction onto a dock rocking the opposite way.

It was autumn now. Every morning, steam rose off the surface of the lake, slightly obscuring the ruggedness of the distant shoreline; frost gleamed like polished silver on the trees in higher elevations until the sun finally conquered the mountain and reclaimed the valley. For several weeks, flocks of geese had been filling the sky, migrating south. Soon, even the loons would make their exodus.

In one week, the season would come to an end. Lou would then make the usual repairs before closing his twelve cottages before the long brutal Canadian winter set in. The only sportsmen with access to the lake were guests who flew in and stayed with Lou at Havre de Poisson.

Two guests had just completed a week of fishing and were standing outside the lodge looking across the clearing at Lou. They would be leaving shortly on the mail plane, making connecting flights to wherever home was – back in civilization. One of the guests called to Lou.

"Was that a wolf we heard howling last night, Lou?"

"No, a coyote," he called back, walking over to them.

"Any wolves around here?"

"There were always wolves in the valley, but they moved further north quite a while back. We've had coyotes around here the last couple of years. Angelo saw one sitting at the edge of the woods the other day - near the hen house."

"They come that close?"

"Once in awhile, but we haven't had any trouble with them . . . not yet, anyway. I'd rather have the wolves though."

"Yeah? Why's that?"

"Wolves are better for the ecosystem."

Lou usually enjoyed the majority of his guests, but was pleased that most only booked for a week's stay. One week was about all he could stand with some of these rich, pampered city folk who came here looking to "check the box" and brag about how they had spent a week fishing with a native guide in the wilds of New Brunswick.

These two guests were different, though, they were true

sportsmen and had been coming to Havre de Poisson for years. He didn't mind at all when they came to stay. "I'm curious fellas, what keeps you coming back here year after year?"

"Well, we were just talking about that ourselves, Lou. It's the fishing that brings us back, 'course, but it's just so damn peaceful here."

"Don't let him kid you, Lou," the other man said. "It's Angelo's cooking that keeps us coming back."

"Yeah, I'll second that, and I don't know how the hell you keep him here. He'd make a fortune down in Manhattan," the first one said. "Yet here he is, in the middle of absolutely freaking *nowhere* cooking up a storm on a wood stove like a gourmet chef."

Angelo and his wife, Alessandra, were the only other year-round residents at Havre de Poisson. A middle-aged couple, they came over from Italy years ago, and never left.

"Angelo is a favorite with everybody, no question about that," Lou said. "He'll transform anything anyone catches, or shoots, into a delicious, mouthwatering epicurean delight like they've never tasted; he's unbelievable."

"And Alessandra is his wife?"

"Yeah, she's our housekeeper, but she works with Angelo in the kitchen as well."

He thought about the couple. Angelo and Alessandra considered him the son they never had and always wanted . . . and that's how they treated him.

As the men continued talking, the serenity of the valley was broken by the sound of a float plane advancing up the lake. The single-engine mail plane usually arrived late in the day, even though schedules in the north country were rarely precise. Gault gestured toward the speck in the sky.

"Looks like you'll be leaving before lunch, fellas. Let Angelo know, he'll fix you up a couple of box lunches."

Having grown up on the shores of this lake, Lou knew

the weather patterns well. The windsock at the end of the dock showed the pilot which direction the wind was blowing. Today, it was coming from the west which meant the plane would circle around and land heading into the wind.

By the time the pilot made his circle and set up for landing, Lou would be down at the dock jockeying around a few boats to give the float plane room to tie up.

When he reached the dock, he was surprised to see two float planes approaching. The first was the mail plane which his cousin, Jake, had flown for the past few years. But he didn't recognize the other one. While it was commonplace for multiple planes to fly in during peak season, it was rare for a second plane to be arriving now.

A few years back, when Lou had started replacing the old dock, he didn't have the time or energy to extend the dock far enough out to allow more than one plane to tie up and unload at a time. Fortunately, there was more than enough sandy shoreline for the second plane to safely ride up onto the beach and unload whatever cargo it was bringing. As the mail plane set down and taxied toward him, Lou expected to see Jake sticking his arm out the window waving hello. But after securing the mail plane's tiedown straps, he realized it wasn't Jake at the throttles. All the same, he recognized two men inside.

Jumping out of the plane dressed as Canadian Mounties, were the same two men who served with Lou in Afghanistan. The three of them had been in the same ten-man squad, slept together, ate together, and fought side by side in the Islamic wars for close to two years. He hadn't seen them since he mustered out.

"Lou, how the hell are you?" one of them called.

"Fletcher?"

"Yeah . . . and look who I brought with me!"

"Duffy, is that you?"

"Hey, Lou!"

The three friends embraced as a brief flash back crowded in on Lou: All three had been on point and fought hand to hand, building by building, to save the lives of their comrades that fateful day. Even though it was years ago, Lou remembered it clear as yesterday.

"So, when did you two decide to put on 'Smokey the Bear' hats and start riding horses for a living?" Lou laughed.

"Not long after we rotated out of JTF2, Lou," Fletcher said with just a hint of a smile.

"Yeah, we took a look at the Mounties and decided it would be a quiet lifestyle," Duffy added. "As if!"

"We both made sergeant fairly quickly," Fletcher said. "However, *Private* Duffy here has been reduced in rank *twice* now. He still loves to play practical jokes on the higher ups, but it's catching up with him. I keep telling him: Once more, and he's a goner."

"Ah, don't listen to him Lou," Duffy said "They'll never get rid of me, I'm one of the few at Headquarters that even knows how to turn a computer on, and they damn well know a good detective when they see one."

"Ah, you're full of yourself."

"Besides, Fletcher's in line for Sergeant Major," Duffy said, "that is, once old Andre Girard finally retires."

"Ha, and don't you go thinking for one minute I'll be able to save your butt," Fletcher said, "if you pull any more of your stunts."

"You'd be lost without me."

"Lou, the only reason he's still got a pension coming is because his brother sits in the House of Commons," Fletcher said, "and has oversight on our budget!"

"I'm glad to see nothing's changed between you two," Lou smiled.

"It never will," Duffy said.

"So, what the hell are you two doing up here?"

Duffy made a face and used his thumb to point over his shoulder to the plane. "Official business."

Chapter

3

Andre Girard struggled a bit to get out of the plane. "All right," he called out. "I need at least *one* of you to help me out of this blasted thing!"

Is that really Andre? Lou thought. *He has certainly aged since I saw him last.*

Fifteen years earlier, Andre Girard had begun recruiting both Lou and his cousin, Jake, to lead search and rescue efforts across New Brunswick for lost hunters and stranded snowmobilers. Girard had immediately taken to young Lou and became his mentor. Jake was another story. But in recognition of both their efforts, Lou and his cousin eventually received lifetime Auxiliary Officer status with the Mounties.

Now, Lou hurried over to the four-seat plane and extended his hand.

"Here Andre, let me help you."

"Thanks, Lou. It's been a long time; really good to see you again, my friend."

"It has been."

"I wish I could say that this was a pleasure trip . . . but it's not." Lou waited for Andre to share more, but he didn't. "Let's go over to your cottage and have a coffee," was all he said.

Lou looked back at the other two Mounties. No expressions to reveal the reason they were there.

"You can catch up with those two later," Andre continued. "They have some gear to unload, and can help the other plane make a shore landing while we talk."

During the walk from the dock and up the grassy incline to his cottage, Lou listened as Andre complained, "It's taken me the whole blasted day to get here, first by car and then by floatplane. You sure live out in the boonies, even by New Brunswick standards."

"Where'd you come from?"

"Fredericton."

"Andre, it doesn't take a whole day to come up from Fredericton."

Ignoring Lou's comment, Andre asked, "Are the trout still as big as they were years ago?"

"They brought in a lot of nice fish this year."

"Did they?"

"Yeah, there's always a lot of catch and release, but the lakers they brought in this time averaged four and five pounds, with a few lunkers. The rainbows were all around three to four pounds each. A lot of happy people."

"Humph," Andre acknowledged.

Since Andre had last visited, the layout of Havre de Poisson had changed significantly. When Lou sensed Andre was looking for the cottage that he had stayed in years ago, he stepped in and pointed to the left.

"You stayed over there, across the field last time," Lou said. "When you were here, all the cottages had that weathered grey look. Jake and I stained them dark green a few years ago."

"Really? I don't remember screen porches. Were they always there?"

"No . . . good memory. I added the porches four years ago; comment cards kept mentioning black flies and mosquitoes. So, I had to fix it. Funny, my customers pride themselves on wanting a rustic experience, but bugs are one rustic touch they can do without."

"My wife gets a shot for the damn black flies every year," Andre said.

"Once I put on the porches, I jacked up the rates to cover my costs and the comment cards have been all smiley faces and exclamation points ever since."

"I see the sawmill is still standing over by the brook . . . still use it?"

"The Abenaki guides used it off-and-on all summer," Lou said. "The village has hired a second teacher, so they're adding on to the old one-room schoolhouse."

Andre's breathing was a little quicker and he was flushed by the time they reached Lou's cottage.

"Have a seat while I make coffee."

Out of the corner of his eye, Lou saw Andre sneer and shake his head when Lou pulled out a jar of the instant stuff. *He's okay,* Lou thought.

In a few minutes, they were sitting across the table from each other cradling two mugs as the steam drifted toward the ceiling.

"A decade ago, we sat at this very same table, after a search and rescue mission. Except it was bourbon then, not coffee . . . and Jake was here, too."

Patient to a point, Lou's patience finally began to run out when Andre was still not forthcoming about his journey here after a couple of sips of coffee.

"Andre," Lou said. ". . . where is Jake?"

"I was hoping you could tell me, Lou. I have a warrant for his arrest."

Chapter

4

Lou took a moment to internalize what he'd just heard. His cousin, Jake, was being charged with assault and they were looking for him. He thought of his cousin who he had grown up with as close as two cousins could be. The thought of Jake being in real trouble bothered him . . . a lot.

"So, let me get this straight," he said. "Jake's wanted on a simple assault charge and the Royal Canadian Mounted Police send New Brunswick's *only* sergeant major all the way up here, with an escort, just to ask me if *I* know where he is?

Andre took a deep breath as he looked down into his coffee cup, saying nothing.

"Andre, I understand cell phone coverage is a little spotty up here at times, but there seems to be more than just a few missing pieces to this story that you're not sharing with me." Andre now looked up but continued to stare at him.

"It's not a simple assault charge, Lou. Jake is being sought in connection with an incident that sent three people to the hospital down in Grand Manan Island." He hesitated. "One of whom is the local constable, Orson Evers."

"Grand *Manan*? Andre, that's down in the Bay of Fundy! Jake stopped making long-haul flights there *years* ago."

"I know where it is," Andre said.

"Jake flies out of Kedgwick, delivering mail six days a week in a radius of seventy-five miles."

"I know that."

"Grand Manan is over three hundred miles south . . . he doesn't fly down there."

"I *know* where it is, Lou,"

Andre took a sip of his coffee.

"Are you *sure* you're looking for the right guy?" Lou said.

Andre nodded his head, but remained silent.

"Andre, level with me, I didn't just fall off the back of a damn turnip truck. You didn't come all the way up here from Fredericton just to ask me if I knew where Jake was."

"Lou, Jake was working for me last week."

"And?"

"And his whereabouts is *my* responsibility. The last time I talked to him, he told me he was 'going to ground,' and I thought he might have come *here.* Don't worry about the warrant, it doesn't mean a thing, it's all bogus."

"So, Andre, tell me the whole truth . . . what's going on?" He watched the man sigh heavily, then begin to talk.

"I agreed to take on one last assignment before I retired. This one. I was told it would be a simple two, maybe three-day investigation leading to an arrest that I could coast through, and then retire. But this whole damn thing has turned into a quagmire. Lou, I could really use your help on this, if you're willing. That's another reason I came up here." Lou could tell the man was being sincere.

"Andre, I have no idea what it is that you're up against, but I'll tell you right now that I don't have a dog in this hunt."

"I know that Lou, but still, I could really use your help. For some time now we've suspected a smuggling ring has been operating out on Grand Manan. We have an idea where the goods are coming in from, but the trail ends at Grand Manan. When several merchant ships bound for the Port of Quebec started losing their satellite tracking signals south of Nova Scotia, we became interested."

Andre paused and took another sip of coffee. "At first, both Canadian and US Coast Guard helicopters were dispatched on search and rescue missions because of the missing transmissions. The ships were consistently found either *at* Grand Manan or just entering the Bay of Fundy. Later, it turned out the ships had been fitted with blocking devices and were deliberately turning off their own signals."

"They can do that?"

"Not legally. That's why the focus has turned to smuggling. Orson Evers is our constable out on the island. He talks a good talk, and makes it look like he's going through all the motions, but he's not really making any effort to help us get to the bottom of what's going on."

Andre paused again for another sip of coffee which had now grown tepid. "In hindsight, we should've been monitoring that island and Passamaquoddy Bay all along. There's a long history of smuggling down there . . . going back to colonial times. It's always been something that the locals have 'winked at.' Evers grew up down there and we now think he's likely involved in what's going on. We've got *him,* and the whole *damn island,* under surveillance. Am I boring you yet?"

"No, I'm okay."

"I needed someone on the ground down there that I knew I could trust."

"So you sent Jake."

"I did. I approached Jake a few weeks back about going down there undercover to do some reconnoitering. Jake wasn't there more than a couple of days when he decided to steal a laptop. He ended up having to fight his way out, and sent Constable Evers and the keeper of the lighthouse over on Passamaquoddy Bay to the local hospital. They airlifted Emmett Davis, the harbor master at Lubec, Maine, over to the States."

"Well, that's no surprise to me," Lou said, leaning back in his chair while chuckling. "Jake was always able to handle himself. He was the martial arts field instructor when we were in JTF2; more than one recruit ended up in the infirmary trying to take him on."

"Yeah, but that's the last time I've heard from him. Here, let me show you the text Jake sent." He pulled out his cell phone and dialed into the message: 'O*n mainland, have laptop, bugged phone, going to ground.*' That's his last message and now I'm really starting to worry," Andre said. "I had a magistrate issue a warrant for him just so I'd have first priority on Jake before INTERPOL got wind of the incident. The challenge now is to find out where the hell he is and get hold of that laptop." Lou sat bolt upright.

"Did you just say *INTERPOL?*"

"Lou, this is now an international operation . . . code name 'Delta-Tango' and it's big. MI6 is running the op on the other side of the pond along *with* INTERPOL. I have the lead role over here. We're just now getting integrated. The States are helping, too. The Brits' MI6 and INTERPOL are focused on finding the head of this snake. Ireland, of all places, seems to be the point where the goods are being moved into and out of Europe. M16 and INTERPOL are keeping tabs on a little fishing village called Portmagee, on Ireland's west coast." Suddenly, Lou stood up somewhat agitated.

"*Whoa,* what the hell am I doing sitting here jabbering with *you*? I have two guests I need to welcome and get settled!"

"Lou. There wasn't anybody on those two planes but

two Mounties, a Yank, and a European. They're all part of my team. We'll be camping out here for a stretch."

"Say, that again?"

"Sit down and think for a second. I had Jake help me set up a fake reservation last week, just so you'd keep the lodge open. Truth is there's a mole somewhere in headquarters who is in bed with this ring and reporting everything we've been doing. I had to move out of headquarters and find a location where I could run my operation with people I could trust. Once I found we could redirect a few communications satellites, Havre de Poisson became the perfect out-of-the-way location."

"Andre! We're in the middle of the damn wilderness up here! We don't even have television reception!"

"I know that . . . sit back down, Lou. That's what actually made Havre de Poisson so attractive. We've brought all the electronic surveillance gear and generators we'll need to run the operation from here."

"I don't believe this." Lou ran fingers through his hair in exasperation. "Here I thought I was going to have a nice quiet final week this season."

"And you will! You won't even know we're around. Come on, I'll introduce you to the rest of the team. We're all looking forward to staying here in all this fresh air. Everybody's a seasoned professional. We'll operate totally independent of you. Just give us the lodge to work in. I've had them load up everything we'll need for four weeks, including food. You can give us a hand if you want, if not, you're free to do whatever you do while we're here. And, just so you know, I've arranged with Ottawa for you to receive your regular rates for as long as we're here." He watched as his friend processed the entire conversation.

"I appreciate that," Lou said, "but just so *you* know, as long as you're here, Angelo will be doing the cooking.

I couldn't change that even if I wanted to." Lou stood up. "Okay, let's go meet your guys." They began walking toward the dock. But Lou's sixth sense told him there was more that had been left unsaid. He didn't have to wait long.

"Lou," Andre said. "I could really use you on my team."

I knew it, Lou thought. *There's always a catch.*

"Andre, I'll do whatever is needed to help make your stay comfortable while you're here, but that's the limit of my involvement in whatever you're doing," Lou said. But then he thought: *That's it, my friend.*

They reached the dock in time to see a man emerge from one of the planes with a satchel of luggage. Andre made the first introduction.

"Lou, this is Clarence James. He isn't staying over in spite of the luggage; he'll be flying your two departing guests over to Kedgwick shortly. Before joining the Mounties, he was a bush pilot in western Ontario, so, until Jake returns, he'll fly the mail plane."

"What about the other plane?"

"That'll stay here. Duffy has his pilot's license, if we need to fly somewhere."

The men made small talk as they walked up to the lodge. Before going inside, Andre said, "Let me introduce you to Matt Dorsey, a U.S. Customs Special Agent assigned to Border Protection Intelligence, based out of Portland, Maine. This is Dorsey's first field assignment.

" Dorsey was chosen because he's computer savvy and highly regarded by his superiors for investigative skills and follow through. But, just so you know, like many U.S. Customs agents, he can come across as very direct, sometimes even rude at times.

"But he has other endearing qualities, too. It would be an *understatement* to say that Dorsey is passionate about the game of baseball. He follows the box scores daily, knows the stats of everybody whose ever played the game, and talks about it incessantly. Good man to have on our team, though."

As soon as they entered the lodge, Andre motioned Dorsey over to them. "Lou, this is Matt Dorsey."

"Welcome to Havre de Poisson, Matt," Lou said while extending his hand in greeting. He could learn a lot about a person from a simple handshake. "Let me know if there's anything I can do to make your stay more comfortable."

"Thanks, will do," Dorsey said.

Lou's initial impression of the man just from his flimsy handshake was that Dorsey was nothing more than a desk jockey, maybe not even a good one.

The remaining member of Andre's team was Lieutenant Kathryn O'Grady, the European contribution to Andre's team. Still out of earshot, Andre told Lou the particulars. "O'Grady lives in the village of Abbeyfeale in County Limerick. She seems somewhat reserved, but don't let that fool you; she can handle herself when necessary." As they approached her, Andre spoke out loud.

"Lou, this is Kathryn O'Grady. She has a number of contacts in both MI6 and INTERPOL that she can draw upon when needed, and she brings a lot of technical expertise to the team."

"A pleasure to meet you, Mr. Gault," she said. "I go by 'Kate.'" Neither her quick smile nor the eye contact that went along with a firm handshake went unnoticed by Lou.

"It's a pleasure to meet you, Kate. I go by 'Lou.' We're a little rustic here, so let me know if you need anything." He was briefly fixated on Kate's chestnut brown hair and hazel green eyes. He also held Kate's hand just a little longer than he had intended to. When she pulled it away, he was slightly embarrassed.

"Seriously, let me know if you need anything."

"I will," she said with a quick smile.

With introductions over, Lou left the team to their task of getting all the sophisticated gear up and running. He headed out to fire up the stoves in the cottages where they would be assigned. He had been surprised that someone who looked as young as O'Grady held the rank of Lieutenant in the Irish Directorate of Military Intelligence. She looked young, but she was only a year younger than Lou. He was surprised that he was still thinking about her.

Once the boats at the wharf were secured, there really wasn't much more for Lou to be concerned about beyond letting Angelo know how many to expect for meals and how long they'd be staying. To the west, the bottoms of huge billowing clouds were turning dark grey, a sure sign that a storm was brewing at the far end of the valley.

Lou had a lot of information he needed to digest and a few more questions still to ask. Foremost on his mind was a big one: What the hell ever motivated Jake to get involved in another man's fight?

Heading over to a small rocky point jutting out into the lake, his train of thought was broken by a flock of geese passing overhead just above tree top level honking like a traffic jam at rush hour.

The rocky point had been Lou's safe-haven ever since he was a boy; it was the spot where he had always gone whenever he needed to be alone or do a little reflecting. It was also the place where he and his wife had picnicked and where they had escaped whenever they had needed solitude. Willow had died from ovarian cancer two years ago. The stage four diagnosis had come as a complete surprise and Lou had been devastated when he lost his soul mate.

The air was brisk today and filled with all the earthy

aromas that abounded in autumn. There was always a breeze on the point and fall had always been Lou's favorite season; it had come late this year, the trees just now nearing peak color.

Lou walked over to his favorite spot, leaned back, and inhaled deeply to clear his head before his thoughts shifted to Jake.

He fantasized a conversation in his head: *Andre, the reality is, if Jake has gone to ground, no one is going to find Jake unless Jake wants to be found.*

Lou and his cousin had been orphaned early in life. The Abenaki village elders decided that the boys would continue to be raised in the ways of the Abenaki people and that they would live with their maternal grandfather. Grey Elk had welcomed his grandsons into his home and treated them like his own sons. It was at Havre de Poisson that he patiently taught them how to hunt, to fish, to learn the ways of the forest, the life skills they would need to embrace, and the values necessary to live an honorable life. The boys grew up like twin brothers and from a distance they were difficult to tell apart. Temperament-wise, Lou had taken after his grandfather and was the more stoic and pragmatic of the two. His cousin, Jake, was more the comic, always going for the laugh, and was an opportunist.

An integral part of their upbringing had been playing the game of "Butterfly Hide and Seek." The game had been originated by the Pequot tribe centuries ago. Over time, the game became a learning exercise for young Abenaki men as they prepared to prove themselves worthy to sit among the warriors. Similar to the children's game of hide and seek, this game was much more involved and lasted for days. It was a test of one's stealth, self-discipline, and endurance. The ability to blend into one's surroundings, remain quiet, and not be seen by others was the very essence of the game.

It was also believed to be good luck if one remained quiet and stayed still long enough that a butterfly would land on them.

Back in those days, whether it was Lou or Jake who chose to hide, they would take enough food and supplies for three days, leave without being seen, and "go to ground." Within twenty-four hours, the "tracker" would pack food and supplies for two days, and use their skills to find their "adversary." Lou had found Jake as often as Jake had found him. They were evenly matched even back then.

Now, directly across the lake from where Lou was sitting, an outcrop halfway up the side of Mount Carleton was visible and had always been known as Pinnacle Rock. When the boys were young, they had hiked there often, and once made a pact that should either of them ever really need to go to ground, they would find a way to reach Pinnacle Rock and send a signal exactly at noon each day until the other saw it, and came to them.

Out of habit, Lou glanced at his watch. It was eleven fifty-five in the morning. At exactly twelve o'clock, Lou looked up at Pinnacle Rock . . . and saw a flash of light.

Chapter 5

Lou returned to his cottage, packed his personal gear, and walked over to the kitchen to provision enough food for a couple of days. Before departing, he went to find Andre.

"Andre, I think I'll head out, I might be gone for a couple of days."

"There's a storm coming up the valley, Lou, why don't you wait?"

"Nah, I'll be fine."

Andre just shook his head wondering why anyone would head out with a storm coming.

"Oh, and Andre, the best fishing from shore this time of year is early in the morning below the sawmill right where the brook comes into the lake."

"Really?"

"Yeah, it's kinda funny, the rainbow have been feeding on whatever is washing into the lake . . . they were hitting on a muddler fly and some wooly buggers a couple of days ago."

"Okay, thanks, I'll give it a try."

Later that morning, Andre's team wasted no time bringing the second floatplane further ashore and unloading the gear. Three portable antennas were easily erected, the satellite dish assembled, the communication gear unpacked, the generators put into position, and their personal gear brought up to the lodge.

Once most of the dining area inside the lodge had been transformed into an actual base of operations, Andre called everyone together.

"Okay listen up; here's the sleeping arrangements: Fletcher, you and Duffy will bunk together in cottage three; Matt Dorsey, you're in four; Kate you're in six and I'll take number five."

"I was hoping you'd give us the cabin down by the lake, Andre," Duffy said.

"Like I said, you and Fletcher are in cottage three . . . these are the cottages Lou gave us to use." There were no further gripes from anyone.

The base lodge and cottages were all in excellent condition and structurally sound, just rustic. The walls and ceilings were all constructed of pine, which over the years had aged to a venerable golden hue. The rafters and wall studs were exposed since none of the guest cottages were insulated. The only negative was that the wide pine floors were somewhat worn near the doorsteps from use. Smoke from the countless wood fires in the stoves has permeated into the wall and the smokey tinge near the stovepipe merely added to the overall rustic ambiance of the cottages.

Alessandra worked hard at keeping the cottages neat and clean; the beds were freshly made, and each cottage had fresh towels and a supply of firewood inside. There were a couple cords of split wood outside under a tarp, with more nearby if needed. A shared bathhouse contained two enclosed outdoor showers, and outhouses were located a short distance from the cottages, more toward the woods. It was all part of the natural feeling of the place. Alessandra routinely put lye down the toilet holes to keep the aroma as palatable as possible which also kept flies to a minimum.

Andre and his two Mounties were fine with the accommodations. This was to be expected for a Canadian hunting and fishing camp. Dorsey, however, expected indoor plumbing and hot running water. Kate had totally expected something more along the lines of a Holiday Inn but, being low maintenance, she had decided to adapt instead.

The only cottages different from the others belonged to Lou and Angelo. Their cottages were triple the size of the others, insulated, and offered indoor plumbing. Such was the privilege of long-term inhabitants.

"Okay, you've got your cottage assignments. Stow your personal gear before the rain hits and come right back to finish setting up this equipment," Andre said.

Fletcher and Duffy began running lines from the antennas and satellite dish into the lodge and getting portable generators up and running. The work went quickly, as the two men had been together for so long, they knew each other's habits, and anticipated the other's needs. The generators fired up on their first try. Given the sensitivity of the electronic equipment, they chained the generators in tandem to provide a fail-safe constant source of power. Before the energy reached the lodge, it traveled through a massive surge protector for added protection.

"Duffy, I know we brought up two auxiliary tanks, but do ya think we'll have enough fuel to run these generators?" Fletcher asked.

"Hey, if we run low, we'll just remove the catalytic converters and go with a 50/50 mix of Avgas in the floatplane until Clarence brings in some more."

Inside, Kate and Dorsey had been arranging tables into individual workstations and setting up the computer equipment.

Dorsey loved listening to an Irish accent and had been attempting to engage Kate in small talk just for the pleasure of hearing her speak. Kate, on the other had just arrived that morning, had a bit of jet lag, and the work at hand was taking up her energy. Small talk wasn't something she was happy to engage in at this time. She repeatedly responded to Dorsey's questions with short one or two-word answers, only causing Dorsey to ask more open-ended questions. He wanted to hear her accent, dammit.

Finally, Kate had enough of Dorsey's questions, "Dorsey, will ya just give it a rest? Can't ya see I'm trying to concentrate on setting up the equipment?"

"Sorry," he said, somewhat chagrined.

Finally, with the equipment up and running, Kate turned to Dorsey. "All right lad, give it a go now, what was it that you were wanting to know?"

Dorsey was pleasantly surprised to find that Kate lived in the same county in Ireland that his people came from. But, she was reluctant to share much about her personal life with someone she had just met. To ward off more questions, she started asking Dorsey questions about himself. It wasn't long before she realized that had been a mistake. She'd had no idea that Dorsey could talk non-stop about himself for hours on end.

After hearing about his family, where he went to school, where he most often fished in the spring and during the winter through the ice, the work he did before becoming a customs agent, why he decided to join the US Customs and ad infinitum trivia about the game of baseball, Kate excused herself and walked over to the kitchen area to make a pot of tea. Dorsey followed her saying, "So, let me tell you why I believe Ted Williams was a better true hitter than Joe DiMaggio ever was."

Totally uninterested in hearing more, Kate, with only a vague understanding of the game of baseball and totally uninterested in baseball trivia, made an excuse to leave. Dorsey, oblivious to her feelings, continued on with his loquacious drivel. Only when the other three Mounties came inside the lodge was she finally able to escape from Dorsey.

"Kate, wait, don't run off," he called after her. "Don't you want to hear how the 1919 Chicago White Sox threw the series and were forever after known as the Black Sox?"

"Hold that one for another time, Dorsey," she called back as she went out the door.

Duffy had suffered through the better part of the previous day being subjected to this obsession with baseball statistics and antidotes and quickly sensed that Dorsey has been bending O'Grady's ear about baseball.

Outside, he caught up to Kate and whispered, "So, have you had enough baseball trivia for today?" Kate just rolled her eyes and sighed.

Elsewhere, Andre was looking around. "Okay, let's do a full test on the system just to verify that everything is up and ready," Once he was satisfied that everything was operational, he laid out the plan for the next few days.

"I think it's best that we work in pairs," Andre said, "Fletcher and Duffy, you'll focus on building a storyboard from what is already known about Grand Manan and later add whatever information can be gleaned from the laptop that Jake is bringing in.

"Dorsey and Kate, I'd like you two to work together and focus on where the goods arriving from Portmagee, Ireland, go once they leave Grand Manan."

"What about time cards?" Dorsey asked.

"Let's not worry about any of that minutia, aye?" Andre said. "We'll begin after breakfast. Take whatever breaks you need, and we'll quit around three-thirty. Everything else is free time."

Other than sleep, the only other free time options were fishing, playing ping pong, or watching one of the only two DVDs at the lodge. Angelo and Jake had watched the James Bond flick *"Skyfall,"* and *"The Untouchables"* with Kevin Costner and Sean Connery so often they knew all the lines from every character. Dorsey has already figured out how to pull in some night games broadcast over the MLB channel through the satellite connections.

Since Kate O'Grady had grown up fly fishing along the banks of the river Feale and in the tributaries that flowed into the Shannon, she planned on fishing in the afternoons once she'd shaken off the jet lag.

Andre's role would be keeping Fredericton, INTERPOL, and MI6 informed of the progress he was making and updating his team on what the other half of Operation Delta-Tango was doing.

Everything was ready now.

Chapter 6

It was well after midnight when coyotes surrounded the outbuildings where Angelo kept the fowl and rabbits that he raised. Earlier, Alessandra had said to her husband. "Angelo, it seems every other day, when I go out to collect eggs, I see one or two coyotes sitting at the edge of the forest watching the pens. At least they seem to be keeping their distance."

"Sooner or later, we'll have trouble," Angelo said. "They're no different than foxes." A heavy rain muffled the sound of the coyotes yipping a little until, finally, they began racing and clawing at the structure frantically trying to find a way in. As their hunger increased, the wild animals began racing around, intense and frenzied. Angelo arrived first, in his slippers, double-barrel shotgun in hand. "Git!" he yelled and fired a shot into the air. The coyotes briefly scattered.

One of the wild dogs had been digging next to the fence, attempting to tunnel under the wired enclosure. The first shotgun blast didn't deter him for long; when he returned, he again clawed at the apron extending a full foot below ground.

But Angelo's perfect aim and second shot brought an abrupt end to that effort.

Duffy arrived next, flashlight in hand, and immediately saw two coyotes standing on top of the screen that covered the enclosure. They had scaled the eight-foot fence. On top of the enclosure was a screen built only to fend off birds of prey, so a much narrower gauge wire had been used. The coyotes had already chewed through the wire on top and were beginning to rip a hole in the screen when Duffy chambered a round, took aim, and fired his shotgun. His aim was true. One coyote rolled off the screen and onto the ground; the other fell forward and lay suspended, trapped halfway through the hole he had made. Those on the ground turned tail and ran. Duffy looked over at Angelo.

"I think we chased 'em off."

"For now."

Anticipating the coyotes would circle back, Angelo reloaded, moved into the shadows, and patiently waited. It wasn't long before they returned. He unloaded both barrels on the pack reducing what was left of the band by half.

"You're pretty handy with that scattergun, Angelo."

"It's all we had in Italy, Duffy."

By the time Fletcher and Andre arrived armed with shotguns, flashlights, and umbrellas against the inclement weather, the remaining coyotes were gone.

"Anybody hurt?"

"Just a few coyotes, Andre."

Angelo counted five dead ones on the ground, and one suspended in the wire. After sunrise, they would find more lying a few yards from the edge of the woods.

The next morning, talk of coyotes and wolves dominated the conversation at breakfast.

"There's been fresh coyote prints every morning down by the lake," Angelo said, as he came out of the kitchen. "My wife saw them every time she collected eggs. I figured it was just a matter of time before they tried to get into that coop."

"Well, it's a good thing they weren't wolves, Angelo," Andre said. "There's no coop or hutch that could ever keep *those* devils out,"

"The very first winter I was here, a wolf pack got into the pens out back, we lost every animal we had."

"Ha! You must have eaten a lot of fish that winter Angelo," Andre laughed.

"Right. Fish and venison, was all we had."

Dorsey was looking at Kate O'Grady. He had little interest in listening to stories of coyotes, wolves, or cooking, and had managed to sit directly across from her at the breakfast table. "So, tell me Kate . . . you like to go by 'Kate,' right?" he asked rather bluntly. "Why do you think they sent you over here to be part of the team?"

Duffy nearly spit out his coffee as he hunched over his plate trying to avoid laughing out loud at Dorsey's directness.

Kate took her time finishing the food in her mouth, used her napkin, took a sip of tea, then looked directly at Duffy and smiled. "Well, initially they *did* consider sending someone else over, but then they found that he already knew a lot about baseball, and I didn't, so they decided to give the nod to me."

Completely missing the sarcasm, Dorsey, replied, "Well, not to worry Kate, I can certainly help you with *that*!"

When Duffy cleared his throat, Kate glanced at him. He nodded his head, as if to say, well done, and she gave him a wink.

Chapter

7

With the storm beginning to move up the lake, Lou quickened his pace, hoping to get around the far end before rain arrived, and with it, a full force wind. As he approached the beaver pond near one end of the lake, he stopped short. Up ahead was an adult bull moose foraging on the near shoreline. Lou hoped he was far enough away that even if the bull did see him, he probably wouldn't charge. He waited patiently until the moose had his head submerged in the shallow water again before moving down the path. Even though every bull reacts differently, attracting the bull's attention could have been as dangerous as getting bit by a rattle snake.

Treetops were beginning to bend now from the wind coming across the lake. Lou heard thunder rumbling in the distance and smelled the metallic odor that always came before a storm like this one. The rain was still almost an hour away from reaching the east end of the lake.

Completely focused now on locating the game trail leading directly up to Pinnacle Rock, Lou unintentionally flushed a pair of ducks feeding in the reeds close to shore. Once the birds took flight, the entire beaver pond seemed to erupt as a huge flock of ducks and geese followed suit.

Then Lou found the animal trail; he entered it and was immediately sheltered from the wind. This trail, more so than others, seemed to crisscross a number of mountain springs. Deer tracks were abundant in the muddy sections; there was even evidence that a bear had recently been on the trail. Since bears wouldn't retreat to their dens for at least another month, he had to be cautious as they were still active. In New Brunswick, the only home to black bears, Lou knew they were rarely aggressive toward humans unless their cubs were threatened.

Lou pushed his pace and reached Pinnacle Rock in just over thirty minutes. The climb had been steep in a few places, but otherwise uneventful. Even though he was in great shape, it took a few moments to catch his breath and orient himself to the surroundings before moving on. Here, the game trail seemed to split off in three directions. An untrained eye would never have noticed where the soil near one of the trails had been disturbed. But he had. Lou smiled and moved forward.

The trail meandered along a ridgeline for a distance. The terrain was flat, except for large earthen mounds created when a tree had been uprooted during a storm. Knowing that Jake would not have gone too far from Pinnacle Rock, Lou decided to stop and scan the area.

"Okay, are you going to show yourself, or do I actually have to say 'ollie, ollie, oxen free?'" he called out.

Not more than ten feet in front of Lou, a camouflaged figure emerged from among the leaves on the forest floor.

"I thought you were never going to ask!"

Smiling, Lou embraced his cousin.

"Welcome to the neighborhood, Lou," Jake said. "The weather

isn't going to hold much longer, so come and see my new digs. It's not much, but it'll keep us dry. Have you eaten? I have some smoked rabbit, but I'm totally out of Grey Poupon at the moment."

The lean-to had been constructed entirely out of natural materials just as Gray Elk had taught them. The frame and lashings would last for some time; it was more than adequate for two people. The opening faced away from the prevailing winds, protecting them from the approaching storm. Lou unloaded his gear, and together, they secured a plastic tarp over the fire pit, finishing just as the rain began to come down with a fury.

"Okay, Jake, tell me what's going on."

"Well, I've been sort of on the run now for a few days, Lou, but no one is on my trail. I've been doing some work for Andre."

"So, I've heard."

"My instincts told me that going directly to see Andre at headquarters wasn't the smartest thing to do, so I came here, figuring you and I could work out a plan."

"Why didn't you just come and see me?"

"I was on my way. But when I was down by the beaver pond this morning I saw those float planes come in. They hung around too long just to be dropping off sportsmen. Given what I've been through, I figured waltzing in on you unannounced wasn't the best move at the time, so I headed up here to Pinnacle Rock. Wasn't sure how long it would take you to start watching this way at noontimes, so I built myself this little starter home to wait. When I finally flashed the mirror earlier today, I was surprised you saw it."

"Jake, I can assure you, it was pure dumb luck that I happened to look up today. Otherwise, you could have been waiting for quite a few days. By the way, that was Andre who flew in. He brought a couple of Mounties and some others with him. He had a suspicion that I might know where you were."

"That's surprising. I didn't expect him to follow me here."

"Well, I was honest when I told him I had no clue where you were. At the time, I didn't, but once I saw your signal, I just told him I'd be off hiking for a couple of days. He's setting up his base of operations here to unravel whatever it is that you're involved in."

"He's going to run a base camp from *here* in the boonies! What is he, nuts?"

"Jake, these 'boonies' are being catapulted right into 21st Century technology as we speak. Andre has brought in a slew of communication gear, and they've jockeyed around a couple of communications satellites out in space just for him. By the way, he also has a warrant out for your arrest, but I think it's more for your protection than anything else."

"Yeah, the warrant was the plan if anything went wrong. I didn't leave Grand Manan on the best of terms the other night."

"So, I heard."

"I had to make sure there wouldn't be any pursuit, then I ran like hell across the harbor to catch the last ferry before it left the island."

"Andre said you snagged a laptop?"

"Yeah, by then they knew I wasn't really who I was pretending to be. But honestly, Lou, the only thing that went through my head was 'drop the gun and take the cannoli.' They didn't have any cannoli, so, what the hell, I grabbed the laptop. I've been on the run ever since. Never even had a chance to fire up the laptop."

"Andre showed me the text you sent him."

Jake didn't respond.

"Let's see if there's any battery life left in this sucker." He reached over and took the laptop out of its case. "Fancy case, huh?"

"Is that real leather?" Lou asked.

"Yeah, these guys spent money on themselves like it was water."

The laptop fired right up, but was password protected.

"Damn!" Jake said. "Okay, not one of those guys struck me as being all that sophisticated. Just in case, I'm gonna have a look. Maybe they wrote the password down somewhere." He rustled through the various zippered pockets.

"Well, what do we have here?" he asked. "Yellow Post-It notes! Ha, bingo!"

Jake scrolled through the file names and realized the laptop contained a mother lode of information.

"Lou, I think I just found my 'get out of jail free card.' We need to get this down to Andre."

"Cuz, that's not happening tonight. No one's getting off the mountain in this storm. Besides, tomorrow will be soon enough. In the meantime, tell me how you managed to send three people to the hospital. Just whatever in hell made you decide to get involved in another man's fight in the first place!"

"Ahh, the night is long," Jake said. "Want a cigar?"

Chapter 8

The storm raged through the valley most of the night. Jake's shelter kept both men dry and shielded them from howling winds. By morning, the storm had moved on and the forest was beginning to come back to life. In the distance, the rhythmic drumming of a woodpecker made the morning come alive. Chickadees and titmice began flitting from tree to tree directly above the lean-to, curious to see who it was that had spent the night in their domain.

When Jake returned from the nearby spring, he could tell from the aromas drifting his way that Lou had coffee brewing and had brought bacon. Both men worked quickly around the fire; soon a few slices of bread were hanging over the coals on skewers, slowly toasting.

"Lou, did you bring any lemon curd with you?"

"No, I didn't. Just finish your breakfast so we can dismantle everything, and not leave any evidence that we were here."

"Want more coffee?"

"No," Lou said. His thoughts were already on their next moves. "Jake, the trail I came up will be too muddy after this rain. Let's take the trail on the backside of the mountain going down, it's a little longer, but it'll be dryer and the footing safer."

"I was thinking the same thing."

Hiking down the backside of the mountain, the air was crisp and invigorating, quickening their pace. By the time they circled around the base of the mountain and reached the beaver pond, they were surrounded by thick fog. It was not unusual to have an early morning fog on the lake this time of year; the water temperature being warmer than air caused steam to rise off the water until the sun came up. Passing the beaver pond, Lou held up his hand and whispered, "Someone's coming; let's step off the path and see who it is."

Fletcher Martin emerged from the fog. In the habit of taking early morning walks for the past few years, he was out for his morning jaunt. An avid hunter, Fletcher usually walked with his head down looking for signs of wildlife on the trail. He was following a well-used trail that would eventually loop back around to the cottages once it crossed over the old logging road.

Lou signaled for Jake to remain quiet as they waited for Fletcher to pass.

"Who was that?"

"An old friend. He's okay, I just thought it best for you to stay out of sight until we've met with Andre."

As Lou and Jake approached Havre de Poisson, they noticed someone standing on the shore near the mouth of the brook totally absorbed in fly fishing. Their approach went unnoticed, masked by the noise of the water flowing into the lake, and the heavy fog. They both recognized the fisherman was Andre Girard. Rather than interrupt Andre's concentration, they took a seat on a fallen tree directly behind him to wait.
Andre misplayed landing a couple of trout, then turned to change a fly he'd been using on his line. That's when he realized

he had an audience.

"How long have you two been sitting there?"

"Long enough to see you'd make out better going to the fish market, if *that's* what you wanted for breakfast," Jake said.

"Humph," Andre managed. "I wondered how long it would take you to get here. Are you okay?"

"Yeah, ribs are a little sore, but nothing I can't live with," Jake said. "I brought you a present."

"I saw the text you sent me Jake. Anything of value?"

"Andre, how do you say, 'treasure trove' in Pig-Latin?"

"Let's go; the cook can serve some of that canned hash we brought with our eggs this morning!"

Walking toward the lodge, Lou moved closer to Andre. "Hey, just a word of advice, while you're here, don't ever refer to Angelo as a 'cook' to his face; it's *Chef* Angelo, *Chef,* or just plain 'Angelo.' Trust me on this one."

Meanwhile, the trail that Fletcher Martin had been following, brought him to the old logging road at the back entrance to Havre de Poisson. He stopped to inspect a moss-covered wooden gate in the road that separated the land leased to the logging company from property owned by Lou Gault. He chuckled at the lock on the gate, given how far he was from anything even remotely resembling civilization at the moment.

What did impress Fletcher, however, were all the fresh deer tracks and rubbings that he had seen this morning, especially here around the gate area. New Brunswick's gun season would begin shortly, and Fletcher had brought his hunting license with him when he flew up . . . just in case. Over the next week, he planned to continue scouting the area before deciding exactly *where* he would be on opening day.

Back at the lodge, Jake had already fired up the laptop. It had belonged to Emmett Davis. Now, as Jake walked them through the files, it was obvious they were getting a firsthand glimpse at how things operated on Grand Manan.

"Okay, here's a file that lists the names of every ship's captain that has ever been involved, including the dates when they moved goods for them. Here's a file listing how much everyone was compensated. This file contains the names of merchant ships that brought goods into Grand Manan, along with the name of the port from which they originally sailed. This one here is a file listing the names and phone numbers of dockworkers and how much they were compensated. Are you impressed Andre?"

"Very much so!"

As they poured through the files, Portmagee, Ireland appeared to be the primary port from which these merchant ships were sailing. Tralee was mentioned a few times, too.

Constable Orson Evers appeared to be coordinating everything when goods came into Grand Manan. There was a file detailing what had been moved into a warehouse and when it moved out. Entries listed were as current as four days ago. A man named Felix Lajoie appeared to be the one who took charge of moving goods over to Passamaquoddy Bay. Even the names of the docks where goods were offloaded on the bay were listed. Everything that the ring has smuggled in and out of Grand Manan for the past three years was listed. Emmett Davis appeared to be the bookkeeper, and paymaster, for the group.

"Where the contraband goes once it reaches the mainland still remains a mystery," Jake said. "The roles of these three men seem to be compartmentalized," he finished and looked up.

"Jake, I am *extremely* impressed," Andre said. "This is going to help us piece a lot of information together."

"I thought you'd be happy."

"However, there's just *one* little problem," Andre said,

looking at him intently. "Because you *stole* the damn thing, we'll never be able to introduce it as evidence! I'll have Duffy summarize what's on the laptop so we can at least share it with INTERPOL and MI6."

"Yeah, but Andre," Jake protested, "is the information in the laptop sufficient to rescind the warrant on *me*, or am I still a wanted criminal?"

Andre smirked and patted Jake on the shoulder. "I'll make a call today and have the judge rescind the warrant but stick around and try to behave. We need to uncover a lot more before any raid on Grand Manan can happen. You'll get your job back delivering the mail when this is all over. But for now, Jake, you're on *my* payroll."

Part 2

Chapter

9

Portmagee, a small fishing village in County Kerry, Ireland, was located on the edge of the Iveragh Peninsula just south of Valentia Island. The harbor was one of the most western points of land in all of Europe.

The village was named after an 18th-century sea captain, Theobald Magee, who was a smuggler of various forms of contraband and who managed to marry the rebellious daughter of a member of Parliament representing County Kerry. Legend had it that his new father-in-law was livid when he learned that Magee was a pirate. He became instrumental in both Magee's exile and ultimate death in a foreign monastery. After Magee's death, the pirate's young wife quietly carried on her former husband's nefarious business interests.

Once a bustling harbor filled with merchant ships that sailed to America and Australia, the boom days ended when the deeper ports of Cobh and Cork became accessible for transportation via the railroads.

These days, Portmagee was just one of many quaint fishing villages. If not for annual festivals held at the port, it would have completely fallen off the map. Still, upon occasion, a large merchant ship would arrive to unload or take on a shipment. These merchant ships usually departed in predawn hours leaving whatever paperwork the harbor master needed to sign off in the shack that he used as an office. The harbor master was a direct descendant of Theobald Magee. If asked, he'd tell you, "We're just a wee port; there's no need to get ourselves wrapped around our undies over all these maritime regulations, we leave that to the big ports." But what he wouldn't tell you was that smuggling was still a very large part of life in Portmagee.

Portmagee's population numbered barely in the mid-hundreds and could easily have been classified as merely a hamlet. Since no schools existed in Portmagee, children were bused over an hour away back and forth to the county seat of Tralee.

For years, one such youngster was Sean Tinker, an only child and direct descendant of Theobald Magee. When Tinker's father died, Sean became the man of the house at an early age. To help his mother make ends meet, Sean worked as often as he could on the docks with his uncles. Many a morning, Sean would sleep during the hour-long ride to school after having helped unload a late-arriving merchant ship the night before. It was always assumed that when Sean graduated from secondary school, he would join the family business.

To everyone's surprise, Sean Tinker proved to be his own man. On the day he graduated from secondary school, he announced: "The sergeant over at the Irish Defense Services office said that they'd have me. So, I'll be saying goodbye to you, one and all."

Even Sean's mother was surprised. "Sean, now don't be going off and doing that; it's here with the family where you belong."

"Ah, it's a grand deal they've given me, Mum," he said. "I can live on base, learn a trade, and be able to send most of my pay home to help you. It's a win for the two of us!" And off he went.

Sean Tinker made a career out of logistics. He served for twenty years before mustering out with the rank of company quartermaster sergeant, the highest possible non-commissioned officer rank.

There were also many love interests in Tinker's life, however he never married. His career came first, and after a while, he was no longer seen as the young eligible bachelor as he once had been.

During his tenure in Defense Services, he became masterful in the art of managing supply and demand. As he rose in rank, his abilities and sense of loyalty attracted the attention of three commanding officers in the British Army's logistics group, who invited him to join them in trafficking government supplies into the black market. Over time, Tinker was able to quadruple his monthly income, and eventually amassed a significant nest egg. Upon his discharge, Tinker returned to Portmagee with full intentions of settling down and enjoying the good life at a leisurely pace.

The pension for a retired sergeant was more than adequate for one person to live on. But with the nest egg that Tinker had accumulated, it allowed him to build a grand house with a commanding view overlooking Portmagee's harbor.

Tinker never had time for hobbies, nor did he have any interest in traveling the world or socializing with relatives whom he hadn't seen in decades. And he certainly didn't have any desire to pursue renewing relationships with old friends.

So, when he moved back to Portmagee, his relations encouraged him to get involved in the family's maritime shipping business. The business had been floundering and the expertise Tinker had in logistics was sorely needed. His oldest cousin had actually asked him to come in and run the entire operation. On rare occasions Sean would get involved, but only to help resolve a specific problem.

But after living such an active work life for twenty years, the idleness and lack of purpose, which can often appear in retirement, eventually overtook Tinker.
It wasn't long before he reached out to his former military higher ups and began exploring how he might again play a role in their import / export operation.

The low-key profile of Portmagee was quickly seen as the perfect out-of-the-way location to move goods in and out of Europe. Tinker was flattered with the generous proposal he was presented, and immediately accepted the offer. The decision to bring Tinker onboard had little to do with him personally, and everything to do with the attractiveness of the harbor.

"If I'm to be successful in this, Tinker thought, *I'll need to control these docks."* The following day, he approached his family. "I've had a change of heart," he said. "I'm willing to step in, if you'll let me, and turn this business around."

The family had prayed this day would come and gladly relinquished control of the operation to Tinker. Within a matter of months the business was once again thriving, and Portmagee had become the primary point of entry for contraband entering and leaving Europe.

Tinker shied away from personally touching anything that passed through Portmagee, and only rarely did he appear on the docks. His role was wheeling and dealing in the background; scheduling, warehousing, and greasing the palms of the local constables and politicians. His organization consisted entirely of trusted family members; one was his stevedore; another was the bookkeeper; two were warehouse workers, and the rest were the longshoremen who worked the docks whenever a merchant ship arrived.

Tinker was totally in his element, and confident that the higher ups, or 'Imperial Trading' as they were known, would run interference for him if it was ever needed.

One of the few pleasures in life that Tinker allowed himself every day was sitting on his porch, looking out across the harbor, watching the sun sink into the ocean. On one particular evening he thought: *"There's a few clouds, but with luck, maybe tonight I'll see a flash of green on the horizon, just as the sun kisses the ocean."* As the sun went behind the clouds, Tinker stood up thinking, *"Well, maybe my luck will change tomorrow."*

Tinker had no idea that his luck was, in fact, about to change, only *not* for the better. Portmagee had captured the attention of INTERPOL. Nor was he aware that at the very moment the sun was setting, INTERPOL agents were seeking access to his phone records.

Chapter 10

Three friends sat on the deck of the Upper Thames River Yacht Club, under the stars with cigars and brandy in hand, listening to the sounds coming off the river. Even with seat cushions, the sturdy handcrafted teak benches were a little uncomfortable, but the breeze off the water was refreshing and just enough to keep the pesky mosquitos away.

The friends' wives had given them permission to disappear during the speeches at this year's Lords and Ladies Charity Dance, with the understanding that they promised to *reappear* once the orchestra returned to the stage.

Inseparable since their early teens, the three men had boarded together at The King's School in Canterbury, and all through their undergraduate years at The University of Cambridge. After graduation, they went separate ways but had remained close friends.

Richard More enrolled at Imperial College to study law; Clark Hastings followed in his family's tradition and went to Oxford, while Herbert Maxwell decided to remain at Cambridge to further his studies in Banking and International Commerce.

After graduate school, the three friends honored the expectation placed upon male members of their social class, and served a tour of duty in the military, as junior Logistics officers. Military life proved not only boring but extremely confining for these young men. To amuse themselves, they dabbled in the black markets of Europe and profited on the sale of the very government equipment and supplies they had been entrusted to safeguard.

Once their military obligations were satisfied, all three reentered the world of endless social events available only to England's elite aristocracy. It wasn't long before the young, extremely eligible bachelors, were engaged and married. Richard More and Clark Hastings pursued the hands of the twin daughters of Aaron Yardley, the Earl of Surrey. They married Anne and Beatrice Yardley in a double-ring ceremony the following spring. Herbert Maxwell succumbed to the charms of Evelyn Tinsley, eldest daughter of Baron Gilbert Tinsley, president of the prestigious Royalty Bank and Trust Company. He followed his friends to the altar one month after their wedding.

Like their husbands, the Yardley twins and Evelyn Tinsley had grown up as a threesome, attending the same finishing schools, traveling in the same social circles, and involving themselves in the same charitable causes.

Every one of the families had been members of Britain's aristocracy since the sixteenth century. The three young men could actually have lived quite handsomely just on the trust funds established for them. However, since childhood, their fathers had lectured them: "Life is to be lived, not just experienced." It was also understood that they were expected to pursue excellence in whatever their chosen purpose in life might eventually be.

Over time, they each became quite influential in their professional worlds, as well as in the world of international commerce. Herbert Maxwell became a senior vice president at his father-in-law's bank, Richard More became one of the more notable solicitors in London, and Clark Hastings became a junior member of The House of Lords after inheriting his family's title of Earl.

Now they all lived within a quarter-mile of one another in the town of East Molesey, Surrey, in extravagant homes located on the bank of the river Thames. Their daily commute into London was relatively easy either by car or train. They belonged to the same social circles; the same athletic clubs, and often entertained each other in their homes. Even by the standards of the elite aristocracy, the life they led at this young age was quite privileged.

By the time they reached their thirties, the three friends had begun to lament about how boring and predictable their privileged lives had become. To break the monotony, they began meeting at the exclusive Garrick Club on Friday afternoons, before leaving the city, to enjoy a cigar, a little brandy, play a game or two of billiards, and engage in some stimulating conversation.

Quite often the conversation drifted to their desire of adding some excitement to their lives.

"I say that we should start looking for opportunities to push the envelope a bit," Solicitor More suggested at one such gathering. "Just to see what might happen." He offered nothing specific, and the conversation shifted to other subjects.

The following week when they gathered, Lord Hasting shared a little about a conversation that was going on in Parliament. "We're entering a new trade agreement with Canada. Perhaps we should try to get in on that act."

After various discussions on which businesses might be worthwhile investments, Richard More asked, "I say, why are we looking at investing in someone else?" The discussion quickly turned to how they might run their own show.

During the third week, Maxwell researched how they might get into the game. Once he shared the tax implications and oppressive regulatory requirements that would result, their enthusiasm was squelched, until Solicitor More said, "I'd bloody well rather operate in the shadows, and take my chances in the black market."

As soon as More said that they each recalled the rush of adrenalin that always came with their forays into the black-market years earlier. Maxwell suddenly slammed his open palm on the table. "I'm in, legal or not!"

"I'm with you Max," said Hastings. "Hell, everything's legal until you get caught, right?" As he raised his glass, he offered a toast. "Here's to not getting bloody caught."

"Here, here!" the others agreed.

Discretion was actually an art form taught in the upper levels of British society, and from a young age, the three men had learned to play the game extremely well.
As Maxwell slowly swirled the brandy around in his glass, he said, "We'll need to protect our true identities, or there'll be hell to pay."

"That goes without say," Hastings said. "Do you agree, solicitor?"

"It's a fool's game, if we don't," More agreed.

As such, it was decided they would operate in the shadows exclusively through intermediaries and would be only known to others as "Imperial Trading."

In the beginning, they were extremely cautious. But as their operation expanded, the markets they served began to look for different merchandise. What started out as a lark, slowly evolved into a major operation, modeled after the British Government's very own military logistics system. It took over a year to establish a solid network and an infrastructure to move illicit goods from Europe into the black market of eastern Canada.

As much as they enjoyed knowing how it all came together, the three men continued to discipline themselves to remain beyond arm's length from day-to-day operations.

Sean Tinker was the only individual in the entire operation who knew their true identities. Tinker had earned their trust years ago when they were all in Logistics units, siphoning off their own military supplies and selling them on the black market. Tinker proved himself to be discrete, loyal, trustworthy, and, most importantly, he appreciated the special status that he was allowed in their organization. Tinker aspired to someday be invited into their elite world, but that would never happen.

Within a year, the profits the three friends realized were beyond obscene. The staggering additional income allowed them to be overly generous with those who were loyal to them. They began to live an extremely extravagant lifestyle, even when measured against the standards of the wealthy British aristocracy. Yet, no one noticed.

As time passed, the thrill of merely diverting goods lost much of the excitement that it once held, and like drug addicts, they began to look for a bigger rush. Trips to gaming tables in Monaco, and occasionally, to Las Vegas became commonplace, as well as the competition among the three vying for who could score the biggest and most ingenious deal.

There came a time when Solicitor More scored a huge coup on his partners through one of his clients, BMW, one of the most popular luxury cars in Eastern Canada. The demand for new BMWs far exceeded the allotment of cars shipped to Canadian dealers. As a result, servicing older models was a huge segment of the dealership's business model. BMW engineers in Germany determined exactly what parts and how many parts needed to be shipped to Canada twice a year. The dealerships tended to run lean on spare parts toward the tail end of the cycles and, for years, had lobbied for more frequent shipments, to no avail.

Then Solicitor More arranged a deal that would divert the next shipment of BMW parts destined for Canada into the clutches of Imperial Trading. The biannual shipment was worth in the neighborhood of four million pounds sterling. Once the demand for BMW parts in Canada exceeded supply, they would figure a way to move the parts into the black market in Montreal. More's present challenge was to get the parts through customs and off the dock once they reached Canada.

Simultaneously, Lord Hastings had worked a deal to funnel the much-needed laser equipment and satellite receivers being made in Canada over to eastern Europe's black market.

Pleased with themselves, the three friends decided to fly to Vegas with their wives and spend a week trying their luck at the tables. The way things were going . . . they couldn't lose.

Chapter 11

For several days, Andre's team integrated the information they found on the laptop with what they already knew. The picture of what was happening down on Grand Manan was becoming clearer, but there were still a lot of unknowns.

Kate could only take being paired with Dorsey for just so long before she made it known that she needed a break from his constant chatter. Andre had no other choice than to have them work solo. Things quieted down after that.

Satellite photos showed a large structure close to the docks on Grand Manan, which was believed to be the warehouse that Constable Evers was using to store goods coming into the island.

The information on the laptop revealed that an individual named Felix Lajoie, was apparently acting upon instructions from someone else regarding what goods needed to be moved to a dock over on Passamaquoddy Bay, and when. Whatever happened to the goods after they left the bay was still an unknown. But, somehow, the stolen goods were reaching a market in Canada. How it happened, which market it was, and who the fence was still evaded the Mounties.

Jake managed to bug a phone before he left Grand Manan, but it had yielded nothing of value. Warrants were being sought to access the landline phone records of all incoming and outgoing calls for Constable Evers, Emmett Davis, and Felix Lajoie.

Andre's team reached out to all cell carriers servicing Grand Manan and the Passamaquoddy Bay area to find out which carrier the three men were contracting for cell phone service. Once they knew who the carriers were, they could obtain a file with all text messages and calls made by and received on each phone.

Kate was being kept apprised by INTERPOL and MI6 regarding which ships were believed to be heading west from Portmagee. The work Andre's team was involved in was tedious and mentally draining. By the time three-thirty rolled around each afternoon, they were all ready to unwind and relax.

Lou and Jake spent their days readying the empty cottages for winter, storing boats, winterizing outboard motors, splitting, and stacking firewood, and doing anything else that needed to be done before the snow arrived. It was only during breakfast, dinner and in the evenings that the two men mingled with Andre's team.

Every day after work, Dorsey commandeered the satellite link and was glued to a baseball game. Jake and Duffy challenged each other to a nightly game of ping pong before watching either the movie *Skyfall* or *The Untouchables* with Angelo. Fletcher and Andre usually relaxed at the cribbage board, and Kate would grab a fly rod and fish over by the brook before dinner.

One particular afternoon, Lou was sitting by the rocky point near where Kate was fishing, deep in thought. This was the time of year he contemplated changes that he wanted to make during the offseason. He was brought back to reality when Kate began talking out loud to a huge rainbow trout she'd hooked, that was continually breaking the surface and dancing on top of the water.

Finally, she called out, "Lou, get the net! I've only got a four-pound leader on, and this one's a fighter." Lou walked over and picked up the net, then expertly hauled the trout in when it made a pass close to shore.

"That's a nice fish you brought in, Kate. Would you like me to release it?"

"He put up such a fight, I really should," she said. "but I promised Angelo that I'd bring him a fish today."

"Okay, I'll leave him in the net. You handle a fly rod really well. Where'd you learn to fish like that?"

"From my dad. He was a grand one with the fly rod; loved to fish. The poor man had no sons, so he'd often take me with him when he fished the Shannon or the River Feale."

"So, you've done a lot of fishing."

"A bit, for sure. This fish put up a nice fight, but nothing like an Atlantic salmon does. Now *that's* a powerful fish if you're looking for a fight. It's not that difficult to hook one, it's keeping them on the line and the landing that's the challenge. It takes a lot of patience to play them out before you can net one," she hesitated. "But listen to me, going on about fishing and all."

Lou smiled, "Do you find it helps if you talk to the fish when you have them on the line, like you were doing with this one?"

"Well, it certainly does help to let them know early on that I'm not one to be trifled with."

Lou enjoyed listening to Kate's lilting brogue and her phrasing. Her honesty and spunk reminded him just a little of his wife, Willow.

"Kate, if your intention is to give this fish to Angelo, you'd best hurry while he's still in the kitchen."

"Oh, you're right," she said starting to reel in the line. "I thank you for the help, Lou."

"Here, Kate, just take the fish. I'll take care of the gear for you."

"Well, I thank you again, Lou," she laughed and started off for the kitchen. Lou watched her until she was out of sight before he began reeling in the line. It was the most conversation he'd had with anyone of the opposite sex, besides Alessandra, since Willow had died.

The next morning everyone sat down to a hearty breakfast of trout fillets, crispy potatoes, sauteed spinach and creamy eggs. At the opposite end of the table from Kate and the others, Lou and Fletcher were deep in conversation about deer hunting. While Kate was half listening to Dorsey telling Duffy about the ball game he watched the previous night, she was looking down the table at Lou. She was more than a little surprised that Lou had been so friendly toward her last night, yet he hadn't even acknowledge her existence with a simple nod or hello this morning.

When Andre noticed Alessandra standing by, waiting to clear the table; he pushed his chair back, cleared his throat and announced, "Okay, let's get to work people. Lou, I'd like you to join me for another cup of coffee." The two men walked over to the kitchen, refilled their cups, and headed out the back door

Outside the lodge, the air was brisk; the sun wouldn't peek over the mountain for a while yet. The surface of the lake was as smooth as glass, the only disturbance was an occasional ripple when a fish surfaced to take an insect that had hovered a little too close to the water.

Lou followed Andre down to the dock area where

they'd be away from the noise of the generators. Andre took a seat on the bench next to the boathouse and shifted over to make room for Lou.

Andre took a few moments and inhaled deeply before he began to speak. "Lou, I need to know more about what's going on down on Grand Manan Island. There are way too many missing pieces to this puzzle. We're only going to learn so much looking at data files, satellite photographs, and searching the internet."

"I won't argue that."

"Right. I need to send someone down there to bring back more information. With hunting season coming up, the whole damn division will be shorthanded. Every year it seems to get more challenging to cover the shifts with so many people taking time off to go hunting. After what Jake pulled, I obviously can't send him back down there."

"Nope, Jake's out, that's for sure. He burnt his bridges when he left."

"What I had in mind was sending a couple of people there posing as tourists to look around and come back with some firsthand information on what's happening when a merchant ship comes into port and unloads."

"That would give you better intel on how they're running their operation."

"That's what I figured."

"Who are you planning to send?"

"I was thinking of sending Kate O'Grady down with someone else, that way they'd look like a couple on vacation."

"That could work. So, O'Grady and who else?"

"You."

"Whoa, Andre, I am definitely *not* your man. I've got work to do around here . . . I have a *lot* to do to prepare for winter. Secondly, like I said, I'm not getting involved. Send one of the others down there with her."

"The two of you could pull it off."

"Send her down with Fletcher."

"Ah, come on, Fletcher couldn't pull it off, he's too much of a stiff. No one would believe Kate would be attracted to him."

"So, have her go down with Duffy."

"I can't, Duffy's too critical to the investigation."

"Then send her down with Dorsey."

"Ha, there's no way in *hell* that Kate would agree to go down there with Dorsey."

"Then *you* go with her . . . make it a father and daughter on holiday trip."

"Lou, give this some consideration. We've got a few days before INTERPOL says the next ship from Portmagee will be docking at Grand Manan. Jake could fly the two of you down. You'd have separate rooms on the mainland and could take the ferry back and forth to the island. Then Jake would pick you up and bring you back. One and done, simple as that!"

Lou breathed in the crisp air a few times before shaking his head. "Andre, this is not my fight, and my anchor is holding fast on that. You're my friend and you're welcome to stay here, but that's the extent of my involvement."

"Lou, you wouldn't actually be joining the fight, I'm just asking you to go and look around. It would only take a day, maybe two days, in and out. I know you can do this. You're still on the books as a reserve Mountie. Just give it some thought. Sleep on it, if you have to, and get back to me in the morning."

For the rest of the day, Lou's mind shifted back and forth as he considered helping his friend versus honoring his decision to stay out of any fight that wasn't his own. He'd never done any undercover work before and was uncomfortable with the whole idea of trying to play-act at being someone's significant other on vacation.

By the next morning, he still hadn't come to any decision.

Chapter 12

Early on, Emile Baker, owner of one of Quebec's more profitable container transport companies, took a chance and made a significant investment in his storage facilities near Quebec's port. Soon after, transporting containers to and from the port became his primary business.

Baker's business model was quite different from his competition and had proven to be quite successful. He didn't leave containers sitting at the dock until they were inspected, rather, upon a ship's arrival, Baker's trucks were dispatched to pick up the containers and haul them over to his own facility. Upon arrival, they were held in a secured area until inspected and subsequently scheduled for delivery to their final destination. His schedulers were quick to work out a pickup and delivery plan. As a result, Baker consistently freed up limited dock space at the old port faster than anyone else.

Because of Baker's ingenuity, he enjoyed a larger share of the market as a quid pro quo. His growing fleet of trucks would pick up and deliver pallets and loose freight throughout the provinces of Quebec and New Brunswick and were seen everywhere.

Baker was a serial risk-taker, it was actually a character flaw that he had always had. Growing up, Emile was the kid who was always willing to take a chance on any "dare" or challenge made by a friend. No matter how many times he took a chance and got caught skipping school, he'd chance it again. So, it was only a matter of time before one of his friends nicknamed him "Chance" Baker. The moniker stuck. When Baker graduated from secondary school, he proudly inserted "Chance" in quotes as his middle name in the yearbook.

When he started his business, though, he went with his given name, "Emile". Only those who grew up with him still called him Chance Baker.

After secondary school and a mishap with the law, the judge presiding over Baker's case offered him a choice. He chose to enlist in the Canadian Army Service Corps for four years to avoid jail and have the court expunge any record of him dealing in stolen goods. It was while in Army Service Corps training in *Saint-Jean-sur-Richelieu,* Quebec that he first met Felix Lajoie.

Following training, Baker and Lajoie were both assigned to the same supply unit and tasked with overseeing stores and the daily unloading and distribution of supplies. Working side by side, in roles that were at the bottom rung of the ladder, it didn't take long for them to become friends. At the end of the third week, Baker sat on his bunk, looked over at Lajoie, and said, "I've just about had it with sleeping on a bunk bed, in a military garrison, for minimal pay. This is no life we're living."

"Ha, and throw in all the inefficiencies in this operation and it's a bugger. Ya know, we could easily "game" the system if we wanted to, and make some serious money."

"Yeah, we could, but I just want my life back."

"Well get used to it…we're stuck with this for now."

They talked a good game, but they routinely followed orders, played it straight, and learned the realities of supply and demand, along with hedge buying, and the challenges that go along with backorders.

A few years later, when the Canadian military needed to trim its budget, Emile Baker saw an opportunity to escape the life he was living.

As a cost-saving measure, non-essential first-term enlistees were given the opportunity, under certain conditions, to convert from a four-year active commitment to a two-year active/two-year reserve commitment. Baker just passed the two-year time requirement and jumped at the chance to regain his freedom. Lajoie followed suit. The two pals mustered out together and decided to share an apartment on *Rue Saint-Paul* in the Old Port section of Quebec City, at least until they could figure out what they wanted to do next.

Baker immediately began canvassing the docks looking for work. He was able to secure a job driving a truck with a small local company that showed promise and was willing to take him on. Lajoie was more interested in finding a government job, one where he wouldn't have to work hard.

When the "Keepers" position for the light station on Campobello Island at the mouth of Passamaquoddy Bay in New Brunswick opened up, Lajoie applied for it. Lajoie's active military service was just enough to edge out other applicants and placed him at the top of the list.

The night before Lajoie headed off to New Brunswick, the two friends went bar-hopping. As the evening was coming to an end, Baker raised his glass, "Felix, let's make a pledge that no matter what, we stay in touch with one another."
Lajoie, clinked his glass against Baker's saying, "Let's drink to that."

Over the years, Baker paid attention to detail and continually moved his way up the ladder from driver to assistant foreman, to foreman to general foreman. His career success was largely a result of his unique insight on how to satisfy customers and invoke loyalty from others; marrying Simone, the owner's daughter, also helped. When his father-in-law decided to retire, Baker decided to take a chance and the company became known as E. Baker Trucking.

Baker and his old friend Lajoie managed to stay in touch, and Lajoie steered business Baker's way whenever he heard of some freight on Passamaquoddy Bay that needed to be brought up to Quebec. Eventually, E. Baker Trucking began to enjoy a significant share of the freight being hauled from the bay area.

On Thursday mornings, Baker could be found at the local Tim Horton's having coffee with a few buddies. Along with jokes and good-natured jabs that only good friends can get away with, that was where Baker usually found out what was happening around town.

On this particular day, talk centered on conditions at the port and news reports condemning the number of container ships waiting at anchorage, creating a hazard in the Saint Lawrence River. In between laughing at jokes made about the government's inability to manage things, Baker listened with interest.

During his days in the Quartermaster Corps, Baker had become well acquainted with ferreting out bottlenecks in the system. Upon hearing news of difficulties at the port, Baker decided to go down to the docks to see for himself exactly what was going on.

After a few visits to the port, Baker thought, *No wonder they're backed up. The containers I saw two days ago are still sitting on the docks.* Baker walked back to his pickup shaking his head, thinking, *You'd think they'd be trucks coming and going all day.*

Later that day, he reached out to a friend who had a connection at the port. "I need a favor," he said. "Arrange a meeting with the port authority's chief logistics manager for me."

Baker always believed if you wanted to go big, you needed to act big from the start. He invited the port logistics manager to lunch at *Le Chateau Frontenac.*

They hit it off immediately and during the course of their conversation, the logistics manager unloaded all his frustrations about the containers sitting at the port.

"Our biggest challenge," he said, "comes from having no room for expansion. Secondly, there aren't enough trucking companies to keep up with demand and those that are available seem to take forever to pick up."

The more the logistics manager shared, the more Baker began to see a solution. What came to mind would be a huge risk for him, and he needed time to work it out. Before lunch was over, he presented a suggestion.

"I have an idea on how I could solve your problem, but I'll need a couple of days to work out details. Can I drop off a proposal the first of next week?"

"If you think you have an idea that'll help, I'm all ears!" said the chief. If nothing else, Emile Baker was a smooth talker and had always been able to solicit trust from others.

E. Baker Trucking was located just outside Quebec City in Saint Foy. His facility wasn't exceptionally large; however, it was surrounded by acres of unused farmland, some of which was in receivership that he could easily acquire.

Baker knew the key was moving containers off the dock as soon as they were inspected and released. Scheduling deliveries to the ultimate destination could be accomplished just as easily once the containers were moved over to his yard. The only question was how fast could the Canadian Border Services Agency Inspectors clear and release the containers.

He calculated the number of additional trucks and

drivers he would need to constantly have a truck at the port picking up a container, another enroute with a container to his yard, and another one on the way back to the port. He then factored in the number of additional trucks needed to haul containers to their final destinations. It was a huge business risk that would require an immediate ramp-up. The upside was huge, something that always motivated Baker to take a chance.

By week's end, he had the plan worked out. All he needed was agreement from the port authority, along with a lot of cooperation from the Canadian Border Services Agency (CBSA) that they would add more inspectors to clear the containers on the docks faster.

Baker's proposed plan and bid to the CBSA was received with mixed reviews. The positives were apparent. The negatives were primarily due to the size of his company and that he was relatively unknown. Ultimately, Baker was awarded a six-month trial contract.

He wasted no time pulling in favors to acquire additional land and fast-tracking the installation of fencing to secure the yard. He leased additional trucks and began staffing up for this new business model. With the contract in hand, he had absolutely no trouble arranging for financing and a line of credit. Before the year was out, Baker's approach proved to be so remarkable that the port authority unilaterally converted the contract to an open-ended agreement with E. Baker Trucking.

In gratitude, Baker personally worked each of the relationships with CBSA inspectors and higher ups. Birthdays were recognized with tickets to Montreal Canadian hockey games, or generous gift certificates to the restaurant at Le Chateau Frontenac.

At Christmas, Baker hosted an annual holiday party for all his workers, their spouses or significant others, and anyone else who even remotely helped his business run smoothly, and helped make it the great success it had become.

As years went by and traffic coming into the port increased significantly, Baker presented a new plan designed to clear the docks even faster. It all hinged on whether he would be allowed to transport *uninspected* containers from the docks to a secured area, that he would construct inside his yard. The area would become a CBSA impoundment and be under full control of the inspectors. Nothing would move from the special impoundment until an inspector released a container.

If accepted, this change would not only eliminate containers resting at the dock awaiting inspection, but Baker's schedulers could also get a head start on scheduling delivery to the final destination. Baker felt certain this would be seen as a win/win. So did the port authority which was immediately onboard with the idea. It took CBSA Officials a little longer to approve the change, but with some modifications, it was approved by Ottawa, primarily on the basis of need, but Baker's successful track record was also a factor.

The work environment for inspectors at Baker's yard was far more relaxed than conditions over at the port. It didn't take long for inspectors with the most seniority to negotiate permanent assignment to the yard at E. Baker Trucking. The new model proved to be extremely efficient and integrated the inspectors and Baker's personnel so well that on any given day, if it wasn't for the inspector's uniforms, it would be difficult to distinguish Baker's men from the inspectors. The inspectors assigned to Baker's yard rarely went to the port themselves. Their paperwork was delivered to Port Quebec by Baker's drivers. Any supplies they needed were sent back in a Baker vehicle.

Baker spared no expense taking care of the inspectors' needs. He constructed a building specifically for their comfort. The building was designed to include a washroom with showers, lockers, a kitchenette, television, lounge chairs, a computer, a printer, a desk for writing reports, and file cabinets, all for the exclusive use by the inspectors. Additionally, there was plenty of storage for the official seals they applied to the containers after they were inspected, as well as trash bins to dispose of seals that were removed from containers upon inspection.

The CBSA annual onsite audits consistently showed no irregularities or issues with adherence to regulations at the Baker site. In addition to carting the containers from the docks and ultimately to their final destination, Baker's share of hauling containers going to the port shot up like a hockey stick.

E. Baker Trucking eventually caught the attention of the port authority in Montreal. The logistics manager at Montreal called several times seeking to set up a meeting with Baker to discuss how he might be able to add value for Montreal's port. His company had seemingly become the preferred carrier for everyone who used containers to ship goods out of Quebec's Old Port.

The previous year had been a very profitable year for E. Baker Trucking, so good that for the first time in his entire life Emile Baker felt he could take an entire week off and enjoy a vacation with his wife. During that same time period, E. Baker Trucking also caught the attention of Solicitor Richard More who had been actively searching for a way to get six containers of stolen BMW parts into Canada. When he learned of Baker's unique arrangement with the port authorities, he became even more interested.

Chapter 13

Charles Teal was a low-level member of the Royal Canadian Mounted Police Fredericton administrative cadre. Physically, he was the polar opposite of what most people envision a Mountie to look like. Short and underweight, he walked with a round-shouldered slouch, and although his clothes were clean, he often looked like he was wearing hand-me-downs that he hadn't quite grown into.

Perhaps the most annoying thing about Teal was that he habitually bit his fingernails, often down below the quick, which caused them to bleed. More than a few times he'd been spoken to about leaving bloody fingerprints on paperwork that he passed along.

Day after day, he sat at an old gray metal desk next to a wall of dull gray file cabinets, reviewing and coding every incoming invoice before forwarding it to accounting for payment. The job was extremely repetitive and uninspiring, yet he willing tolerated it because it allowed him to work independently.

Teal has been shuffled around from one dead-end

position to another and passed over for promotion several times before 'time in grade' finally forced his promotion to corporal.

When Teal received an employee rating of "fails to meet minimum requirements" and was placed on probation, his first cousin, Felix Lajoie, stepped in to become his mentor. Lajoie began helping Teal prepare the weekly report that he was required to send to upper command summarizing the prior week's expenditures.

Even before Teal was placed on probation, and before Lajoie began helping, Lajoie had begun discreetly quizzing Teal on certain investigations being conducted by the Mounties. Granted, the conversations were open-ended, but Lajoie often dove deeply into investigation details on the premise of "helping" Teal precisely word his upcoming weekly report.

To amuse himself, Teal liked to keep score on who the big spenders were in the building. Every week he and a few others placed bets on whose project would spend the most money. For the past several weeks, a project led by Andre Girard had been the top spender. Then, Girard's project slipped to third place until a huge cross-charge came over from Canada's National Space Agency.

Lajoie began pushing for more clarity and information on Girard's project, under the premise that the more he knew, the more he could help Teal appropriately phrase it in his report.

"Felix, I can't finish my report this week until I speak with Girard to get more information about what this charge is all about," Teal said. "To say: 'For services related to Slant Range Adjustment and Low Orbit Enhanced Spillover' actually means nothing to me. This sounds like one of those expenses that will never fly under the radar."

"I agree," said Lajoie, "It does sound like an item that

will need more clarification. When can you get to Girard so I can help you word it?"

"He stops off at a Tim Horton's on the way to work for coffee, I'll catch him there. That will be easier than trying to get time on his calendar, his admin is an unyielding gatekeeper. I think he may be on vacation now, though, I haven't seen him at Horton's for a few weeks.

Teal was completely unaware that Lajoie had an entirely different purpose for wanting to help him with his reports. Lajoie had found the perfect opportunity to manipulate his cousin for his own selfish purpose.

When Teal failed to run into Girard for yet another week at Horton's, he approached Girard's admin to get on his schedule.

"Sergeant Girard is not in now, and I'm not able to schedule any appointments for him presently," the administrator said.

"Could you ask him to call me?"

"I'll relay the message, however, to my knowledge he is not returning calls."

Another week went by and Andre Girard's special project topped Teal's private list of big spenders. By midweek, Teal phoned Lajoie.

"Felix, I just don't get it. Everyone is extremely tight-lipped about Girard's project, even my usual 'go to' sources are in the dark on what Girard is up to. I've never had a problem until now obtaining whatever information I needed to know about a project, regardless of the security classification that's been assigned. But I can't get to square one, and I can't get in to see Gerard either."

Felix Lajoie's instincts had been on alert the past few weeks due to his cousin's ongoing frustration with confidentiality surrounding Girard's project. Bureaucratic behavior had always mystified Lajoie, but this "blackout" appeared to be limited to just this one project. He thought to himself, *I suspect far more is going on than my dear cousin is aware of.*

As days passed, Lajoie became even less comfortable not knowing exactly what Girard's project involved, so he decided to take a different tact with his cousin.

"Charles, you're struggling way too much trying to pull everything together on this Girard project. You're also not getting anywhere *near* the support you should be receiving. Here's an idea that could really help you stand out. Why not go on the Internet and pull down a data visualization software application."

"A what?"

"A data visualization software application," Lajoie said slowly. "Then load every expense that Girard's project has ever incurred into it. The software will provide you with a virtual picture of what's going on. Then we can analyze it."

"I've never heard of that. I'll have to check with the data center first."

"No, no, no . . . you won't need to do that," Lajoie said quickly. "It'll be safe to download yourself. Just give it a try. I can help if you need me."

Soon Teal had downloaded the software and begun keying in every expense related to Girard. It didn't take long before the software developed a conclusion on Girard's project.

Speaking to no one in particular, Teal whispered, "So, the software says that Girard is off site running a live operation. But why is he wasting money on that? Everything he needs to run an op exists right here at headquarters? What's he really up to?"

Teal generated a full report from the software and emailed a copy over to Lajoie. Once Lajoie reviewed the report he called Teal. "Charles, I believe you've nailed it. He's offsite somewhere running up a lot of unnecessary expenses.

We'll have to work on finding the right words so you can diplomatically question the purpose of these unnecessary expenses in your next report; maybe then you'll get some answers."

Over the next few days, Teal got wind of a rumor that Girard's team was operating in conjunction with MI6 and INTERPOL regarding a smuggling operation. He tried reaching Lajoie, but Lajoie's phone was busy. It was close to lunch, so he just left a voice message for Lajoie to call and he headed down to the cafeteria.

When Lajoie learned about the rumor that MI6 and INTERPOL were involved with Girard, he instantly connected the dots and passed word along to Evers on Grand Manan about the secret project and the rumors. Evers tried reaching Sean Tinker, in Portmagee, but Tinker wasn't answering his phone. All he could do was leave a voice message. When Tinker picked up the message, he immediately called Evers back.

"Orson, thanks for the heads up! Stay on top of this; we need to know everything these Mounties are doing. If anything changes, call me; I don't care what time it is."

Sean Tinker then summarized the information he had received in an email and forwarded it to the three principal members of Imperial Trading.

Chapter 14

When the three principals of Imperial Trading next gathered at the Garrick Club for their weekly repartee, Solicitor More casually mentioned that he may have found a way to get the BMW parts past the Canadian customs inspectors.

"You're among friends, my good fellow, do tell us more, Solicitor!"

Richard shared the unique arrangement that E. Baker Trucking seemed to enjoy with the port authority at the Old Port of Quebec. "What I haven't figured out is how we might turn Baker into an Imperial Trading player, either willingly or unwittingly," More said.

"Well, we'll just have to make him an offer that he can't refuse!" Herbert Maxwell offered.

"I'm afraid that only happens in the cinema, Max," Clark Hastings, the third partner, said

By the following week, both Maxwell and More had made a number of inquiries on E. Baker Trucking and had a pretty comprehensive profile on both the company and Emile

Baker. However, there was no indication that Emile Baker was anything other than a straight shooter who played by the rules.

"Didn't one of you say that his mates nicknamed him 'Chance' at one time?" Hastings asked.

"Yes, but that was years ago," Maxwell said.

"No matter, have someone interview a few of those chaps; tell them *Business Matters Magazine,* or *British Economy,* or someone is doing an article on him and they're interested in how the nickname 'Chance' came about."

Once it was known that Emile Baker had a penchant for taking risks in his earlier days, ideas on how to compromise him begin to take shape.

"Sounds as though he likes to gamble," Hastings said. "We should be able to parlay that into something. Maybe he wins our 'Vendor Appreciation Award', which just happens to be an all-expense-paid trip to Vegas, where he'll meet the principals of Imperial Trading and receive a handsome amount of chips to play."

"Nice idea Hastings, but we don't have an award like that, and we don't actually do any business with E. Baker Trucking, that I'm aware of," Maxwell said.

Hastings looked at him for a long moment. "We can *start* doing business with Baker. Hell, we ship enough bloody stuff over to Canada, and an award is nothing more than a participation trophy anyway. We can position it as a lottery; every vendor that we've successfully done business with gets their name thrown into the hat, and this year's lucky winner will just happen to be Emile Baker! Airfare, hotel, gambling chips for him, and spending money for his wife; first-class all the way, all on Imperial Trading!"

"Think he'll bite?"

"Richard, if we make the invitation fancy enough, he should. Hell, we're playing to his ego . . . don't all those types like to feel they're up on a pedestal now and again?"

"Okay," Maxwell said, "so how do we play the mark? What's the sting?"

"Well, I think we stick to him like glue; let him think we're his long-lost best mates, all four of us out to have a good time, one for all and all for one! One of us will always be with him. Let him win at the tables a few nights, get a feel for how he plays his hands; then one night, he'll, unfortunately, lose big. We'll push a pile of chips in front of him, so he stays in the game, then we'll clean him out again. Once that happens, we'll own him!"

"Hastings, that is brilliant!"

"Max, didn't we do something similar with that French inspector in Monaco a few years ago?"

"I believe you're referring to the investment scam that we set up," Maxwell said. "That was different, but greed is such a wonderful thing when it's manipulated appropriately, isn't it?"

"We'll have to put some parameters around when this occurs, of course, otherwise we'll never be able to coordinate calendars among ourselves and our wives. Clark, when does Parliament recess? We should offer him some dates during that window."

Within two weeks Emile Baker received the following overseas cable:

Congratulations to E. Baker Trucking. Stop. You have won Imperial Trading's Annual Vendor Appreciation Award. Stop. Further information to follow. Stop.

Two weeks later, a very impressive-looking package was hand-delivered by courier to Emile Baker, personally, for his signature. Inside were details explaining the award:

Our sincere congratulations to Emile Baker.

The Annual Vendor Appreciation Award is being presented to the president of E. Baker Trucking and is non-transferable. The Award Ceremony will occur in Las Vegas, Nevada, U.S.A.

Transportation to and from Las Vegas will be provided by private jet. Hotel accommodations for one week at the Hotel Bellagio are included.

Upon arrival Mr. and Mrs. Emile Baker will join the owners of Imperial Trading, and their wives, for dinner that evening, followed by a formal presentation of the award plaque along with ten thousand dollars in chips, good at all tables in the Bellagio Casino and two thousand dollars in 'Vegas Money' good anywhere on the strip.

The remainder of the week will be yours to enjoy.

RSVP within two weeks indicating which of the three weeks offered in the accompanying document you are selecting, so that proper arrangements may be made.

Congratulations,
Imperial Trading

Emile immediately called his wife. "Simone, remember that award I said I somehow won a couple of weeks ago?" he asked her excitedly.

"No, not really."

"Well, listen to this: I've just received the details on it. We're going to Vegas for a week, all expenses paid and there's even a cash award! They're putting us up at the Bellagio."

"Can I see this?" Simone said now with interest.

"Yes, yes, of course. I'll bring everything home tonight and we can decide which week we'll go. Ha! talk about timing. We were looking to go somewhere and now we'll get to do it on somebody else's dime!" That was something Chance Baker always believed made him a winner.

Chapter 15

Emile Baker and his wife were anxious to see Las Vegas. "I'm so happy we're flying on a private jet," Simone said. "I've heard story after story about luggage being lost or delayed due to sloppy baggage handling between connecting flights on the regular airlines."

"Let's just relax, Simone. We're going to have a good time."

When they arrived at Quebec City's terminal for private aircraft, Imperial Trading's Gulfstream G650 was sitting on the tarmac waiting to fly them to Vegas. Because the flight wasn't originating from an airport that had a pre-clearance agreement with the United States, Baker, and his wife, would wait on the tarmac in Vegas until customs officials came out to the private plane to clear them for entry into the US.

The flight was smooth and uneventful. Once they reached Vegas, the plane was cleared quickly; Baker and his wife disembarked, and carried their luggage to the east side of the terminal where a limo awaited them.

When they reached the Bellagio, they were told they had already been checked in and were given key cards to their room. As soon as their luggage was delivered, Baker said, "Simone, I'm going to head down to the casino to try my hand at blackjack."

"Okay, I'll unpack and freshened up, just remember we have a five-thirty." Baker's wife had no interest in gambling, she was looking forward to shopping on the strip and seeing a few shows.

Downstairs, the tables were quite full, but after walking around Baker found a ten-dollar blackjack table with an open seat at shortstop. When Baker played blackjack, he preferred to sit at third base, but those seats were all taken. Third base was the seat that often influenced whether the table, as a whole, would win or lose. Even though he didn't play blackjack often, Baker had a fairly decent command of the game, but poker was his real game.

After a few hands, it was obvious to Baker that the guy sitting at first base was not very skilled at the basic strategy of the game. After watching the woman at third base play a few hands, he realized she had absolutely no business even sitting at the table, let alone in *that* seat. When the table stakes were raised to a fifteen-dollar minimum, Baker left and headed back to his room.

At 5:30 p.m., Baker and his wife arrived at the private dining room where they were immediately greeted by Lord Hastings, then introduced to everyone. It was prearranged that the ladies would be seated together during cocktails, as would the men. Baker noted that each group had an open fourth chair.

As soon as Simone sat down, the wives began talking about the shows that were on the strip for the week. As they talked, Evelyn Tinsley Maxwell noticed that Simone Baker had the identical Gucci handbag she had.

"Simone, don't you just love that bag? I love mine, but the strap has a slight tear. I'm dropping it off at Gucci's while we're here; they said they'll replace the strap."

"You've got to be kidding!" Simone said. "The same thing happened to mine a week after I brought it home! My husband wanted to take it to a shoe cobbler to fix it, I said: Hello! Are you out of your mind? This is a *Gucci.* I brought it right back to them and they replaced the strap for me!"

The Gucci connection was enough for the wives to immediately hit it off, and they continued to chit-chat. Talk among the men focused on which form of gambling they would pursue that evening. Baker shared, "I had a bit of a trying experience at a blackjack table earlier tonight. For some reason, I thought that people who came to Vegas knew how to play cards."

Richard More chuckled, "First time we came here, we learned quickly that you need to sit at the more expensive tables; that's where you'll find the *real* players."

When the conversation shifted to poker, Baker was all ears. Poker seemed to be the game of choice for everyone tonight. However, he was unaware there was an unspoken agreement among the other three that they never sat at the same poker table with one another. But he was pleased when the men said that he must join them after dinner in the poker room.

Richard More, stood up, cleared his throat and announced they should all move into the adjacent room where dinner was about to be served. Once Emile entered the room, he realized the background music he had been enjoying wasn't a soundtrack, but rather a trio that had been playing chamber music all the while in their private dining room.

Later, as the table was being cleared of dishes, Richard More stood up again, and using a spoon, lightly tapped his water glass to get everyone's attention.

"Ladies and gentlemen, may I have your attention? Emile, would you come around to me please?" There was a pause while Emile got up and walked around the table to stand next to Solicitor More.

"Emile Baker, it is with extreme pleasure that on behalf of Imperial Trading, I present to you the Imperial Trading Vendor of the Year Award, along with your Bellagio chips and Vegas Money! Thank you for helping us be the success that we are! We look forward to continuing our partnership with you."

After polite applause, Solicitor More continued. "Now ladies, if you'll excuse us, I believe that your husbands and I plan to momentarily adjourn to the poker room."

Before Baker left, he gave his wife a kiss; she wished him luck and let him know that she wouldn't wait up. As Baker followed the three men into the poker room, all four wives headed into the lounge.

Once in the poker room, all three men from the UK headed off in different directions. Baker followed Richard More for no other reason than he was the master of ceremonies at the dinner. The two men traveled to the upper level and took a seat at the same table directly across from one another. The table was a no-limit Texas Hold'em game with a one-grand buy-in. Baker remained at the table until well into the early morning. He'd had a few good hands and was up more than a grand when he decided to call it quits for the night.

The following morning, Baker called down to have breakfast brought up to their room. As he poured coffee, he shared with Simone how enjoyable his night had been. His wife said, "I had a marvelous time with the wives after dinner. We've made plans to go shopping today and take in a matinee." Baker smiled to himself, he was hoping to be able to have a late lunch with the husbands.

He found the men easily and during lunch, the talk was mostly about how everyone did the night before, and what their game plan was for later today. Baker was somewhat surprised he had been accepted into their circle so quickly.

Toward the end of lunch, Maxwell asked, "Emile, I hope you are planning to return to the Bellagio's poker room this evening? They have the best tables in town."

Baker hadn't made up his mind at that point and actually had been thinking that he needed to spend a night out on the strip with his wife.

"Emile," Hastings said, "I know what you're thinking, but listen, our wives are enjoying each other's company . . . how often do we get an opportunity to indulge ourselves? Your place is with us tonight at the Bellagio's tables."

Baker agreed to meet them that evening, but as he walked away, he wondered why he had felt somewhat pressured.
Later, during dinner, Baker listened to his wife's story about her shopping adventures, and the matinee. Again, she gave him permission to gamble to his heart's content that night, but, as before, said that she wouldn't wait up.

After dinner, when Baker entered the poker room, Clark Hastings stood up and waved. When Baker came over to him, Hastings whispered, "The tables were filling up, so I saved you a seat across from me."

"Thank you; it looks packed tonight."

The game at the table was again a high-stakes Texas Hold'em with a grand buy-in. Baker played his hands well and managed to win a few hands early but ended the night on a losing streak. He was down more than three grand when he left the table.

The next morning, Baker was moody and disappointed with himself for taking the foolish chances that he had and staying with a few poor hands. He was determined to not only win *back* the money he was now down but also to come out ahead at the end of the night.

Herbert Maxwell called Baker's room and left a message that there was a nice, high-stakes invitation-only poker game at the Bellagio later that he knew Baker would enjoy. He asked Emile to meet him in the lobby at seven.

These three are really high rollers, Baker thought.

After dinner, Simone Baker joined the other women, and they headed off to attend yet another show. Once more, Baker was free to gamble the night away.

When Emile arrived in the lobby, Maxwell was already waiting for him. "Emile, follow me, the table is on the far side of the room, they're holding two seats for us." After being introduced, Emile excused himself, walked over to the cage, and converted all the cash he had brought to Vegas into chips.

Unknown to Baker, the three principals of Imperial Trading had spent a few hours earlier discussing how Baker tended to play his hands, what facial expressions to watch for when he was bluffing, and how he acted when the hand he held was a decent one. The cards began falling in Baker's favor and, so far, he was up five grand. The table had no limit, and the pots were often extremely rich. Maxwell constantly studied Baker's expressions and movements.

Well after midnight, Baker had been dealt a straight, Jack high, and felt pretty confident. Betting went around the table several times until only he and Maxwell remained in. Baker noticed that Maxwell seemed slightly vexed, breathing a little heavily and nervously shuffling his cards, all of which made him even more confident that his straight was the winning hand. He went all-in with every one of his chips and called. Maxwell met Baker's anti and made his own call. Baker laid out his Jack high straight, a mix of spades and clubs. Maxwell had palmed the cards that he had been dealt and turned over the red flush he had hidden up his sleeve from the beginning. Baker was completely wiped out of every chip that he had won at the table and his entire bankroll.

Knowing he had just cleaned Baker out, Herbert Maxwell pushed fifteen grand in chips over to Baker saying, "Emile, you're keeping this game interesting for me, I'm going to loan you some chips. Please, stay in the game."

"I can't accept that."

"Yes, you can, do it for me, *please,* I'm asking you to stay in as a friend." Maxwell pushed another twenty grand in chips over to Baker. "Please . . . as a favor to me, stay in the game."

Baker paused for longer than a moment before signaling that he would remain at the table. But he was so shaken from losing such a large amount of money that he was totally off his game now. In an effort to recoup his losses, he began taking one risk after another, even when he knew that he should have folded. Baker's body language and facial expressions were telegraphing the strength of his hands to Maxwell.

Over the course of the next half hour, Baker proceeded to lose the thirty-five grand that Maxwell had lent him before finally dropping out of the game.

He apologized for his behavior and retired for the night.

The next morning, Simone noticed that Emile was acting very peculiar. "Emile, dear, are you all right? Is something wrong?"

"No, no nothing is wrong," he lied. "I just . . . I just . . . I think I may have mixed my drinks last night and am feeling it this morning, that's all. Nothing for you to worry about."

"Okay, but you are acting rather strangely. Maybe you shouldn't stay out so late tonight."

Later that day, he again joined the three men from the UK for lunch. The conversation was a bit awkward until Richard More spoke.

"Emile, Max told us what happened to you last night. I want you to know that this has happened to each and every one of us at one time. I know you're concerned, but don't be. We're friends, and we have an idea on how you can settle the debt."

Baker was beyond embarrassed and ashamed of his behavior. He knew Simone would be furious with him, if she ever found out how much he had lost. If this had been a marker that he held with the casino, he could have been brought up on criminal charges. He had never been in a situation where he owed someone thirty-five thousand dollars before. Now, he was all ears as to what they had to say.

Hastings broke the silence first. "Emile, we're in the business of moving goods between Europe and Canada, if you would agree to help us from time to time with our operation, you could easily work off the debt you owe Max."

Richard More went on to explain, "Our operation is small time, there's not a lot of volume; we fly totally under the radar screen, and everybody wins. It's funny, we were actually about to start looking for someone who hauls freight in Quebec."

Baker had always played the game above board, but at this moment, it didn't appear he had many alternatives. He was trapped, and he knew it. Maxwell sensed that Baker was struggling with what he was hearing. "Emile, let me reassure you, we've been doing this for years. There's a number of checks and balances in the system, specifically designed to keep everyone safe and happy. All we're asking is that you circumvent customs on a few overseas cargo containers that we'll send over to you. Simply sit on them for a while."

"Let me sleep on it," he said. "I'm appreciative of your offer." But he knew exactly what they meant, and he didn't like it. Baker's business was highly leveraged, and he'd already used up the full line of credit he had with his banks. He had no personal reserves; everything he had was tied up in his business. He'd even taken the equity out of his home and put that in the business. If he tried to suddenly take thirty-five grand out of his working capital, he'd risk missing payroll and bankrupting the business.

Reluctantly, he nodded his head as he said, "Okay, I'll become a part of Imperial Trading's network, but only until I've worked off the debt I owe."

Hasting smiled. "You'll be fine Emile, trust me."

"One of our senior people will be in touch with you soon to work out the details on the role that you'll play," Richard More said.

Maxwell placed a hand on Baker's forearm. "Emile, as a sign of good faith and friendship, we're going to advance you ten thousand now. We want you and Simone to have enough spending money to enjoy the rest of your vacation."

Three days later, Emile Baker and his wife boarded Imperial Trading's Gulfstream G650 and flew home. Throughout the flight, Baker chastised himself for his stupidity.

Have I just sold my soul to the devil for forty-five grand to save my business?

Chapter 16

On the flight home from Vegas, Emile Baker worked out the approach he would use to pay off his debt to Imperial Trading. The plan had some risks, but Baker was confident the goodwill he had with the Port Authority, and the trust inspectors had in him would provide enough cover for his plan to work. He totally abhorred having to go down this path, but there didn't seem to be another option.

"Emile, are you all right?" Simone asked. "You haven't spoken a single word to me during this entire flight!"

"I'm sorry, Simone, it's just . . . my mind has been totally focused on business."

"Please, Emile, relax. It will still be there when we get back. This was a lovely vacation."

Regardless, Emile went back to mulling over his plan. For the past few years, he had been authorized to remove incoming containers from the port prior to their inspection and transporting them directly to his yard without any problems. Containers that hadn't been inspected were all kept separate in an impoundment area that Baker had fenced off within his yard. Then, once the inspectors cleared the containers, Baker's people were notified, and the containers were moved to the general holding area where they awaited transport to their final destination.

Over a year ago, Baker had his IT support people develop an automated system as a favor for the inspectors, which significantly reduced the time it took them to complete their paperwork. Baker had designed the system himself, and as a result, became intimately familiar with the process the inspectors used to clear incoming containers. Unknown to the inspectors, he still had access to the system.

With this new turn of events, Baker felt it would be too risky to have containers from Imperial Trading brought into his yard, and decided he would look around for another location.

His regular drivers could pick up containers at the dock and drop them off at any location he specified, so that wasn't an issue. But once the "special" containers began arriving, they would be moved from the port and Baker, not the inspectors would log them into the inspector's system as having been cleared. It wasn't complicated, it was just different.

Shortly after Baker arrived home, he heard that a hangar at the airport was available to lease. He immediately took a ride over to Quebec's *Jean Lesage* International Airport to check it out. As soon as Baker saw the hangar, he knew it was perfect for what he had in mind. It was located on the far side of the airport in an area of other air freight hangars. Customs inspectors were only present when a plane arrived, or when they were called to clear outgoing freight. Other than changing out the locks, the building was quite suitable. Once Baker signed the lease, he sent word to the email address he had been provided.

Ready, his text simply said.

He was now operational, and all he would need was the name of the ship that would be docking at Quebec and any identifying markers on the containers. Each container would have its own paperwork specifically stating the container was to be picked up by E. Baker Trucking and held until delivery was requested.

The only thing Baker still needed was a list of unused codes the inspectors assigned when a container had been cleared; he also needed a box of metal seals that inspectors attached to the containers after inspecting them. Baker decided it would be safer, and less noticeable, if he used codes from the series the port used rather than the series assigned at his yard.

The seals proved easy to acquire, as the inspectors carelessly left them hanging around inside the building. They weren't even inventoried, nor did they have specific serial numbers to identify them.

Within weeks of notifying Imperial Trading that he was ready, Baker received a text letting him know that two cargo containers had been shipped with explicit instructions that they were to be picked up by E. Baker Trucking and held until he received further instructions regarding their final destination.

On the day the ship was scheduled to arrive at Quebec's Old Port, Baker was waiting at the docks. Well known by the stevedores, he let on that he was specifically there to pick up two cargo containers. The stevedores could care less which containers were inspected at the Old Port versus over at E. Baker Trucking. And, after Baker greased a few palms, the two containers were located and unloaded. Baker personally drove one truck and had another driver follow him over to his new storage facility near the airport.

Security going into the freight area was pretty much non-existent. Once they arrived at the hangar, Baker opened the huge hangar doors and both trucks dropped off their containers.

Baker then headed back to the yard, satisfied that this approach was going to work. The other driver returned to the port completely unaware that anything unusual had occurred. The driver simply continued hauling containers back and forth to Baker's yard for the rest of his shift.

When Baker arrived at his office, he sent a cryptic text message. *Two boxes picked up, now secured, will clear customs in 24 hours.*

Shortly, Baker received a message back: *Agent in Montreal will contact U soon.*

A few days later, Baker received another message: *More containers arriving soon... details 2 follow.*

It had taken more than several years for Imperial Trading to find the right opportunistic people they could trust to create such an infrastructure across Europe which would enable them to move illicit goods in and out of Portmagee.

Since the overwhelming majority of BMW parts shipped to eastern Canada were made in Germany and sent over from Port Hamburg, Germany, Solicitor More had recently recruited a German Federal Customs Service executive assigned to Port Hamburg to join the network. Both he and the executive inside BMW were anxious to supplement their income.

Until recently, Richard More hadn't known of any practical way to drop BMW parts off in Grand Manan, Canada, and move them over to Passamaquoddy Bay without detection. In the past, Imperial Trading's shipments entering Canada had been small enough that any ship could transport them to Grand Manan, and any Canadian trucker could be engaged to make a pickup on Passamaquoddy Bay.

But now, Emile Baker would satisfy the missing piece to the puzzle Imperial Trading needed to move stolen BMW parts across the pond.

When six containers loaded with BMW parts destined for Canada arrived at Port Hamburg, they were marked as "received" and new documentation was created. The identifying markings on the containers were painted over, and new Bills of Lading were created using a different city of origination. In a matter of days, the containers were traveling to the Old Port of Quebec, each with a new identity, where Emile Baker would warehouse them until delivery was requested.

BMW shipped car parts to Canada twice a year. The biannual shipments had worked well for manufacturing; the only variations to production runs and what was shipped, had been a result of safety recalls.

It usually took about two weeks for the parts to arrive in Canada once they left the factory. German engineering believed they had perfected the art of production planning to the point they knew precisely what parts would be needed in Canada based on the age and models of cars there, and when those parts would be needed.

Imperial Trading's plan was to store the parts with Baker until such time as the dealership's inventory of spare BMW parts in eastern Canada were depleted to the point they were unable to repair their customer's cars. Once that happened, BMW parts would begin to become available on the black market.

When BMW failed to receive confirmation from Port Hamburg that the six shipping containers had been loaded onto the ship they were scheduled for, inquiries were sent out and the port put a trace on the containers. The port's investigators were stymied; they had the documents showing the containers leaving the BMW plant and entering Port Hamburg, but from that point on it was a mystery.

Within a month, the Canadian dealerships began receiving pressure from a few customers about the long lead times to repair their cars. In a gesture of goodwill, dealerships began providing customers whose cars "needed" repairs and were undriveable, with "loaners" while they awaited parts. The dealerships began putting pressure on BMW to send an interim allotment of parts. Every department inside BMW was still pointing fingers. A full month after delivery of the parts should have occurred, BMW still hadn't arrived at a solution.

The Imperial Trading plan was about to succeed.

Chapter

17

As the smuggling operation continued to evolve, it became more about "the rush" and seeing how far the envelope could be pushed without getting caught. Motivation among the members of Imperial Trading was fueled by seeing who could score the biggest prize. Competition became intense, and consequently, members were taking greater risks on a regular basis.

Sean Tinker rarely called Solicitor Richard More, so when More saw Tinker's ID on the phone, he immediately picked up.

"Yes?"

"Tinker here. Word is the Mounties have a base somewhere in eastern Canada tasked with shutting us down."

"Where?"

"New Brunswick, somewhere off the beaten track."

"Well, that's bloody not good enough, old chap. We need to know *exactly* where it is."

"Felix is trying to find out."

"Brilliant. Inform him that *trying* is not an effective strategy!"

"Davis' laptop was taken."

"Should we be concerned?"

"He said it was password protected."

"That's rubbish. It sounds like things have become sloppy in Grand Manan, Sean. We need to nip this while we can."

"I'll keep you informed."

"I expect no less."

Imperial Trading's first priority had always been to protect the three partners, and secondly, if possible, to preserve the game. Solicitor More immediately reached out to his network for additional information.

Over the years, he had meticulously pieced together a network of confidants and reliable sources, every bit as complex as a spider's web. The network deliberately contained duplicate sources for the same information just so Richard More could check the information's accuracy.

Shortly, a small piece of information regarding New Brunswick surfaced.

"Richard, Cecil here."

"Yes, Cecil, what is it?"

"New Brunswick recently came up on the Worldwide Air Traffic Control database."

"And?"

"The Moncton, New Brunswick Area Control Center, has designated a small sector in a remote area of central New Brunswick as a restricted area."

"And?"

"Only pre-approved aircraft are allowed into that sector."

"And?"

"No further information is available. Calls into

Moncton ACC are not being returned."

"I need more on this. Stay on top of it and keep me informed."

Constable Orson Evers faxed Richard More the newspaper article that appeared in the weekly Quoddy Tides about the incident on Grand Manan Island which sent two unnamed men to Grand Manan's hospital, and required a third man to be airlifted to the Regional Medical Center in Lubec, Maine. The article also stated that a laptop had been taken during the altercation. One of More's French contacts faxed him a brief report indicating the possible repositioning of communication satellites over eastern Canada, but it wasn't anything that he was able to corroborate.

Shortly after More forwarded this information to his partners he received a phone call from Herbert Maxwell.

"Richard, I read your message; are we at risk?"

"I don't believe we are, Max. Whatever safeguards we needed to take, were taken. However, we may need to terminate one of our people on Grand Manan."

"Evers is the key man on Grand Manan; he would be difficult to replace because he oversees everything on the island."

"Forget Evers," Richard More growled. "He's in so deep, he's not a risk. I don't believe Lajoie is a risk either, and his contact inside the RCMP is critical if we hope to get to the bottom of what these Mounties are up to."

"I think Davis is a risk," Maxwell said, "one that could result in U.S. Customs getting involved."

"Davis is expendable. I've long thought that he needed to be taken out."

The discussion was over, but it was obvious the

partners needed more information on this temporary RCMP base camp. Within hours, their network produced someone capable of not only discreetly dispatching Davis but was also skilled enough to reconnoiter the Mounties' secret base, and report back.

Chapter 18

Back at the lodge, Kate had received a number of posts from INTERPOL detailing the disappearance of goods in transit, many of which were suspected to have been diverted to Portmagee, Ireland.

The majority of marine traffic going in and out of Portmagee's harbor were small fishing boats. Commercial traffic was handled by a privately owned operation run by Sean Tinker who had shown up a couple of times on radar screens of both INTERPOL and MI6 as a person of interest.

After some searching, Kate was able to match the names of ships sailing from Portmagee against names of ships appearing in several files on the laptop that Jake had brought in.

"Now, that's interesting," she said out loud, "MI6 is matching names of ships leaving Portmagee to those known to have or suspected of having turned off their satellite tracking signals when approaching the Bay of Fundy. They're also back-checking to verify if the ship's captains filed their course before leaving Portmagee and whether it showed them entering the Bay of Fundy."

Constable Orson Evers seems to consistently be unable to offer any information regarding goods flowing into Grand Manan. He and the lighthouse keeper, Felix Lajoie, had now been identified as probable accomplices in the smuggling ring.

Dorsey had tacked a huge map of Passamaquoddy Bay onto the wall and was plotting the known drop-off points with colored tacks. He was only halfway through the list found in the laptop files, but the map already looked like a pincushion. Kate had been going through the files for hours trying to determine what happened after the goods reached Passamaquoddy Bay. All she could see was that the goods were being dropped off at various harbors along the bay, but there was no apparent consistency, and the trail stopped there.

As she pushed back from the table, she said in a voice barely loud enough for anyone else to hear, "From Tinker to Evers to . . . who?"

Dorsey automatically reacted. "To Chance."

"What did you just say?"

"I said 'to Chance.' From Tinker to Evers to Chance." His voice was flat and emotionless as he continued typing away.

"And who, pray tell, is Chance?"

Dorsey sat back, and stretched, "Frank Leroy Chance. He was the first baseman for the Chicago Cubs back in the early 1900's. Anybody that follows baseball has heard the old saying 'From Tinker to Evers to Chance.' They were one of the greatest double play combinations in the history of baseball."

Kate rolled her eyes and dismissed Dorsey's comment as more baseball rubbish, then headed to the kitchen for a cup of tea with Alessandra. Talking to no one in particular, Dorsey continued explaining how significant a double play was in the game of baseball as he typed away on his keyboard.

Duffy overheard the exchange and shook his head, laughing to himself. At that moment, he was focused on gathering information on Felix Lajoie to create a more complete profile on whoever he was; however, the detective in him made a mental note to later google the word 'chance' on the internet, just to see what came up.

As the only two females in camp, Alessandra and Kate gathered each morning and afternoon to chat over a cup of tea. Most days, Alessandra let Kate know when the water was ready for tea; but today, Kate just needed to get away from Dorsey for a while. Lately, she had been savoring her time with Alessandra and listening to stories about the life she and Angelo enjoyed at Havre de Poisson.

Alessandra was impressed with this young, attractive Irish lass and wondered if she might be a good match for her "adopted" son, Lou. During their talks, Alessandra subtly asked a few probing questions. She learned that Kate had once been engaged, but that her fiancé was killed in a hit-and-run accident outside Dublin a few years ago.

Today, their chat was only a short one. When Kate returned to her desk, she had received a message from INTERPOL that six international shipping containers destined for Quebec City had subsequently disappeared after being received at Port Hamburg, Germany. The containers were believed to have been hijacked and possibly had left the port under different paperwork.

Portmagee, Ireland, had been ruled out as a destination since the harbor was far too small for a container ship of the size that sailed from Hamburg to dock.

"So, the question now becomes: If the containers are on a ship, which ship is it?" Kate asked. Officials at Hamburg's port authority were checking destinations of every ship that sailed subsequent to the containers being received at Hamburg. The port authority was already under significant pressure from BMW, and various insurance underwriters, to recover the lost cargo.

So far, only one ship from Hamburg was heading across the Atlantic. Its destination was the Old Port in Quebec City. There was no record of the missing containers being loaded onto the ship; however, Quebec had been asked to compare every container offloaded against the ship's manifest as filed when leaving Hamburg.

Duffy looked at his computer screen. He had pulled together a pretty interesting profile on Felix Lajoie: He grew up on Grand Manan and frequently traveled there; spent two years active duty and two years inactive duty in the Canadian Army Service Corps. He mustered out early, briefly living on Rue Saint-Paul in the Old Port section of Quebec City, and for the past decade, has been the keeper at the Head Harbor Light Station, on Campobello Island. The only criminal record that Duffy was able to find on Lajoie was a misdemeanor. Court records showed that he had been arrested once for public intoxication and firing a weapon within city limits.

After lunch, Duffy decided to google the word "chance" just for kicks. Aside from the definition of the word, there were a few results referencing, "From Tinker to Evers to Chance." Duffy read one entry that said their fame originated from a poem written about them, not from their prowess on the diamond. He decided to tuck that one away and have some fun with Dorsey later. There were eight more pages of results for the word "chance." Strictly out of boredom, Duffy scrolled down to page seven where the word "chance" was connected to a Canadian secondary school's reunion site.

Curiosity made him click on it and he found someone

by the name of Emile "Chance" Baker had served on the class reunion committee. Then, Duffy clicked on the hotlink and learned that Emile Baker currently operated a trucking business serving New Brunswick and Quebec.

His interest was piqued. He drilled down a little further and discovered that Baker had been in the Canadian Army Service Corps and took advantage of a one-time opportunity to convert a four-year enlistment into a two-year active/two-year reserve commitment then briefly lived on Rue Saint Paul in Quebec City. The coincidences between Baker and Lajoie were just too great not to warrant further investigation.

Duffy pulled up E. Baker Trucking and saw the majority of business was transporting containers to and from the Port of Quebec. Baker also had a large share of the smaller freight business coming up to the Port of Quebec from New Brunswick. He read how the company had grown rapidly over the past several years, and that Baker owned a significant property near the Port of Quebec where containers were stored before being released for transport to their final destination. Then he closed off the page, stood up and stretched.

"Dorsey, I think you may have just hit one out of the park for us with this friggin' bizarre obsession you have for baseball trivia!

"What?"

"Never mind."

Duffy sent a text over to Kate: *C me - may have a lead on Chance.*

Chapter 19

By day, Oliver Clarke worked for a street vendor at London's Whitecross Market. There was nothing memorable about Clarke; he blended into the busy marketplace so well that most people walked right past him, day after day, and never noticed him.

Every day from eleven until two in the afternoon, Clarke stood behind a glass case of pork pies, and when people pointed to one, he would wrap it up and ring up the sale. The pay was minimal and his tips usually exceeded the wages he was paid. But Clarke didn't mind the low salary as the owner allowed him to take as much time off as he needed, whenever he wanted.

In a previous life, Clarke had been a highly decorated member of Britain's Special Reconnaissance Regiment. A little over five years ago, he had retired from government service, and since then had occasionally freelanced as a "soldier of fortune" provided that the assignment was interesting enough, and he was well-compensated.

Sean Tinker was told to go to London and meet with Clarke. Then, if he was satisfied that Clarke was the right man for the job, to engage his services. The assignment involved a quick trip to New Brunswick, a stop across the US border for some "wet work," then back to New Brunswick for some reconnaissance work and a full report.

Tinker was impressed with Clarke, and Clarke was willing to take on the assignment for his usual fee.
Within twenty-four hours, Clarke was walking toward the Avis rental desk after stepping off a plane at the Greater Moncton International Airport, in New Brunswick, Canada.

Clarke has several aliases; on this trip, he traveled as Thomas Green, the eccentric owner of an exclusive specialty shop in London offering men's socks and ladies' hosiery. He was pleased that the Avis representative was able to provide a non-descript black 4WD SUV on such short notice.

The ride around Passamaquoddy Bay from Moncton was pleasant, and he had no problems crossing the border at Saint Stephen's, New Brunswick, into the States. When questioned on the purpose of his visit he said, "I'm on my way to the Moosehorn National Wildlife Refuge to take some pictures of birds migrating down the Atlantic flyway we never get to see in the UK."

A cautious man, Clarke believed in planning ahead. Pictures of the birds he would likely see this time of year had already been downloaded to the digital camera that was in his luggage. Should he be questioned upon his return, the pictures would support his reason for the brief crossing.

Soon afterward, a morning edition of the Machias Valley Daily News carried a small notice that Emmett Davis, harbormaster at Lubec, Maine, died from an apparent heart attack while convalescing at his home from injuries sustained in a mugging.

Back in New Brunswick, Clarke's initial search of

possible locations the RCMP might be using within the sector of restricted air traffic yielded four possible locations: The Franquelin Campground in Eldon Parish on Nictau Lake, The Canadian Sportsman Lodge in Nictau, and the Nictau Inn, all of which were just off route 385. A fourth possible location was a fly-in sportsman's lodge called Havre de Poisson. An old map showed a logging road off route 385 that traveled right up to Havre de Poisson's property line.

The Canadian Sportsman Lodge and the Nictau Inn were privately owned. When Clarke called them and learned they both had vacancies, he put them at the bottom of his list. He now sensed the odds-on favorite was Franquelin. It was remote, owned by the province, and would have a limited number of campers this time of year. He headed there first.

The sign at the campground's main entrance said that the park was closed for the season, which only piqued Clarke's interest. He parked the SUV and hiked in to have a look around. It didn't take long before it was obvious that the park had in fact truly been shut down for the season.

The Mounties are somewhere else, he thought. Clarke stopped off at a country store to pick up various items he might need to clear the old logging road to Havre de Poisson anticipating that it might be overgrown or blocked with windblown trees. The elderly storekeeper was little help with directions to the isolated sportsman's camp located deep in the woods.

"I can tell from your accent that you're not from around here," the shopkeeper said. "There's old logging roads all around these parts, young fella, take your pick. They've been logging these woods off and on since before I was born."

"This map says there's one leading to Havre de Poisson."

"Lived here all my life, and I ain't never heard of any road that went over to Havre de Poisson. Course, I could be wrong. But as far as I know, the only way folks get there is by float plane."

Finding the logging road off Route 385 proved more challenging than Clarke had anticipated. When the sun began to set, he pulled off the road and put up for the night.

The following morning, after going down several dead ends, Clarke was finally certain he was on the abandoned logging road that led to Havre de Poisson. Several stops along the way were required to clear a few windfalls that had blocked the road since Lou Gault had last used it in the early spring. It took Clarke the better part of two hours to reach what must have been a loading area for the loggers. The road continued beyond an old gate with a sign indicating that the rest of the way was private property. The gate had a lock on it with a mechanism that Clarke easily defeated.

As he continued driving up the road, he noticed this particular leg of the road was in much better shape than the previous section. There were a few stretches of mud, caused by surface springs, but nothing blocked the road. Aware that the noise of a 4WD could travel quite a distance and being uncertain of just how much further ahead the camp was, Clarke decided to kill the engine, change into his camo gear, and proceed on foot.

Not more than a mile further, Clarke noticed a slight trace of wood smoke in the air. Now on full alert, he carefully moved off the road and proceeded forward. Not long after that, he heard the sound of gas generators.

Havre de Poisson appears to have a lot of activity going on this late in the season, Clarke thought, feeling more and more confident that he was on the right track. Continuing to work his way forward, he reached a vantage point with a fairly good view of the area. His first thought was, *It looks like the boats have all been stored for the winter. So whoever's here didn't come to fish.*

A few of the cottages appeared to have been boarded up for the winter; a float plane was pulled up onto the beach, and smoke was coming from a number of the cottages. A large antenna and a temporary satellite dish had been erected outside the largest structure. *That must be the lodge,* he thought. Clarke observed two people wearing some type of uniform who were walking from the cottages toward the larger building.

Six cabins seem to be occupied, maybe two people to a cabin. Total head count could be twelve, he thought, *but I can't know exactly how many people are present.* As he moved about the perimeter, he was surprised there was no evidence of patrols. His presence, apparently, hadn't been detected by any surveillance equipment.

This part of the contract was only to reconnoiter. Clarke knew he had enough information to report back on the remote location the Mounties were using. He took a few pictures of the area with his cell phone, marked the GPS coordinates, and headed back to his SUV. Now, he needed to travel quickly if he hoped to make the "red eye" back to Heathrow. In a rare act of carelessness, Clarke forgot to close and lock the old wooden gate before he left.

When Clarke arrived back in Fredericton, he drove behind a Walmart supercenter, changed into his street clothes, dumped the gear he had purchased and the camo outfit into a dumpster; then he drove to the Avis return lot at Fredericton International Airport. Once inside the terminal, Clarke purchased a ticket to Toronto and a ticket on the 'red eye' flight from Toronto to London.

Clarke transmitted his report to Tinker while he waited to board the "red eye." Within an hour, payment was wired over to the account Clarke had provided. The next day, Oliver Clarke was back behind the meat counter at Whitecross Market, wrapping meat pies that people had pointed to, totally unaware that he had left a calling card behind.

Chapter

20

Fletcher Martin was up early. Like every morning, he was out walking the trails around Havre de Poisson just as dawn was breaking. This was the time of year that Fletcher enjoyed - the air was crisp, the fallen leaves created a nice woodsy smell in the forest, and the bucks were in rut. Fletcher looked forward to deer season every year. He had decided that on opening day, he'd take a stand near the deer trails that crossed down by the old logging road, close to the wooden gate.

Fletcher had seen plenty of fresh deer tracks on his walks; however, he hadn't seen any deer until this morning when he "jumped" two down by the beaver pond. The wind was blowing toward him, neither the yearling nor the doe had caught his scent. He hadn't seen any "rubbings" near the beaver pond, but there were quite a few down by the wooden gate, so he knew at least one buck had been in that area rubbing the velvet off his antlers.

As he continued along the trail, he smiled when a pair of squirrels gave him his daily scolding for, yet again, invading their space. It was a perfect morning for people like Fletcher who love traipsing about in the woods.

When he reached the old logging road, he noticed the gate was open and fresh tire tracks in the mud. *Hmm, I didn't hear a vehicle leave camp this morning, but maybe Lou or Jake left when I was down by the beaver pond,* he thought. Returning to the lodge, he was surprised to see both Lou and Jake walking up from the dock area.

"Morning guys," he said. "I thought for sure one of you had gone into town, but here you both are."

The puzzled looks on their faces surprised him.

"Well, the gate to the logging road was open and there's a fresh set of tire tracks. I just figured it was one of you."

"That road hasn't been used since last spring, Fletcher," Lou said. "You sure there were fresh tire tracks down there?"

"Yup. Gate was wide open. The lock was just hanging on the eye bolt and I sure as hell know what fresh tire tracks look like. Trust me, they weren't there yesterday. I figured for sure one of you had driven through."

"Jake, give Andre a heads up, then meet me down by the gate. Sounds like we've had a visitor that we didn't know about. Thanks, Fletcher, good catch."

Lou headed directly to the gate area. He carefully stayed to the side of the fresh footprints that were going toward the lodge. Based on the sole imprint, he figured those tracks belonged to Fletcher Martin. But about a mile further down the road, a different set of footprints appeared heading *away* from the lodge. Whoever left those prints was in a hurry; the imprint of the toe was much deeper than the heel. A short distance further, tracks from that same second pair of shoes appeared again, this time they were heading *toward* the lodge. Another mile down the road, Lou found the set of tire tracks Fletcher had mentioned. The unknown footprints he had been following suddenly disappeared.

Well, whoever was here on foot got out and back into a vehicle here, Lou thought. There were also tracks indicating the vehicle had made a three-point turn before heading back down the road. The only set of footprints visible now, were Fletcher Martin's … coming up from the gate area.

When Lou finally arrived at the old wooden gate, he could see where a vehicle had come to a stop in front of it, someone got out, walked over to the gate, "jimmied" the lock, walked the gate open, returned to the vehicle and drove forward. He knelt down to get a closer look at the footprints.

Odd that they didn't bother to close the gate when they left, he thought. *Why? Why would they leave the gate open?*
Lou looked up just in time to see both Jake and Andre hurrying down the road.

"Andre," Lou called out. "Someone paid us a visit in the last twenty-four hours. They jimmied the lock, drove about a mile further up from this point, then went up toward the lodge on foot."

Jake walked over to check out the lock, "A lot of good this old lock did. It couldn't keep anyone out, and it's so rusty, you couldn't lift a set of prints off it if you tried."

Andre knelt down to look at the tire tracks. "Will you be able to track where they went after they entered the woods?"

"Sure, for all the good it will do," Jake said. "Whoever it was, they got what they came for and are long gone now. We'll take a look to see if they left anything behind." Then, for what it was worth, Jake closed the gate.

"Let's go back," Lou said as he stood up. When they came to where the second set of prints heading toward the lodge left the road, Lou and Jake followed that trail while Andre continued up the road.

Lou and Jake had absolutely no difficulty following the path of the intruder. It was obvious from the trampled grass and disturbed leaves that whoever it was, the intruder had stopped quite a few times, and waited, before moving on. They carefully searched those immediate areas for anything that might have been left behind, deliberately, or not. On the way back to the lodge Lou and Jake kicked around what they'd seen.

"Lou, what are your thoughts on what this visit means?"

"Clearly, someone wanted intel on what the set up was here. Anyone willing to go to all that trouble wasn't just looking to gather data for the sake of it, Jake."

"Any thoughts on who it was?"

"It has to be connected to whoever Andre is going after. Now that they know where he and his team are hiding out, I suspect a strike force will be sent in to take them out. We probably have only a few days to take countermeasures before any attack comes."

"I'm thinking the same thing."

"We're damn lucky that Fletcher takes those morning walks of his, otherwise, we'd never have known we'd been scouted."

"Ya, I'm glad Fletcher and Duffy came up with Andre too. The other two may be good people, but they're desk jockeys. The team that's coming here will be playing for keeps."

"Let's go have a talk with Andre."

When they arrived back at the lodge, all three men walked over to the rocky point area so they could talk privately.

"So, what do you make of all this Lou?" Andre asked.

"We're going to have to start watching our back door," Lou said. "Someone went to a lot of trouble coming up that road. Whoever it was won't be the only visitor we're going to have."

"Then our cover's blown. I'll need to pack up and relocate."

"Hold on Andre," Lou said. "All that will accomplish is changing the location of the firefight that's going to happen."

"Whaddya mean?"

"I mean, they've found you. If you run now, it'll only be a

matter of time before they find you again, and you'll be sending a clear message that you're onto them. But if you stay put, *we'll* have a better chance of owning the element of surprise."

"Lou, I'm a policeman. I'm not a product of JTF2 like you are, and I'm too damn old for something like this. What the hell are my chances if I stay here, in the middle of nowhere?"

"You're right, Andre. What's coming at us isn't police work. But I think our chances are pretty damn good here. We know the terrain; we have a small window of time to develop a plan and prepare. I would say chances are better than eighty-twenty in our favor. Hell, you flew up here in a friggin' *float* plane with a similar percentage risk."

"Lou this is becoming far more complicated than I ever thought it would be."

"Andre, I'm telling ya', you've got a far better chance if you stay put here than if you go back to Fredericton. You go back to Fredericton and they're liable to blow up the whole damn building."

"I can't put that many lives at risk, it'll have to be someplace else."

"Where?"

"I don't know."

"Look, all we're going to need is some special equipment, nothing that someone with your influence can't easily have flown in."

"Yeah?"

"Andre, the better move is for you to stay put."

"I'm not so sure."

"Andre, we don't know how many bad guys will be coming at us, so I'm going to ask you to assign Fletcher and Duffy to me. Having a couple more former JTF2 types like them working with Jake and me will make a big difference."

Andre finally picked up on the inclusive words and phrases Lou had been using.

"Lou, I thought you said you didn't 'have a horse in this race,' or something like that, and you weren't getting involved?"

"I didn't . . . until now."

Andre frowned looking at Lou.

"Andre, you know I wasn't looking to be part of this damn fight, but they just *made* this my fight. I dismissed the telltale signs of danger once in Afghanistan, and that mistake cost people their lives, I'll be *damned* if I'm gonna let that happen again!"

"Lou, this isn't Afghanistan."

"Makes no difference. Whoever these people are, they'll be coming here with the intention of taking out your team. It won't be a surgical strike, Andre, they'll take out anything and anybody that gets in their way. I saw enough collateral damage to last me a lifetime, and I'm not going to sit by and allow that to happen here on my watch. From this point on, you and I are partners . . . you've got responsibility for your damn investigation, and I'm taking responsibility for our safety and repelling whatever it is that's coming at us."

Andre paused a few moments and looked out at the lake. "You're right Lou; if they found us once, they'd find us again."

"Exactly!"

"It's that damn mole working somewhere inside headquarters. We just can't figure out who the hell it is." Andre paused again and kept looking at the lake.

"All right, I'll bring headquarters up to speed on what's happening and that I'm staying put and bringing you onboard. Now, what kind of special equipment are you talking about?"

Lou relaxed his jaw. He was ready for this. "For openers, we're going to need a couple dozen surveillance cameras to monitor our perimeter, especially down around our back door."

"You think they'll come at us from the lake?"

"No, sound travels too far on the water, I doubt anyone would try to hit us from that direction, but we'll monitor it anyway. The Internet connection that you already have should be sufficient for us to upload and then backhaul camera feeds from the satellites down to a single screen. We'll set it up like a regular security monitoring system."

"What else?"

"Night vision goggles would help and some military-grade bullet proof vests, some flashbangs, a dozen hand grenades for trip wires, and wireless personal communicators for all of us. Duffy and Fletcher will each need a compound bow, we'll need a few dozen 340 spine arrows with fixed blade tips."

Andre's eyes bugged out. "You're going to defend us with friggin' bows and arrows?"

"It'll give us an edge; they won't know what's hitting them."

Andre shook his head, saying, "This is crazy."

"No. it's not, we'll know when they're coming and we'll be waiting for them."

"Okay, it's your call; anything else?"

"Yeah, it'd be best to bring in some field hospital trauma supplies, too, and maybe have a military Medivac stationed nearby on standby, just in case we need to evacuate one of us quickly. The question is, how soon can you release Fletcher and Duffy to work full time with Jake and me on this?"

"That's a hell of a shopping list, Lou, but why no guns or ammo?"

"Well, I was thinking of using compound bows to maximize the element of surprise, but that's a good point. Add four carbines and four side arms with suppressors to that list."

Andre thought about what Lou was asking for a few moments before saying, "All right, let me go to work on this. You can have Fletcher and Duffy immediately."

"Before you go, Fletcher is the only one on your team who's aware we had a visitor last night. We'll bring him and

Duffy up to speed on what the plan is, but it's your call when you decide to bring Dorsey and Kate up to date on what's happening. Matter of fact, while I think of it, you should get some fire power up here for them too. In the meantime, Jake and I have a lot to do before we can properly welcome the visitors I'm expecting."

Within an hour, Lou and Jake met with Fletcher and Duffy and appraised them of the situation; both men were immediately all in. Working in pairs, they set out to identify where the surveillance cameras would be placed and where trip wires would work.

Jake began drawing on his commando training and constructed a few tension spear point traps in the woods. Once he was satisfied with those traps, he set out a few antique iron bear traps in the woods directly behind the lodge.

Andre's rank held a lot of influence. By late afternoon, most of the gear Lou had requested was on its way up in floatplanes. The trauma supplies would take another day to arrive.

By nightfall, cameras had been installed in every location Jake and Lou had designated and successfully linked to the satellites. Now they had the ability to monitor any and all movement within two miles of their immediate perimeter, in any direction, from inside the lodge.

Everyone on Lou's team was a skilled archer and regularly took a deer during bow season; however, in the morning, in-between monitoring camera feeds, they each spent time practicing their archery skills and getting familiar with firing their bows from various positions.

Fletcher has belonged to a competitive pistol team for a few years. He quickly became comfortable with the suppressor and was firing a tight pattern with the sidearm that Andre had sent up. Everyone else practiced firing the carbines and sidearms to get a feel for the suppressors. Later in the day, Jake brought everyone through a refresher course in martial arts.

Andre included Angelo and Alessandra in the briefing when he brought Dorsey and Kate up to speed on what was happening. Everyone, but Alessandra, carved out time to practice with the close-range weapons on the firing range.

Kate proved exceptionally accurate with the pistol and carbine. She chose not to share that she had competed in various shooting contests with pistols and rifles in Ireland since the age of twelve and had twice been named to Ireland's Olympic pistol and skeet teams.

Angelo also proved to be quite a marksman.

Andre smiled. "Well, I guess when the enemy's coming over the hill, even the cook needs to grab a rifle."

"Andre, I tell you this one time . . . you call me a cook, you insult me, and you insult what I do! I let it go this time, but only this *one* time."

"Point noted, Chef Angelo, my apologies," Andre said.

That evening, everyone was feeling comfortable that a plan was in place for whatever would be coming at them. Now it became a waiting game.

Duffy modified some software for the surveillance cameras so they'd send a series of beeps whenever movement was detected by any of the cameras. From this point on, the camera feeds would be monitored around the clock. Only Dorsey was disappointed that he wouldn't be able to watch any more baseball.

That night, Fletcher slammed his fist down on the table while monitoring the camera feeds as a huge buck came into view down by the old wooden gate.

As Lou drifted off to sleep, he kept thinking about that open gate. *Why did they leave the gate open? Was it a mistake, or was it deliberate? Did they think they'd been seen? Did they have to meet someone? Did they have to be somewhere else? Did they just not care*? He rolled onto his side. *Would knowing the answers to any of these questions even make a difference?*

But the most important question still hung on his mind: Would they be ready?

Part 3

Chapter 21

When word reached Imperial Trading about the location of Andre's secret base, they decided to take immediate action. Their first and only concern was – as always -- to protect themselves, and secondly, to protect the game, if possible.

Choosing Oliver Clarke to lead a strike force made the most sense to them. Clarke knew exactly where the Mounties were; he was discrete, a proven commodity. But most importantly, should anything go wrong, the principals of Imperial Trading had never had any direct contact with him.

Clarke agreed to take out the Mounties with a force of eight, including himself. With little negotiation, Herbert Maxwell transferred sufficient funds to Clarke's bank account for travel expenses and outfitting the mission, along with a sizable good faith advance.

Clarke also agreed to send a message to Tinker when his team was ready to depart the UK, and another when the mission was completed. Once Tinker received the second message, the remaining funds would be transferred to

Clarke's bank account, which he could then disburse among his team as he saw fit.

The man Clarke chose to be his second-in-command for the mission was a man he knew from the Victory Services Club in London. Both men were seasoned operatives for hire; between them, they quickly assembled six additional "soldiers of fortune."

Once his team was in place, Clarke held a team meeting to brief everyone on the mission logistics. "All right, everyone knows what the mission is, and I think you'll agree this will be an easy op, once we're in-country. So, let's talk about logistics."

"Are you going to tell us exactly where we're headed or is that something we find out once we get there?" he was asked by a burly member of the team.

"We're traveling to New Brunswick, Canada. Our target is located way out in the bloody boonies and believe me when I say 'boonies.'"

"Are we bivouacking?"

"No, we're not roughing it. Our travel cover, should we need it, is that we're employees of AstraZeneca on our way to a team meeting in Canada. To attract the least amount of attention, we'll be traveling in groups of two, and we'll be taking different flights into Halifax."

"What's the deal on ID's?" another asked. "Do we use our own?"

"No. Everyone will be given a new passport, matching Canadian eTA Visa, and an AstraZeneca employee badge - yours to keep. Be sure to memorize your new names, and answer to them."

"What about weapons?"

"I'm taking care of all the gear that we'll need for this mission. The client is transporting everything over for us; all I need do is text them where they can pick it up, and they'll get it through customs."

The briefing lasted about half an hour. Each man was a seasoned combat veteran and had few questions beyond when Clarke planned to pull the trigger and take off.
Six days after their gear was shipped out, Clarke and his team arrived at Heathrow and boarded their flights to Halifax without incident. Once in Halifax, they proceeded to the Air Canada desk in pairs and purchased tickets to St. John, New Brunswick.

When the team gathered in St. John, they picked up two non-descript black 4WD SUVs and traveled to pier 47 in St Stephens, where their gear was waiting in a secured overseas container.

Clarke's plan was to spend the night in St. John, then strike the Mounties the following night. Ever cautious about details, half of Clarke's team checked into the Hilton; the other half stayed at a local inn.

The following morning, everyone checked out and met in a conference room that Clarke had reserved for breakfast. He walked them through the plan in greater detail and gave each one a hand-drawn detailed map of the area where the Mountie base was located and where their targets would be found.

Toward the end of the meeting, there was a knock on the conference room door and the lunch Clarke had ordered from the hotel was brought in.

By early afternoon, the team was on the road. It would take hours to reach the old logging road, which aligned well with Clarke's plan for a surprise night attack on the Mounties. By nightfall, the eight-man team arrived at their destination. The logging road was literally a back door into Havre de Poisson. When they arrived at the old wooden gate, they positioned both vehicles facing outward and began their wait. The time was just approaching 2200 hours; Clarke's plan was to begin moving forward at midnight.

The fact that the gate was now closed, didn't register on Oliver Clarke as anything to be concerned about. He had no memory of having left the gate open when he checked out the area over a week ago.

The moon was full and the sky was crystal clear as if he had planned it. To lighten everyone's load, Clarke told his men, "The moon is bright enough tonight, leave your night vision goggles in the vehicles; it's one less thing for us to deal with."

At midnight, they opened the gate and began walking up the logging road until Clarke gave the signal to halt. Once the signal was given, a three-man team whose focus was to take out those in the lodge headed left into the woods. The three-man team whose objective was to take out everyone in the cottages headed off to the right. Clarke and his second-in-command continued traveling straight up the road in the dark.

The dense underbrush and fallen trees littering the forest floor slowed forward progress of Clarke's team considerably. It took well over half-an-hour for his men to travel a mere five hundred yards.

Too late to make a change now, Clarke thought. *When we return, we'll take the easier route and use the road.*

Chapter 22

From the very moment that Oliver Clarke and his strike force arrived at the wooden gate on the logging road leading to Havre de Poisson, their presence was known to Andre's team. Kate O'Grady had been monitoring the surveillance screens for just under an hour when their images appeared. Word of an imminent attack spread quickly.

Not realizing it, Clarke's decision to delay deploying his forces until midnight had provided Lou and the rest of Andre's team more than enough time to move into position.

The four former JTF2 commandos grabbed their compound bows and the rest of their equipment, then disappeared into the woods. Dorsey positioned himself by the woodpile near the cottages; Andre burrowed in over by the front of the lodge. Both men were equipped with carbines, night vision goggles, and wireless communicators.

Kate remained inside the lodge monitoring the camera feeds and sharing what she was seeing via wireless communicator. Andre had rigged a tent over Kate so that the light from her monitor couldn't be seen, thereby, placing the lodge in total darkness.

Angelo was Kate's first line of defense and sat quietly inside the lodge near her. Alessandra was safely sheltered down in the root cellar below the lodge. Once Clarke and his people began moving forward, Kate shared the info with everyone on their communicators.

"It looks like eight intruders. Two are traveling straight up the road and three are on either side of it spread out into the woods. They all appear to be heavily armed, but no one seems to be wearing NVGs."

The night was cold with temperatures in the upper thirties making it hard for the men to stay still while waiting for the intruders to advance. Dorsey, who was most sensitive to cold weather, began moving about attempting to keep warm. Andre saw him and broke radio silence.

"Dorsey, stay still! You'll give away our position!"
Kate broke in: "An intruder on the left has just been taken out by one of Jake's tension spear point traps!"

Clarke and his strike force were still well over a mile from the lodge when another of his men stepped on a tripwire and detonated two hand grenades.

Kate spoke again: "One intruder on the right now down."

The explosion eliminated the element of surprise that Clarke believed he had; he signaled his men to begin moving forward with greater purpose.

"Two intruders still on the right have split further away from the road," Kate reported. "Two on the road seem to be holding back."

Lou turned his communicator from listen to broadcast. "Duffy, fall back and take a position closer to the lodge."

"Copy that."

Lou and Fletcher moved to opposite sides of the road

and waited for the two on the road to advance toward them.

Jake had positioned himself about a mile from the lodge behind a windfall off to the left of the road. At last he heard the sound of someone advancing toward him. Through his NVG's, he was able to make out two forms approaching.

I'll take out the one furthest away first, then deal with the closer one, he thought.

Once the furthest target was within effective range, Jake silently rose up, pulled back on his bow, and quietly released an arrow. His first shot hit a branch and deflected. Quickly, he notched another arrow and released it. The second arrow found its mark. However, when he stood up, the intruder nearest to Jake had seen his silhouette in the moonlight. He immediately fired a burst from his AK-47 at Jake, then instantly rolled to the side.

Multiple bullets flew inches above Jake's head as he dove for cover. The close muzzle flash briefly blinded him and he wasn't able to see which direction his adversary had taken. Ripping off his NVG's, Jake hoped for better eyesight, but it took several minutes for his eyes to fully adjust to the dark. Meanwhile, off to his right, Jake heard the distinctive "click" of a weapon jamming.

Suddenly, from out of the darkness, the assailant hurled himself at Jake. The impact forced him backward. Intentionally, Jake fell onto his back, lifting both feet and vaulted his assailant over his head using the man's own forward momentum. An instant later, Jake had rolled over scrambling to his feet.

Now, in the moonlight, he could see the glimmer of a knife in his opponent's hand; he was crouched and ready to strike. The assailant charged and tried plunging the blade into Jake's chest. But the blade struck Jake's Kevlar vest and slid across the front to the left, slicing open his forearm.

Looking to end this sooner than later, Jake drew his

sidearm and fired three successive shots point-blank at his adversary. Then quickly reached into his knapsack for a bandage to stop the flow of blood. As he was applying the cloth to his arm, he mouthed one of Sean Connery's memorable lines from *The Untouchables*: "Ya don't bring a knife to a gunfight!"

With all three intruders on the left now down, Jake broke radio silence. "The woods left of the road are now clear; I'm circling back to the lodge."

Oliver Clarke and his second-in-command were huddled off to the side of the logging road whispering how to proceed forward. They were completely unaware their strike force had already been reduced by half.

Kate broke radio silence: "One of the two on the road has moved into the woods on the left. The other is still on the road now moving forward."

Lou knew Jake was headed back to the lodge and believed the road was the easier position to defend, he left Fletcher to cover the road while he moved left into the woods.

Meanwhile, the two remaining intruders on the right were moving forward and were now less than a quarter mile from the lodge. The forest close to the cottages had been thinned out and the underbrush cleared. In the bright moonlight it was easy for the intruders to clearly see the building's outline in the distance silhouetted against the lake.

Duffy had taken up a position near the lodge outside the perimeter of the cameras. With Kate's help, he spotted the two insurgents coming in on the right and began tracking their movements. He notched an arrow into his bow, and as soon as they came within range, released it. The intruder nearest Duffy cried out in pain as the arrow struck him in the upper thigh. The man snapped off the shaft at the point of entry and attempted to move into deeper cover, but cried out in total agony as he stepped into one of the enormous rusty antique bear traps that Jake had set out.

The other intruder immediately dropped to the ground and began low crawling toward the lodge. Duffy's attention was momentarily drawn to the man caught in the bear trap thrashing about in agony and lost track of the second intruder.

Meanwhile, Kate was able to put Lou on a path where he would eventually intercept the man she saw moving toward him in the woods.

"Lou, you're still a good half mile apart; the intruder is much further into the woods than you are."

"Roger that."

Back at the logging road, Fletcher noticed movement in the shadows further down the road and repositioned himself to get a better angle. Instantly, a spray of bullets flew his way. Fletcher took a hit in the chest and one in his right shoulder. The impact knocked him onto the embankment alongside the road. His body armor absorbed the impact from the shot to the chest. The bullet that entered his left shoulder missed the bone but ripped an ugly hole through the muscle. Fletcher no longer had the strength to use the compound bow.

Ignoring the shooting pain in his shoulder, Fletcher low crawled up and over the embankment alongside the road and moved several yards away from where he had been. Now, cupping his right hand, he hoped to throw his voice; he moaned just loud enough to be heard by anyone who might be approaching. A second burst of automatic fire hit the area he had just left. Now readying his side arm, Fletcher leaned back against a tree trunk and patiently waited for whoever was still advancing up the road.

Kate whispered into Fletcher's earpiece: "The man on the road should reach your position momentarily."

Meanwhile, Duffy was unaware that the second man

had managed to get behind him and had now reached the edge of the woods. The intruder paused to scan the area before moving into the open. The building closest to him was the largest of the structures. A satellite dish out front and the generators indicated this was his target. Noticing movement in the shadows next to a large woodpile, he suspected someone was positioned there. In an instant, he decided to retreat back into the woods and come out further down which would place the building between him and whoever was hiding near the woodpile.

Kate was blind to anything within fifty feet of the lodge. Once the second man had low-crawled past Duffy, she lost all visibility on the whereabouts of that intruder.

Andre was stationed over by the outhouses and had a clear view of the front entry to the lodge. Jake still had a distance to go as he continued to work his way back to the lodge from where he had initially positioned himself. Duffy remained in place and was searching the area in front of him with his NVG's, trying to relocate the remaining intruder who had slowly low-crawled across the open area and had now reached the side of the lodge.

Unaware of Andre's position, the man knew that whoever was over by the wood pile had a clear view of the front entry to the lodge. The side of the building where he hid, and the rear of the building, were both in shadows. Cautiously, he moved along the side of the building toward the back. The noise from the generators covered any sound he might have made. As he suspected, there was a back entry to the lodge and he tried the screen door, It wasn't locked. He propped the screen door open, crouched down, and peered through the bottom glass window pane in the door.

The moon was shining through the windows on the opposite side of the building, which gave him just enough light to see the door led into a kitchen area. He watched patiently but saw no movement inside. Next, he tried the knob on the inside door and smiled when he realized it also wasn't locked. He stood up next to the side of the door, and mentally readied himself to turn the knob before entering the building.

Back in the woods, Lou was beginning to close the gap between himself and the last intruder who was heading his way. Lou still hadn't been able to spot him, but Kate was keeping him appraised of the man's position. Concerned about the automatic weapon fire that he'd heard twice now from the vicinity of the old logging road, Lou thought about Fletcher.

He's a big boy, Lou thought. *He should be able to take care of himself.* Lou pushed all thoughts of Fletcher from his mind, including what might be going on at the logging road and began concentrating fully on what lay ahead of him.

"You're going to see movement at two o'clock, coming directly your way," Kate shared with him. "There's quite a lot of underbrush in that section of the woods." Lou decided to scale the roots of a large windfall to improve his field of vision. Within minutes, he was able to detect movement off in the distance, but the individual was still out of bow range.

At the logging road, Oliver Clarke was moving forward. His focus was on the spot where he had aimed his shots, expecting to find a body at any moment.

As he passed the spot where Fletcher was hidden, Fletcher sat straight up and using a combat grip, fired three successive shots into the back of Oliver Clarke's head. Clarke's body fell forward with a quiet thud.

Kate saw Clarke's takedown and shared it with everyone, "The lone intruder on the road is now down, only two intruders remain active."

Fletcher broke radio silence, "I've taken a hit."

Back at the lodge, the intruder slowly turned the doorknob and pushed opened the door with his carbine. When he stepped into the doorway, he was immediately silhouetted against the moonlight that was shining on that open area behind the building.

Angelo emerged from the shadows and pulled both triggers of a 12-gauge shot gun, literally blowing the man out the door. Quoting a line from his favorite James Bond movie, *Skyfall,* Angelo said to no one in particular, "Welcome to Scotland!"

Hearing the shotgun blast, Kate dropped to the floor, grabbed the carbine she had been issued and rolled away from the equipment.

"All clear Kate," Angelo whispered in a voice just loud enough for her to hear.

Slightly shaken, she returned to her station and transmitted: "The intruder near the lodge is now down; lodge is clear."

Hearing this, Andre, Dorsey, and Duffy emerged from their positions. Jake immediately began to circle back to provide backup for Lou.

Knocking on the door of the root cellar, Angelo let Alessandra know it was safe to come out.

Kate was able to guide Duffy to Fletcher's position. Duffy quickly applied a field bandage to slow the flow of blood from Fletcher's wound and told Kate to call in the medivac. Using a fireman's carry, Duffy headed back to the lodge with his best friend over his shoulder.

Andre was on the phone in a heartbeat with Fredericton RCMP Headquarters relaying that his team had sustained two injuries, one of which required emergency transport to a medical facility. Fredericton made the call and within moments the medivac that had been on standby was airborne.

Back in the woods, Lou was now able to see the last adversary approaching head on. The gnarled root system Lou had been using for cover had completely disguised his silhouette; he was virtually invisible as long as he remained motionless.

When his adversary was forty paces away, Lou fired an arrow into the man's right shoulder; he immediately notched a second arrow and let it fly. The impact of the first arrow caused the attacker to turn in such a manner that Lou's second arrow struck the man's neck instead of the opposite shoulder. Lou took his side arm out and cautiously walked toward the intruder, hoping to find out his identity and who had sent him. By the time Lou reached him, the man was gasping for air and choking on the blood from his neck wound. Within minutes, the man's struggle to breathe was over.

"Final intruder down," Lou transmitted. "Returning to lodge."

Hearing the transmission, Jake turned around and headed back to the lodge. Andre and Dorsey went to search for the intruder who had stepped in the bear trap with hopes of getting information from him, if he was still alive.

When they reached the man, it was obvious he had lost a lot of blood and was unconscious.

"I'll go back for a stretcher," Andre said. "See if you can release his leg from that bear trap."

The men manage to transport the injured man back to the lodge; however, within less than half an hour, he died without ever regaining consciousness.

Duffy had been a corpsman in the JTF2. Once he had Fletcher back at the lodge, he cleaned the gunshot wound the best he could and applied a sterile dressing. The bullet had gone clean though; however, extensive contamination had also entered the wound when Fletcher crawled to higher ground after being shot.

Having lost a good amount of blood, Fletcher was in danger of going into shock. Duffy elevated his friend's legs and covered him with a few blankets to keep him warm. Then he turned to check on Jake whose wound wasn't deep. Still, after properly cleaning the area, Duffy stitched Jake up as well as any surgeon would have done, then applied a sterile dressing and fresh bandage.

Andre's phone rang; it was Fredericton.

"Hello, Andre?"

"Speaking."

"In the morning, we're going to send three float planes up with body bags to take the intruders back for identification. Also, we're sending two investigators up to help you complete your report."

"More damn paperwork."

"Sorry, you're breaking up. What did you say?"

"I said: Sure, fine . . . thank you."

In the distance, the sound of an approaching medivac could be heard. Lou and Andre each grabbed a couple of lanterns and headed out to illuminate the landing area.

Once the chopper landed, it only took a few moments before Fletcher was strapped in, and the medivac lifted off again. As the eastern sky began to turn gray, everyone's adrenalin was still running high from the fire fight.

Alessandra emerged from the kitchen with a fresh pot of coffee, laced with anisette, and a tray of biscotti that Angelo had made the day before.

"Mangia, mangia!"

No one refused.

Chapter 23

Andre's team was physically and mentally spent from the ordeal they'd just been through. "All right, listen up! Today will be a day of rest for everyone except those I'm assigning to monitor our perimeter," he announced.

Everyone was calmer now and Dorsey's bravado returned. "We've earned it. We definitely kicked some butt tonight!" he responded enthusiastically.

"We only won a skirmish tonight," Lou said. The room went silent. "Whatever is going on is *far* from over; we were lucky tonight and caught them unaware, that's all. Now they know we'll fight back. Next time they'll come at us with more; it won't be so easy."

"He's right," Andre said before heading off for a couple hours of sleep. He anticipated that, shortly, his day would be totally consumed collaborating with the Mounties he knew would be flying in,

Lou and Jake also headed off to grab some shut-eye. All too soon, they would be guiding Mounties through the woods to retrieve bodies, mainly so no one else would get tangled up in any passive defensive mechanisms still in place.

Dorsey, mentally exhausted now, went to his cottage and hit the sack.

Kate made plans to meet Alessandra for lunch, then headed over to her cottage to get some rest. *Later in the afternoon,* she thought, *I might do a little fishing over by the brook.*

Duffy volunteered to take the first shift monitoring the cameras. *That way,* he figured, *I can call the hospital to check on Fletcher.* A few years ago, Fletcher's wife had died and he lived alone now. Duffy decided that he'd maneuver it so that when Fletcher was discharged from the hospital, it would be into his care at Havre de Poisson.

Andre requested that Fredericton send up another resource while Fletcher Martin was recovering, specifically someone with both field and investigative experience.

Later that day, word came that the last three months' inbound and outbound phone records for Orson Evers, Emmett Davis, and Felix Lajoie had been received in Fredericton. Once the files were fully loaded into the RCMP database, access codes to the files would be set up for Andre's team to access the files.

That afternoon, Lou and Jake decided to make the necessary repairs to the damaged kitchen door. Portions of it were in splinters from when Angelo blew the assailant to smithereens. While inspecting the damage, Jake asked Lou, "Have you made up your mind about going down to Grand Manan with Kate yet?"

Taken aback, Lou wondered, *How the hell does Jake know about the conversation I had with Andre?* Then he realized that Jake would have known, as he was going to be flying them down and back.

"No, I haven't Jake."

"He's looking for an answer."

"I've been a little preoccupied with other things lately, if you haven't noticed."

"What's bugging ya' about this Lou?"

"Nothing."

"The couple-on-vacation setup that Andre is proposing for you is a hell of a lot better cover than the flimsy one he gave *me*."

"I don't know, I'm just not sure about it."

"Not sure about what?"

"What he's asking me to do."

"He's only asking you to go and check out the island."

"That's just going to pull me deeper and deeper into this."

"If you don't mind my saying, last night you got about as deep as anyone could in *this*."

"Yeah, well, the whole play-acting thing with Kate bothers me."

"How?"

"It's gonna feel as awkward as being on one of those lame blind dates that you always seem to fix me up with."

"Whoa."

"Whoa, yourself."

"Lou, when you found out the bad guys were coming to 'storm the castle' you said this was 'now your fight.' What's the matter, are you afraid of *Kate*?"

"Don't be a jerk! I'm not *afraid* of her, hell I don't even know her."

"So, what's the problem?"

"Nothing."

"Nothing?"

"All right, so I'm not sure I can pull off faking that I'm her 'significant other' well enough so that it's believable. But I'll be damned if I want to feel like I'm a fish-out-of-water, and if I mess it up, I'll blow our cover and put the both of us at risk."

"Well, speaking of fish, Kate's over by the brook fishing right now," Jake said. "Might be a good time for you to grab a pole and go over and start getting to know her."

"Let's finish what we're doing."

"Go on, I can finish up here."

Lou inhaled deeply a couple of times, shook his head, put his apprehension aside, then reluctantly headed over to have a talk with Kate. He didn't want to admit it – even to himself - that he was apprehensive. Or was it more than that? He saw her by the water as he approached and shuffled his feet a little so his footsteps would be heard. He didn't like surprises, so why should she?

Kate turned, "Oh, hi, Lou. Well, I don't think the fish are very hungry just now. Maybe once the sun sets their dinner bell will start ringing."

"They can be finicky," Lou said. "Sometimes it's the choice of fly, sometimes it's just the time of day." He paused a moment. "Kate, I was wondering if we might have a talk?"

"Sure Lou, what would you be wanting to talk about?"

"Let's walk over to the point. There's a couple of smooth rocks over there we can sit on."

Arriving at the point, they sat diagonally across from one another. Lou paused, trying to find the right words to begin talking about what was on his mind, which resulted in a bit of awkward silence. He didn't know quite how to start.

Finally, Kate spoke up. "Lou, what was it you were wanting to talk about?"

"Kate, I'd like to talk to you about Grand Manan. Andre has approached me with this wild idea of his that the two of us could go down there posing as a couple and do some reconnaissance work for him."

"He approached me about that too," she smiled. "I told him that I'm open to the idea, but definitely *not* if he's thinking of sending me down there with Dorsey."

"I doubt Andre would ever put Dorsey in the field."

"I hope not."

"Besides, he'd have to get clearance from the Yanks anyway."

"Good point."

"Kate, listen . . . I've never done any undercover work before, but I'm willing to go down there with you as a favor to Andre, provided you think that we could pull it off. It would be strictly two professionals on assignment covering each other's back." He looked at her trying to gauge her thoughts. "I'll tell you though, I won't be able to handle it if it feels like I'm on a blind date that isn't going well the whole time we're down there."

"Lou, I've had my fill of those blind dates too, so we're in agreement there," she smiled, again. "We'd *definitely* have to work on building the chemistry between us though, get to know one another, you know . . . figure out how to act as a couple in public. What do you think about that, Lou?"

"Sounds like you've had a few undercover assignments like this before, Kate."

"Aye, actually, I have. It's not a big deal. It's no different than playing a role in live theatre, actually. You rehearse, and for the run of the show when the curtain goes up, you step into character. At the end of the last act, when the curtain goes down, you step out of character."

"You make it sound like there's a playbook or a script somewhere that I should be reading."

"Hardly. For the most part, it's basically just paying attention to your instincts and the rest is all improv. You just need to stay calm, trust your intuition and when things show up, stay in character."

Lou found himself listening to her soft lilting Irish brogue as much as to her words."So, how would you suggest we start working on 'developing our chemistry' and acting like we're a couple?"

"Well, if we're hoping that others will see us as a couple, we should start practicing *being* a couple."

He hesitated. "And how do we do that?"

"We could start by sitting across the dinner table from one another and acting like we actually liked each other . . . you know, like we're together. Rather than just reaching for the salt and pepper, ask one another if they would 'please pass the salt and pepper.' When I get up to get another cup of tea, I'll ask you if you'd like another cup of coffee. You can ask me how I liked my meal. Things like that. It's really not all that difficult, Lou, it's just showing others that you care about the person you're with. Does that make sense?"

Lou paused a moment. "I was in a relationship like that once; it was taken away from me way too early."

"I lost someone a couple of years ago, too . . . my fiancé . . . it was a hit-and-run driver," she said. "I never even had the chance to say goodbye to Liam. I know the feeling."

"I'm sorry, I didn't know."

"Well, it looks like we've already found a little more common ground to build our characters upon. All we had before was that the two of us knew how to fish," They both laughed.

"Lou, we're both professionals. I'll certainly let you know if you're doing anything that makes me feel uncomfortable, and I'll expect you to do the same. That said, I believe we can pull this off, provided we're both committed to it."

"Well, Kate, if you're game for it, you've got yourself a partner . . . or a boyfriend, or whatever the hell I'm supposed to be," Lou said.

"Great. Angelo must be just about ready to serve dinner. Let's head back and let Andre know," she hesitated. "On second thought, let's just start play-acting now, and have some fun watching everybody's reactions."

"Yeah, let's have some fun with this. Here, I'll give you a hand with that gear!" He helped her gather everything up and they began walking back to the lodge together.

"It's lucky you have both hands full carrying the gear," Kate said along the way, "Otherwise, I'd expect you to be practicing lesson number one."

"Lesson number one?"

Laughing, Kate replied, "Yes, you should be holding my hand!"

Everyone was milling around talking when Lou and Kate arrived at the lodge. While waiting for Alessandra to finish setting things up, the couple walked directly over to the table and Lou pulled out a chair for Kate, helped her get seated, and laid claim to the chair directly opposite her by placing an open napkin on the plate.

"Kate, would you like coffee or tea tonight?" he said in a voice just loud enough for all to hear.

Kate held back a smile as she noticed more than one head turn to look at them with curiosity.

"Oh, tea will be fine, thanks," she said. Throughout the meal, Kate and Lou constantly engaged in polite chit-chat.

"How's your meal?"

"When you have a chance, would you please pass the salt?"

"Have you tasted the broccoli yet?"

Duffy and Dorsey began sneaking side glances at the two of them. Alessandra overheard a little of what was being said and had a smile on her face.

Finally, Andre connected the dots and looked over at Jake. "Hey, is there enough gas in the float plane for a flight down to Grand Manan?"

"It's all fueled up and raring to go, Andre," Jake

answered. "All that's left for me to do is to put a chilled bottle of bubbly in the back for Romeo and Juliet to enjoy."

Kate broke out in laughter, and Lou leaned back in his chair shaking his head.

"Andre, have your fun now, my friend, you'll be crying when you see the trip expenses we turn in."

Dorsey leaned over to Duffy. "Ha, it was all play-acting; I knew it all the time."

The next morning, Lou and Kate walked into the lodge for breakfast together. There were no two seats available opposite the other.

Lou cleared his throat. "Duffy would ya' mind moving down a seat? I'd like to sit opposite my lady friend."

Duffy muttered a comment about "Romeo and Juliet" as he picked up his plate and moved over one seat.

After breakfast, Kate and Dorsey started digging into the phone records. Dorsey was looking at Felix Lajoie's cell phone records, while Kate focused on Orson Evers' file.

It didn't take Dorsey long to notice a pattern of numerous calls from the same number made to and from Felix Lajoie. Dorsey ran the number, and it came back as an RCMP number in Fredericton. He figured that couldn't be right, so he ran the number a second time. Again, it returned as an RCMP number in Fredericton. It made no sense to Dorsey.

"Andre, come here a minute."

"What?"

"This number that Lajoie calls a lot keeps coming back as a RCMP number."

"So, call the damn number…let's see who answers."

Dorsey dialed the number and put his phone on speaker. The line was in use and the call immediately went to voicemail.

"Hello, this is Corporal Charles Teal. I'm not able to

take your call right now, leave a message and I'll get back to you."

Andre smiled. "Well, we've finally caught the bastard!" he said softly. "Nice work Dorsey, you've just uncovered the mole inside headquarters."

"Are ya gonna bust him?"

"Nay, we'll have to decide how we're gonna play him first," Andre said. "For the time being, leave the phone records alone and see if you can find out how Charles Teal is connected to Felix Lajoie."

Andre went back to his workstation and immediately placed a call to Internal Affairs at Fredericton.

Chapter 24

The next morning after everyone had finished eating breakfast, Andre asked them to remain at the table. When he was ready to speak, Andre cleared his throat, took a sip of water, and called out to Angelo.

"Chef Angelo, please join us; I'd like you and Alessandra to hear this too." He waited while those sitting around the table made room for two more chairs.

"All right, here's what we've learned, what we think we know, and some of what we know we *still* don't know:

"First off, Fredericton has identified all the bodies from fingerprints. Everyone is former UK military; some have a rap sheet for minor stuff. They've all served in different units. The only connection among them, at this point, seems to be that MI6 believes they all belonged to the same veteran's organization. The bodies are going back to England under tight security and will be literally kept on ice for a while. The SUVs they used have all been searched; nothing of value was found. With not much more to go on, MI6 and INTERPOL will take it from here, and they'll let us know if they find anything else.

"As you can imagine, this has stirred up quite a hornet's nest, for sure. Ottawa is viewing what occurred here as an international terrorist attack on Canadian soil. As a result, Canadian Border Services is on high alert, the Air Transport Security Authority has initiated new procedures at all airports, and the Security Intelligence Agency is overseeing the entire effort. Special surveillance teams have been deployed to Fredericton International Airport and to every border crossing. All of what Ottawa is doing . . . should bring comfort to us.

"Now, I agree with Lou's assessment that we were *very* lucky the other night. But let's not kid ourselves that we've seen the last of whoever it is that's trying to put us out of business. We represent a bona fide threat to these smugglers; how they come at us next is anybody's guess. Headquarters will be working on an overall strategy with Ottawa to stop anyone from entering the country who they suspect might be intent on coming at us. Lou and Jake will be designing a more comprehensive defensive strategy for us to use here. This is still a semi-restricted air corridor, so it's unlikely that we will see anything coming at us from the air," Andre finished and looked around.

"What about Fletcher?" Dorsey asked, "Are you going to replace him?"

"I've asked Fredericton to send up a replacement for Fletcher, and one additional resource. Duffy, you've worked with Arnold Cunningham before . . . he's one who will be coming up, most likely later today."

"He's a good choice," Duffy smiled.

"Cunningham spent a few years in a 'special ops regiment' before becoming a Mountie. He's been in the field for a number of years now, and he's a damn good investigator. If there's another attack, he'll certainly be a welcome addition. Lou, we'll need to put Cunningham, and whoever else is coming up, in their own cottage."

"Not a problem."

"Now, here's the news on Fletcher," Andre began again. "They've given him a couple pints of blood and he's doing okay. He'll need therapy to regain full use of that shoulder again, but they expect to discharge him in another day or two. When that happens, he'll be coming here to convalesce, under the capable hands of Duffy. At some point, when he's up to it, I'll put him on light duty.

"We've also identified the mole inside the RCMP whose been feeding this ring information about us. Seems he's quite chummy with Felix Lajoie. We're going to play him for a while just to see what else we might be able to uncover.

"From now on, don't call or email anyone down at Headquarters. We've started a rumor down there that we were attacked, and we've been wiped out. Finance has been told to close out the discrete file for our project and as I speak, they're actually taking up a collection for *flowers* for the lot of us." Snickers from everyone ran around the table before quieting down to let Andre continue.

"We believe the mole will share that information with Lajoie and this will give us a little more time to prepare for the next visit, but not a lot. When whoever sent those killers over here fails to receive confirmation that the attack was successful, the ruse will be blown."

"Andre, let them know that I don't care for chrysanthemums," Jake called out.

"I will."

"Andre, can you us tell us who the mole is?" Duffy asked.

"It's Charles Teal, but Duffy, that information goes

nowhere, understood?"

"I know that bastard; we got rid of him as soon as we could . . . nobody liked him."

"All right, enough on Teal," Andre shifted in his seat. "Now, we know that goods are being hijacked from various parts of Europe, and funneled into Portmagee, Ireland. From there the goods are being shipped to Grand Manan down in the Bay of Fundy. Everything is stored there until someone directs that specific goods get dropped off at various docks on Passamaquoddy Bay. We have some data on the ships that are moving the goods over to Passamaquoddy, but where the goods go from *that* point, we don't know. Duffy here is pursuing a lead he's uncovered on E. Baker Trucking. Baker seems to have a connection to Lajoie. Lajoie is the lighthouse keeper over on Campobello Island and the same guy the mole is talking to."

"I put Lajoie's sorry ass in the hospital."

"Yes, we know that, Jake. But let's stay on topic. Baker may be transporting the goods from Passamaquoddy, but, again, where *to* is what we don't know," Andre continued.

"As soon as Lou and Jake feel confident that we have a secure perimeter in place, they'll bring the rest of us up to speed on our defense strategy.

"Shortly, Lou and Kate will be going undercover for a couple of days down on Grand Manan, only to gather information on how they're using the warehouse and the docks. Then they'll spend some time going around Passamaquoddy Bay before coming back. Jake will fly them down and back. The cover they'll use is that of being a *loving couple on holiday,* just so you all understand."

Jake smirked upon hearing that.

"INTERPOL is reporting that six cargo containers destined for Canada are missing. They're believed to be headed this way under different paperwork. The ship MI6 believes those containers are sailing on is destined for Quebec City. Both MI6 and INTERPOL believe this heist is connected to the ring that we're after. If that's true, our scope has just grown exponentially.

"That's about it in a nutshell for now. If you have any questions, see me later, individually," Andre said.

Everyone pushed back their chairs, and headed for more coffee as they left the table. Only Lou hung back until he caught Andre's attention.

"Andre, take a walk down to the dock with me."

"Sure, Lou."

Once Andre and Lou were at the boathouse, sitting on the bench up against its wall, Lou began sharing his ideas on a perimeter defense plan.

"Andre, I'm convinced next time we'll more than likely find ourselves up against a few lightweight vehicles, potentially armored, with some serious firepower coming up the old logging road. I won't rule out the possibility of drones. The next attack won't be stopped with commando warfare and bows and arrows, or bear traps." Andre's face was anything but calm.

"Lou, I'm questioning the wisdom of staying here. I think I need to move my operation to a safer position."

"Andre, this *is* a safe position. We just need to prepare differently this time; we need a different defensive approach, that's all."

"Like what?"

"For starters, we'll need an anti-drone system to knock out any drone attack. Maybe two Drone Guard Systems, actually . . . like the ones they use over at the airports."

"Why two?"

"Technology isn't absolute...we need the fail-safe assurance of redundant coverage."

"Point taken."

"Those things will detect and defeat incoming drones three miles out and jam their signals. We'll also need to set up an RF Sensor and a small radar system so we can accurately pinpoint where any drone may be controlled from. Once we know that, we can call in an airstrike of our own to take them out."

"Lou, this is New Brunswick, not friggin Afghanistan."

"Andre, we need to prepare for the worst-case scenario."

"Okay, okay."

I'll need a dozen anti-vehicle mines to spread out along that old logging road. That should stop anything that tries to come up the road. In the unlikely event that something did get through, we can take it out with a rocket launcher, so get one of those for everyone.

Andre nodded in agreement. "There's a chance that they could come at us on dirt bikes hoping for a quick 'snatch and grab' strike, but unless they want to travel through some pretty heavily wooded terrain, they'll be coming up that road."

"So, what else do you need?"

"Regardless of how they get here, at some point they'll be on foot. So, I'll need some fragmentation grenades and blast mines to set up trip wires in the woods, especially around where we've cleared the brush in back of the cottages, and on the road. If they come in on bikes, it'll be close work. But they'll be heavily armed with automatic weapons, so we'll all need assault weapons. We could also use a few more cameras, so add a dozen more of those to the order. Oh, and every one of us will need to be wearing vests."

"Lou, you're making me nervous . . . this sounds like we need a battalion up here."

"Andre, we've got enough people, but we need to be armed. The only way anyone is getting in here with anything heavy is up that road. We need to be ready for them."

"And if they outnumber us?"

"It won't be a large force coming here; besides, Cunningham brings us back up to four former special ops guys. Whoever the other guy is that's coming up, make sure he's former special ops, too. That will give us five defenders focused on the road. If we can defend the road, we'll succeed. If anyone gets *behind* us, we can easily fall back. You and Dorsey will be the rear guard, and Kate will stay in the lodge monitoring the camera feeds for us."

"Lou, me and Dorsey represent an awfully weak rear guard if they do breakthrough. Maybe Duffy should stay behind with me, and the other fella that's coming up here, too."

"Andre, I'm gonna need at least one of them upfront."

"How soon do you suspect something will happen," Andre asked.

"Most likely they're just now realizing the team they sent wasn't successful. They'll need a little time to pull another team together, develop a plan, and get over here. If they're Brits, I'd say we have a week, maybe two, before anything happens, but we need to stay on constant alert."

Andre flared his nostrils and breathed heavily a couple of times. Lou's confidence about repelling another attack began to calm him down to the point he could think better.

"All right, I'll contact headquarters about getting this new shopping list filled. How long will it take you to get everything in place?"

"If you loan me Cunningham when he gets here, then between him, Duffy, Jake, and me, I think we could get everything put together in a day."

"Okay, you can have Cunningham, but in exchange, I want you and Kate to fly down to Grand Manan *tomorrow.* When you come back, all the gear you want will be here."

"Fine. I'll let Kate know."

Chapter

25

When Oliver Clarke failed to send a "mission accomplished" text in a reasonable amount of time, Herbert Maxwell sent a message to Tinker telling him to put the squeeze on Felix Lajoie for information.

Lajoie immediately contacted his cousin. "Charles, I was just thinking that perhaps an interesting piece of information for your next weekly report might be to compare how much Girard is spending offsite that could be avoided if he was onsite."

"Felix, I was just going to call you. The word going around the building right now is that Andre Girard's entire team has been totally wiped out."

"Are you serious?"

"Yes, they're taking up a collection for flowers, and accounting has just told me to process anything I have for Girard because they're closing out his project file."

Lajoie passed the word along to Tinker with the caveat that it was uncorroborated information at this time, and nothing had appeared yet on any of the news stations. Being cautious was the reason Lajoie had survived this long.

Once again, Imperial Trading's first and only concern was to protect themselves and their identities. Oliver Clarke had no direct connection to any of them, so there was little concern that their identities would be at risk should Clarke, or anyone else on his team, have been taken into custody,

Still, Maxwell had been uneasy all day waiting to hear something positive about Clarke and the mission. That evening, he called for an emergency meeting at his home. By the time everyone arrived, Maxwell was in an agitated state.

"Clarke has failed us. We all know that now. And these Mounties, or whomever they damn well are, *haven't* given up. They're still coming for us and now they're deliberately releasing fake information just to throw us off. They need to be taken *out*!"

In a very matter-of-fact tone, Solicitor More spoke up. "We've tried that already my good fellow. Apparently, it didn't work."

"Richard, we can't ignore this threat," Maxwell railed. "Everything, *everything* that we have, everything that we've built, is at stake here!"

"Max is right, Richard," Hastings spoke. "I seriously doubt that merely fading into the woodwork for a while will make a difference. It appears we did send the wrong people over there."

Conversation among the three principals turned to what a more serious assault team might look like.

The next morning word went out to the Imperial Trading's network that there was a need for someone to lead a tactical strike force. Within days, two names had surfaced. One was Dimitri Bihar, a rebel fighter with strong references in the Middle East; the other was a soldier of fortune known only as "Q" who lived north of London.

Dimitri Bihar's Middle Eastern heritage was an automatic red flag for Solicitor More. "Let's not waste our time even thinking about this Dimitri chap; he'd be profiled as soon as he stepped foot in Canada. Let's see what this other fellow is about."

Hastings agreed. "Max, you're the one pushing for another strike, so take the lead on this."

Later that night, Maxwell connected with Sean Tinker and told him to set up an exploratory meeting with Q and act as the intermediary. Tinker had no difficulty reaching the man. When Q arrived at the regional airport just outside Surry, he was frisked before boarding a Gulfstream G650. The window shades had all been drawn down, but there was enough light coming in from the door for him to find a seat. Surry's regional airport was never extremely busy and the plane received clearance in short order.

About an hour after the plane was airborne, the pilot began making his descent. Before exiting the plane, Q was blindfolded. When he stepped off the plane, the salt air immediately hit him in the face. He had no idea which direction they had flown. However, he thought to himself: *If they flew north, I'm somewhere on the coast of Scotland; if they flew east, I'm on the coast of France; if they went south this is Spain; and if they had flown west, I'm somewhere on the coast of Ireland.*

Given this was a high stakes contract, Q was not surprised that the meeting was being held at an undisclosed location. A Mercedes was waiting to take him to the meeting location.

Tinker had elected to meet with Q at his home in Portmagee. Once Q was seated in his living room, Tinker said, "Q, you may remove the blindfold now."

As he did so, the sudden bright light momentarily distracted Q, but something told him that Tinker was only an intermediary; that alone drove the price up in Q's mind.

After a few brief informalities, Tinker began the serious conversation. "Tell me about the types of operations that you've run in the past." He made a few notes while listening to Q's deep voice. The conversation then shifted to back-and-forth questions.

When Tinker shared that a previous attempt to take out the Mounties had already failed, the price went up even further in Q's mind.

"This time, a fast-in-and-out strike is what we desire," Tinker said.

"I'd like some time to review Oliver Clarke's initial reconnaissance report," Q said after a number of clarifying questions, "so that I fully understand the layout. Once I've seen that, I'll let you know what approach I would use." With that, Tinker provided him a copy of the report, excused himself, and went into another room.

He had installed listening devices prior to Q's arrival, which had enabled the three members of Imperial Trading to hear everything that had been said so far. Now Tinker thought to himself: *This one is a hard case, but I think he's the real deal.* Imperial Trading's only interest was in hearing what his proposal for taking out the Mounties would be.

After a good half hour, Q called out to Tinker, "I'm ready."However, before Tinker returned, he placed a receiver in his ear so that Herbert Maxwell could communicate with him privately. Then he re-joined his guest.

Q began the conversation. "The earlier raid on this location is most definitely being viewed as an international terrorist attack on Canadian soil. You've put the entire country on high alert, which makes a second mission far more challenging. Entry into the country will be more difficult, as will be getting the ordinance in the country that will be required. The restricted air corridor rules out approaching their base by air. They'll most likely have drone surveillance in place, so drones are out. You're looking at another ground assault."

"Really?"

Dismissing Tinker's inexperience, Q continued. "No one's going to get up that logging road . . . soon it will be a minefield, so the road is out. The only way anyone is getting close to that base and back out now is through the woods."

"And?"

"And you want fast-in-and-out, the only way that's going to happen is on dirt bikes. A dozen dirt bikes, spread out approaching through the woods, would give us the maneuverability and speed to get in fast, eliminate the target, and get out."

"They'll hear you coming."

"Can't be avoided. By the time the Mounties realize what is making the noise, I'll be on them."

"I would think that any noise would put them on alert."

"It would, that's why I would arrange for some logging to be done in the area a few days prior to the attack. Once they're used to hearing noise coming from the land that the logging company leases, they'll let their guard down just enough."

"A dozen bikes makes a helluva lot more noise than couple of chain saws."

"I'll fit the bikes with exhaust silencers. Remember, we're going in *fast* which means we'll be well ahead of the noise by the time they hear it."

"What about weapons? What are you bringing in?"

"Assault rifles, hand grenades and handheld rocket launchers should be sufficient armament."

"You're confident this approach will work?"

"There's not much else you can carry in while riding on a dirt bike."

"I was talking about the ground assault."

"There's no other way to get in there, it has to be a ground assault. You said you wanted fast in, and fast out, the bikes will allow us to accomplish that. The actual fighting will all be done on the ground; there won't be any survivors."

Maxwell whispered into Tinker's earplug: "Ask how long it will take him to organize a team and strike the Mounties."

"How long before you'd be ready to go?"

Q noticed a distant look on Tinker's face and a brief hesitation before he asked the question and surmised that Tinker was wearing an earplug.

"I could actually have a team ready to go within a week's time. The challenge and the delay will be getting the armaments and the bikes into Canada."

"I'm in the shipping business. I'll get whatever you need into Canada."

"As long as the equipment is in-country when I arrive, I won't have any trouble filling the contract."

"Once you acquire the armaments you want, the bikes, and the modification kits, let me know where to pick them up, and they'll be in Quebec City within seven days waiting for you. What's your price?"

Without any hesitation Q said, "Half a million British pounds, half upfront."

Maxwell whispered into Tinker's earplug: "Tell him Three hundred thousand pounds and 15 percent up front."

"Too much. Three hundred thousand pounds and fifteen percent upfront," Tinker said to Q. "You'll get the balance when you text 'mission accomplished.' We'll transfer the funds directly into your bank account."

"Half a million British pounds, half upfront," Q repeated without hesitation.

Maxwell whispered into Tinker's earplug: "Three

hundred thousand, *twenty* percent up front."

"I'll do three hundred thousand pounds, *twenty* percent upfront," Tinker repeated.

Q looked Tinker straight in the eye and calmly said: "Half a million pounds, half up front."

Maxwell again whispered into Tinker's earplug: *"Four* hundred thousand, *thirty* percent up front."

"Four hundred thousand pounds, thirty percent upfront," Tinker said.

"Four hundred fifty thousand pounds, *half* up front."

Maxwell whispered into Tinker's earplug, "Say nothing . . . let's see if he blinks, if he doesn't, put him back on the plane."

Chapter 26

Lou woke up early, packed a small valise, and headed over to the lodge. He was surprised to see Andre and Kate already eating breakfast. Kate was dressed as if she was on vacation. The only other people in the lodge were Angelo and Duffy who had been on perimeter surveillance duty since midnight and was anxiously awaiting Dorsey to relieve him. Now, hungry, he was looking for food.

Lou went into the kitchen, grabbed some breakfast and sat down next to Kate. Andre cleared his throat, "All right, the two of you are masquerading as a couple visiting the island to do some hiking and bird watching."

Lou put down his coffee. "That's it? Our cover is looking at *birds*?"

"Lou, birding is a very popular tourist activity on the island. People come from all over to do that. The majority of visitors will be using binoculars, cameras, and backpacks; you won't attract anyone's attention."

Kate placed her hand on Lou's forearm. "It'll be fine

Lou, we'll blend in."

"You're traveling under your own identities," Andre said. "Lou, the only identification you should be carrying is your driver's license; Kate, just your passport. Here's a Glock 43 and a shoulder holster for each of you."

"Nice hardware."

"Don't let anything happen to these . . . the paperwork is brutal if you lose one."

"Got it."

"When you land at Blacks Harbor, go directly to the Ocean Breeze Inn and check-in. They know you're coming early. You've each got a room and you can leave your luggage there before taking the ferry over to Grand Manan."

"This is beginning to sound like the lecture I got from my parents when I first left for college," Kate smiled.

"I also need to stress to each of you that the only reason you are going down there is to observe the docks and report on how goods are being moved in and out of the port," Andre said. "No heroics, like Jake tried to pull. Speaking of Jake, he'll be waiting in Blacks Harbor early on the morning of the third day to bring you back here."

"Got it," Lou said.

"By the way, timing is actually perfect. INTERPOL believes the merchant ship 'Prentice' that set sail from Portmagee five days ago will be arriving in Grand Manan today."

Just as Andre finished speaking, Jake poked his head into the lodge; he'd just finished his preflight inspection. "I'm ready to go whenever you two are."

As everyone stood up, Andre said, "Remember, under no circumstances are you to do *anything* that will bring attention to yourselves or put you at risk. I've cut through some red tape and received clearance for an early morning landing at Black's Harbor. Good luck."

"Thanks," Lou said as he and Kate stood to leave.

When Angelo heard the door open and close, he looked out the window, and watched them travel down to the dock area. It was chilly, but the lake was calm, which meant they'd have a smooth take-off. Within minutes, the engines revved up.

As soon as the pontoons lifted off the water, Jake turned his head to look back at his passengers and smiled. "You are now free to roam about the cabin."

The outside air temperature was close to freezing at the altitude that Jake had leveled off; there was minimal heat reaching the rear of the plane and Lou noticed that Kate was shivering.

"Kate, here, wrap this blanket around yourself."

She smiled and mouthed: "Thank you."

The flight was smooth and when they were twenty minutes out from landing, Jake radioed his approach. Powerful landing lights were soon illuminating the harbor. As luck would have it, they came in on a slack tide.

When they exited the plane, Lou made a show of giving Jake a gratuity in case there were any eyes watching before he grabbed their luggage and walked up the wharf to the taxi stand.

"I'd hold your hand, Kate, but I've got both hands full."

"You're doing fine," she laughed in her soft brogue, "besides, lesson number two is that you always carry your girlfriend's books."

"How many of these lessons are there?"

"Oh look, there's a puffin," she said, obviously avoiding the answer.

Great, we really are watching birds, Lou thought.

When they checked into the Inn, they found their rooms were on separate floors. It was still hours before the first ferry crossing, so they headed over to a restaurant to grab coffee and wait.

About thirty people were already in line waiting for the first crossing. Kate whispered to Lou, "Looks like this is the couple's cruise."

"Yeah, except for the two stiffs by the door."

"Hmmm, I didn't see them."

"They just showed up."

Soon after the ferry left the sheltered harbor, they felt the engines struggle against the powerful tide rushing into the Bay of Fundy. The wind out in the open bay was considerable, but the ferry was designed to handle five-to-six-foot swells and crosswinds with ease.

The sky was still grey and the crossing was pretty boring. The cabin offered Lou and Kate an opportunity to lean against one another and actually get a little sleep, just like every other couple on the ferry seemed to be doing.

When the captain finally announced the approach to North Head Harbor on the intercom, Kate immediately sat up, stretched out her arms, then tousled Lou's hair. "Wake up sleepy head. We're almost there."

Lou straightened and yawned.

Totally in character, Kate said, "You needed that rest, hon."

Lou was surprised before he realized that "the curtain had just gone up." He put his arm around Kate's shoulders and playfully pulled her close to him. Her hazel green eyes widened, then she settled into his embrace. Before long, Kate stood up.

"Come on, let's go outside to watch."

Once ashore, she picked up a map of the island's hiking trails, and they headed down to the wharf. A number of their fellow ferry passengers were already lined up at the whale watch kiosk.

Kate headed toward a weathered picnic table overlooking the harbor at a dockside restaurant that was closed and spread the map out. Lou sat down on the bench seat beside her, took his binoculars out of the case, and pretended to be cleaning them as his eyes scanned around the harbor. To the casual observer, the two of them looked just like any other couple trying to figure out what their game plan was for the day.

"Kate, it looks like most of the fishing boats have left the harbor, but that Gantry crane is active across the way where that merchant ship is tied up."

"What's the name of the ship?"

Through his binoculars, Lou was able to read the ship's name. "Halverson, registered out of Panama.

"That's one of the ships listed in that laptop!" Kate said.

"See if there's a trail that goes along the ridge behind the dock on that map."

"The North Point Trail does, Lou."

"Good, that'll give us a closer look at the Halverson; let's go."

In another twenty-five minutes, they were sitting on craggy rocks looking directly down on the Halverson. Even without the use of binoculars, they could easily observe hand-operated jacks removing pallets wrapped in opaque plastic from a cargo container and dock workers walking the jacks over to the Gantry crane where they were hoisted up and lowered into the cargo hold of the Halverson.

When the container had been emptied, the Gantry moved down the track, picked it up and stacked it next to a few other empty containers at the far end of the dock. Minutes later, another container was brought down to the dock; only a few pallets were removed before the container doors were shut, and a small tractor hauled it back up the hill to what must be a warehouse.

Shortly before noon, the crew of the Halverson left port. Kate sent a text to Andre: *"Halverson now leaving port, pls monitor course."* She received a return text: *'freighter Prentice 4 hours out'.*

They hiked back to their starting point and grabbed the same table they had used earlier. The restaurant was now open with faded umbrellas in the center of each table that hopefully would discourage the cruising gulls from swooping in and trying to take food. As soon as they were seated, a cheerful waitress carrying menus and a tray of condiments approached them. Kate ordered an iced tea as she slipped into tourist mode.

"Tell me, how often do the cruise ships come in and tie up at that big dock over there?"

Laughing the waitress replied, "Oh honey, the cruise ships don't come in here. That's a working dock over there."

"Never?" she said with a disappointed look.

"Well, I've lived here all my life and I haven't seen one yet!"

"Interesting. So, what exactly is a *working* dock?"

"Oh, you know, they service merchant ships that come in at all hours of the day and night. For the most part, it's the smaller ships that arrive in the mornings, they're the ones that bring in everything we need here on the island and they're in and out in no time. But a few big ones will tie up overnight, even bigger than that one." The waitress pointed to the Halverson. "Their cargo goes up into the warehouse and then the ships are gone."

"Well, you certainly do know a lot about shipping."

"Ha! Thankfully it's only second-hand. My brother works across the way on those docks. When he's had a few, all he talks about is life on the docks . . . it's all he's ever done. The wages are good, but it's no life, if you ask me. I hear that another big one is coming in today which means he won't be home now until the morning.

"Now, what'll you two have?" she said, switching her focus. "The lobster rolls are huge, and we have the best clam chowder on the island. Fourth year in a row, now, that we've won the island's annual chowder cook-off. Sam, the barber, always thinks that *his* is the best and expects to win every year, but he skimps too much on the herbs."

Looking directly at Kate, Lou said: "Hon, I don't know about you, but she had me at lobster roll."

"You are so predictable," Kate laughed. "Okay, I'll have a bowl of the clam chowder, please."

When the waitress returned with their order, Lou asked, "Does the island operate the working dock, or is that privately owned?"

"Well, the working dock is privately owned, but we islanders own everything else in the harbor, and that helps keep the cost of running a boat way down."

"Oh, so it's run by a big conglomerate that muscled its way in, huh?" Kate asked.

"Heavens no! It's owned by a consortium of locals. Our constable, Orson Evers and Felix Lajoie, who grew up here but now lives off island, are the majority owners."

"Mmm, this chowder is delicious," Kate said, offering a spoonful to Lou. "Here, give this a taste."

After lunch, they strolled along the wharf that circled the entire harbor, admiring the private yachts that were in port. By midday, many of the lobster boats had already returned to the harbor, unloaded their catch, and were sitting on their swing moorings. The trawlers that had sailed from the harbor earlier, wouldn't return until close to sunset.

As Lou and Kate strolled near the working dock, they noticed a ten-foot-high chain-link fence surrounding it, as well as a guard shack.

Lou held back, but Kate walked right through the gate and headed over to the water's edge. Immediately, the guard was up and shouting.

"Stop, lady, stop! You can't come in here; this is private property."

Kate turned, smiled and said, "Oh, I'm sorry . . . I

was following the dolphins . . . they are just *so* beautiful, we rarely see them at home. Are they here all year?"

The guard was an older man working a lonely job. "Well, that's certainly a nice touch of the brogue that you've got. My folks came over from the 'ole sod,' too. To answer your question, yes, they're here year-round." Then he corrected himself. "Well, not all of them, mind you, most will be migrating south following their food. Now, missy, I must ask you to step back outside the gate. This area isn't open to the public and the insurance company has some pretty strict rules about all of that."

Kate deliberately made a move to lean up against the fence, hoping the guard would warn her if it was electrified. He didn't, and thankfully, it wasn't. Acting startled, she jumped away. "Oh my, is this fence electric?"

The guard chuckled. "No, it's just a plain old fence, but if it was, you can bet those insurance fellas would want a lot more money."

Lou noticed the guard had a sidearm. Whether he could actually hit the broad side of a barn with it was another story. "Come on Kate, let's not get this gentleman in any trouble; he's just trying to do his job," Lou called to Kate,

"Thanks folks," the guard called back. "It's time for me to punch out and go home to the missus, anyway."

Kate took the hint, quickly retreated, and slipped her arm under Lou's, and physically melted into his side as they walked away.

"What did you see?"

"His replacement walking down the hill, I think," Lou whispered back. "I thought it better that he didn't see either of us, if we were planning to come back later tonight."

"Good call."

Later, as they casually walked back along the wharf to the tourist shops, Lou and Kate reviewed what they'd just learned. Since sunset wasn't until six-fifteen, they busied themselves poking around in various shops as the container ship, Prentice, entered the harbor.

When they sat down for dinner, Kate asked, "So, is it lobster again? Or are we venturing out to something else?"

"Actually, I was thinking of salmon cooked on a cedar plank, washed down with a nice glass of Sauvignon Blanc from New Zealand," Lou said. "They raise the salmon in the bay now, you know, but on second thought, I just might be going with the lobster. By the way, did you notice the Prentice had arrived?"

"I *did* know that salmon was being farmed in the bay. Scotland is into that, too. For me, the wild-caught is tastier, and it doesn't impact the environment. And yes, I did notice the Prentice. And on second thought, I'll just go with the haddock." With a smile, Kate leaned across the table. "I think we're going to have the same server that we had at lunch. Order for the both of us, that always gives the impression that we're a couple."

"Is that lesson number three?"

Kate tilted her head, "No, it's more around number seventy-four; it could even be as high as seventy-eight but it's way, way up there."

"You're a piece of work, you know that?"

"My mother always said that I had a touch of the Blarney."

The same server greeted them with a huge smile. "Welcome back, folks! Are you ready to order?"

Lou ordered for them both, along with a bottle of Sauvignon Blanc.

Kate whispered as she looked over her wine glass, "I wonder what's being offloaded from that ship?"

"I'm more curious to see what Constable Evers has

stored up the hill in that warehouse of his."

By the time they finished eating, the sun had set. They nonchalantly got up from the table, put on their backpacks, and moved over to the rail by the water's edge, where they could discuss their plan away from any listening ears. Shortly afterwards, they began strolling along the wharf holding hands in the twilight, stopping ever so often to look out across the harbor.

As they approached the working dock's gate area, Lou broke off to the right while they were still in the shadows. The hill Lou had to climb was steep; fortunately, the perimeter fence wasn't illuminated much beyond the area around the dock. Lou looked for a place where he could easily scale the fence from either direction without being seen.

Kate continued forward on the road, intent on attracting and occupying the guard's attention. As she neared the gate, the guard emerged from the shack saying, "Sorry, this is a restricted area."

"Really? Now that seems odd, what could possibly make this a restricted area?"

"I don't make the rules. I just do what I'm paid to do."

Moving closer to the gate, Kate looked up at him invitingly. "Well, there must be some explanation that you can share with me."

"No admittance without a pass. That's the rule, now please back away."

Kate stood her ground.

"I asked you to move along."

Deliberately standing with one foot inside the restricted area, she said, "Well, what goes on over here that nobody's supposed to see?"

"Look miss, I don't make the rules. Just turn around and go back to the public area."

"Well, maybe, I'll just stand here and watch for a while."

The guard returned to the shack, and Kate overheard him talking to someone on the phone. "Mac? Yeah, listen, I got a situation down here. Some nosey broad is giving me a little crap about this being a restricted area. No, she's still outside. Yeah, it looks like she's alone. Okay, okay, will do."

The guard emerged from the shack again. "You can watch all you want from *outside* the gate area, now be a good little girl and move back."

Kate bristled at being called a "little girl," but let it pass.

By now, Lou had scaled the fence and was inside the restricted area. As he moved toward the warehouse, he carefully circled away from the halogen lights staying in the shadows. The further up the hill he proceeded, the more often he was forced to wait in the shadows as dock workers constantly traveled up and down the roadway.

When Lou was finally able to peek around a building, he could see the doors to the warehouse were wide open. He heard footsteps coming his way and barely managed to slip back into the shadows as someone in a security guard's uniform passed only a few feet from him heading down the hill toward the gate area. He, also, saw quite a few people hanging around the warehouse's open doorway. The better view for observing inside the warehouse was on the opposite side of the narrow street.

Lou tossed a rock onto the metal roof of the warehouse, creating just enough of a distraction to dart across the road into an alley without being seen. He squeezed around a couple of putrid dumpsters for a better line of sight into the warehouse and was now close enough to hear someone with a clipboard directing which containers needed to be opened and which pallets needed to be taken out and placed inside another container to be brought down to the dock.

Having seen enough, he was concerned about a second guard who had gone down to the gate area where he had left Kate. As Lou began to work his way back along the dumpsters, a worker carrying a trash bucket rounded the corner and entered the alley. Lou pressed further back into the shadows, but the worker had seen the movement.

"Hey, who's in here?"

Lou had no option but to take the guy out, which he did with ease, but it delayed his ability to return to Kate. He quickly put on the man's hat and coat, then switched his backpack around to his front and zipped the coat over it. He resembled a man with a pot belly. He headed out. The fastest way to the gate was straight down the road.

In the distance, he could see the two guards talking to Kate. He narrowed his eyes as he watched her beginning to back further away from the gate.

Lou quickened his pace.

Chapter 27

The two men sat staring at each other in silence for nearly three full minutes before Q smiled a frozen, lopsided grimace. "Four hundred twenty-five thousand pounds, *half* upfront." Maxwell whispered into Tinker's earpiece, "Four hundred twenty-five thousand, *twenty percent* upfront . . . final offer."

Tinker relayed the message as if it was his own.

Q repeated, "Twenty-*five* percent upfront."

After a lengthy pause, Maxwell whispered, "Go with the twenty-five."

Tinker inhaled deeply. "Twenty-*five* percent upfront."

"Good," Q smiled, this time for real.

"Tell me where to pick up what you want shipped over and everything will be in Quebec waiting for you within two weeks."

"Agreed."

"Let me know what flight you'll be taking into Quebec City and someone will meet you at the airport with directions to your armaments and the bikes," Tinker said.

"Anything else?"

"Yes, I want a text when you leave for Canada and another when the mission is completed."

"Fine."

"Once I receive your final message, the remaining funds will be electronically deposited into your bank account."

"You won't be disappointed this time."

"I had better not be. I'll need the bank's routing number and account number where you want to receive the upfront funds."

Q reached for his wallet, took out a blank check, and handed it over. "Use this."

"Thank you."

"Oh, by the way, you can tell whomever it was on the other end of that plug in your ear . . . it was nice negotiating with him."

"What?"

"Your body language gave it away, old chap. I bloody well knew it wasn't *you* I was negotiating with." The insult pissed Tinker off. "Put the blindfold back on; you're going back to London."

"I'm going to need a place to modify the bikes once they're in Canada. Can you arrange for that?"

"We'll take care of that."

"Good."

When Q left Tinker's house, he smiled when he overheard him say: "He's a cocky one."

Based on Tinker's accent, Q figured they had flown him to Ireland to make this deal, not that it made any difference to him.

As Lou approached the gate leading into the working dock on Grand Manan, he could clearly hear the guards telling Kate she was under arrest for trespassing.

He pulled the peak of his hat down a little lower,

walked over to the gate, and stood directly behind the two guards about to take her into custody. "We got a problem here, guys?"

"Nothing we can't handle," the first guard replied without turning around. "Just go about your business."

Immediately recognizing Lou's voice, Kate released the tension in her face. Lou pulled out his Glock. The guards heard the click as he chambered a round. "Okay, fellas, nice and easy now; hands up and kneel on the ground."

"What?"

"Just do as I say. There's no need for anyone to get hurt."

Kate backed up a few more steps. Once the guards were kneeling on the ground, Lou removed their sidearms and discretely tossed them into the field next to the guard shack.

Now, what to do with these guards, he thought. Then switching to an authoratative voice, Lou asked, "Young lady, did either of these men threaten you in any way at all, or cause you any harm?"

"Well, sir, I was very concerned, and *did* feel threatened, but no, sir, they did me no harm."

"All right you two. Constable Evers will have my report on this in the morning. I'm officially releasing you from duty for the rest of the night. Get up slowly, go punch out, and go home. You'll be paid for your full shift, and you'll get your sidearms back tomorrow."

"Who the hell are you?" one of them growled.

"Someone you don't want to mess with," Lou said. "The Constable has a few of us working undercover for him, boys. Just do as I say. I'll put in a good word for you, that way you'll only get a reprimand from Evers. Go along now; I'll see to it that this gate is staffed until your regular relief comes on duty. Oh, and the less said about this to anyone else, the better it will go for you. There's one of us working this gig for Evers on every shift. He'll be in touch, boys, in the meantime, come to work tomorrow for your regular shift, and remember, keep your mouths shut about this until you speak with Evers."

"Why'd you pull your weapon on us?"

"I've been in this business long enough to know that disarming someone is the very first thing you do. Ya just never know, my friend. Okay, get up, and don't turn around . . . you don't need to see my face. In the future, be gentler with the tourists. The Constable doesn't want them to be afraid to come over to the island."

Lou waited for both guards to get up and start walking up the road. He assumed they were headed to their lockers. Once they were out of sight, Lou shed his coat and hat and they moved quickly along the wharf, staying in the shadows as much as possible as they headed to the ferry landing.

"Where did you ever come up with the undercover work for Evers?" Kate chuckled.

"Like you said, there's no script for this, it's all improv."

"I'm impressed," she laughed. "If you had told me to get down on my knees and put my hands up, I would have!"

"Well, you had me wondering this afternoon, if you really were seeing dolphins."

When they reached the ferry landing, the ticket office was dark. A sign taped to the window read: "Due to mechanical problems, ferry service has been discontinued for the night."

"Now what?" Kate asked.

"Looks like we're spending the night on the island. Let's get some accommodations, if we can." They headed to the nearest hotel.

"Sorry folks, we're completely booked, but the Compass Chart might still have a vacancy."

"Could you call ahead and inquire?"

"Sure."

Shortly after placing the call, the desk clerk put his hand over the receiver. "They have one room left, a queen bed. Will that be all right?"

When Lou hesitated, Kate spoke up, "That will be fine; we'll take it!"

With directions, they headed to the Compass Chart and checked in. Entering the small quarters,

Lou let out a sigh.

"One bed. This is going to be interesting."

Kate squeezed his arm. "If you were any kind of gentleman, you'd forgo any thoughts about 'choosing up' over who gets the bed and who gets the floor."

Lou walked over to the couch. "Well, look-y here. This converts into a bed. Lucky me."

Surprisingly, the Prentice was still sitting at the dock the next morning. Rubbing his back, Lou grabbed the binoculars and took a closer look.

"There's a lot of people just standing around over there; one guy is waving his arms. Something's up. I'm going to rent one of the kayaks and see if I can slip under the dock to find out what is going on."

When the attendant brought out a bright yellow kayak, Lou said, "Sorry buddy, yellow isn't my color. Let me have the camouflaged one leaning against the wall, and one of those green life vests."

As he approached the working dock, Lou heard a voice call out on a loudspeaker: "This is a restricted area; please remain outside the buoys."

Lou waved in the air acknowledging their instruction and backpaddled beyond the buoys. Then he pointed his kayak parallel to the Prentice. Once alongside the ship and out of sight to anyone on shore, he paddled around the stern and under the dock.

The tide was in, and there was little head clearance under the wooden dock. Lou stowed his paddle and life jacket and worked his way hand over hand past the barnacle encrusted pilings and around support braces until he reached the cement base for the Gantry crane. He could hear a few voices and pieces of conversation.

After a while, it was clear that the Gantry had broken down, and that the Prentice should have been fully loaded and gone hours ago. The problem now was that smaller freighters would be entering the harbor shortly and expecting to be able to tie up.

Lou slowly worked his way back along the underside of the dock and paddled across the harbor to return the kayak. As soon as he hauled the kayak out of the water, Kate was beside him, giving him an enormous hug.

"What's up?" he whispered in her ear.

"Just wanted to show a couple charming characters who made me feel undressed several times, know that I'm not a colleen out on my own."

"Either one of them a guard from last night?"

"No, I would have recognized them if they were."

"Let's get some breakfast 'to go.' We can hike back over to where we were yesterday. Seems like the Gantry is broken, and pressure is building to get the ship out. It'll be interesting to see what they do."

By the time they reached the high spot on the trail immediately above the working dock, things seemed to be in motion again. A gangway had been erected and individual pallets were being hauled aboard using electric hand trucks.

"Kate, I'm not sure how much more we can learn about this operation without putting ourselves at risk. I think it's time we head over to the ferry landing before our luck runs out. Once we're back on the mainland, we can get a car and drive around Passamaquoddy Bay. Maybe we can even find out where the Halverson is docked."

"Let's go," she said.

When they reached the public landing area, the ferry was just arriving in port.

"Good timing, huh?"

"I'll say. Get in line for the ferry. I'll go over to the ticket window."

There was already a decent line of passengers waiting to board. When Lou returned with two tickets, Kate gave him another huge hug and whispered, "It seems we have a tail. The two men busy undressing me with their eyes earlier are standing directly behind you."

Lou removed his backpack and discretely put the Glock in his right cargo pocket of the khakis he was wearing. Then he turned and made a show of putting his backpack on to get a good look at both men before they turned away.

"We've attracted someone's attention, that's for sure," he said. "I hate having to watch my back. The landing is pretty crowded; I doubt they'll try anything here. Lemme go find out who they are."

"I'll have my Glock in the ready if you're wrong," she said. Lou blended into the crowd and was amused when he saw the two men desperately trying to locate him. Within minutes, he was standing directly behind them. He loaded his own Glock's chamber.

"Both hands on top of your heads, boys, and stay facing the way you were." Lou heard one sigh, as they both complied. "Mind telling me why we have a tail?"

"Can I show you my credentials?" the taller of the two men asked.

"Where are they?"

"Left front pocket, my coat."

"Use your left hand and keep your right hand up; no

funny business."

"My partner's credentials are the same."

Lou looked at the folder. "Special Agent, INTERPOL."

"Okay, fellas you can turn around."

Lou introduced himself. 'So, why the tail?"

"We thought we recognized one of our own earlier, a Lieutenant O'Grady. But she isn't supposed to be here. We uploaded a photo to verify that it was her; but no one's gotten back to us yet. We thought if it *was* her, we'd be able to trade intel. Then you showed up and we backed off."

"Well, it *is* O'Grady. So, if you're interested in going for a boat ride, you can join us. We're headed back to the mainland."

"We can't leave the island; we only arrived yesterday. Tell her I'll get word to her through INTERPOL's database on anything we uncover."

Lou noticed that passengers were beginning to board the ferry. "Nice to meet you both, but I gotta run." He caught up with Kate just before she would have needed to step out of line. Quickly, she slid her arm under his, leaned close.

"And the mystery men are . . . ?"

"INTERPOL," he whispered back. "They thought they recognized you and are going to compare notes with you through normal channels."

Kate found it interesting that she wasn't advised from INTERPOL that they were sending agents over to Grand Manan. But then, again, she hadn't let them know she would be traveling to the island either.

When they reached the mainland, Lou went into the only car rental office and secured the last vehicle available in Blacks Harbor. As he headed out the door, he called out, "Come on Kate, we're renting from National. Like their ad says, you can pick out any car on the lot you want. And, hey, today it's ladies' choice!"

The car lot was directly behind the building. As they

rounded the corner, Kate realized that Lou was having a little fun with her, as there was only vehicle on the lot, an old Jeep Renegade with five on the floor.

"Well, at least it green!" Kate said as she jumped in, started up the Jeep and turned to Lou. "Buckle up, cowboy, this will be interesting. This will be my first time steering on the left, shifting with my right, and driving on the wrong side of the road."

She slammed the vehicle into gear, burned more than a little rubber as she scrubbed out of the parking lot, narrowly missing a head-on with an oncoming car.

"Right lane! Kate, we use the *right* lane over here!" Lou's eyes were wide with panic.

"Right lane! Got it."

"Damn, that was close!"

By the time Kate reached third gear, she'd managed to hit every possible pothole and bump in the road at top speed. Lou was jostled around so much he tightened his seatbelt and began holding on to the grip over the door. When Kate blew through a stop sign and took the corner on two wheels, a vision of "Mr. Toad's Wild Ride" filled Lou's thoughts.

Pulling up at a stop light, Kate let out a deep breath. "Well, it's got some guts to it, but it pulls wicked to the right." She glanced over at Lou.

"Hey, pal you look a little pale over there. You need to get out in the sun some more."

"You ever think about driving a cab?"

"Nah, that's no life."

Their first stop was Beaver Harbor, one of the few ports actually deep enough in the bay for the Halverson to possibly have docked there. It also had a Gantry crane. The only person who seemed to be around was an old timer sitting on the dock enjoying a pipe.

"Sir, could you tell me if the Halverson docked here recently?" Kate asked.

"And why would you be wanting to know that?"

"Well, my brother crews on that ship, and I was hoping I might be able to see him."

"Well, you're too late. They left this morning on the early tide.

"Are you sure?"

"I've been sitting here on what they unloaded waiting for it to be picked up ever since. Darn trucker was due here hours ago; the misses will be wondering where I am, *that's* for sure."

"Who's the trucker?"

"Baker, it's always E. Baker Trucking. They're usually on time, too, but not today."

"Does Baker pick up a lot down here?"

"Like I said, it's *always* E. Baker Trucking. Used to be others, but Baker picks up most of the cargo around the bay now. He hauls some of it all the way up to Quebec! Lordy, he has to be earning a hefty shipping fee on that."

Kate smiled at Lou. "Sweetheart, I think it's time for us to go home."

By the time they returned to Blacks Harbor and dropped off the rental, it was dinnertime. Sitting across from one another in a candlelit restaurant, they unwound a little from the last two days. Kate looked up from fiddling with her wine glass.

"Lou, I wasn't exactly sure how this whole thing was going to turn out when we committed to do it, but I have to say, you really made it work for me on a number of levels. I want to say, 'thank you.'"

"Well, if we're being honest," Lou said, "you made it easy for me, too, Kate, and you're right, it did work. And it was fun, except when those two guards were trying to arrest you. I can do without *that* feeling again."

The rest of the evening, they relaxed over a second bottle of wine and shared a few personal stories with one another. Lou found himself more than once sneaking a glance at this attractive young woman, with chestnut brown hair, who sat across from him. Until then, he had only seen the professional side of her. He hadn't expected to find the fun-loving side that her devilish sense of humor had brought out. A few times, he saw her looking at him with a steady gaze and wondered what she was thinking.

When they'd had enough wine, they retired for the night. But he slept on the couch again.

The next morning, when they reached the harbor, Jake was already waiting. Lou greeted his cousin.

"I see you're up bright and early."

"Ya, well, I had to stop off and pick up a hitchhiker along the way."

"Oh?"

As if on cue, Fletcher Martin poked his good arm out the side window of the plane and waved. "Hi, guys!"

Chapter 28

When Lou and Kate returned to the lodge, everyone listened as they debriefed Andre on their observations from Grand Manan and Passamaquoddy Bay. Andre was especially interested in the working dock and warehouse.

"Grand Manan doesn't produce anything that's exported," he said. "So, clearly, whatever the Halverson and Prentice picked up or dropped off were goods smuggled in." After listening further to the debrief, Andre was satisfied he now had enough information to act. "But the island is only one piece of the puzzle," he said.

Given Duffy's investigative work and the debrief, E. Baker Trucking had now become a prime suspect for how illicit goods were being moved further into Canada. Exactly *where* they were going was still an unknown. *How* Baker kept the illegal goods being moved separated from everything else constantly moving in and out of his yards was a mystery, too.

Andre sensed an undercover expedition to E. Baker Trucking in Quebec was needed, but it would have to wait for now. In the meantime, he would reach out to Bob Newton, an old friend who retired from the Mounties a few years ago, and now lived in Quebec City.

As a Mountie, Newton had been well-liked. He had been everyone's 'go-to' guy whenever they needed to book off a shift. He'd work a double any day of the week and was always volunteering for special details. One night, he'd flipped his cruiser on an icy stretch of road racing to respond to a call for backup. The injuries he sustained were serious enough to force him into early retirement, a retirement he was reluctant to accept.

As soon as they finished the debrief, Kate hurried over to her computer to check for incoming messages. She found two emails from the INTERPOL system. The first verified that INTERPOL did have agents on Grand Manan Island; the second contained a file listing Canadian phone numbers that Sean Tinker had either called or received calls from during the past three months. Interestingly, the majority of calls were to or from the same number, however, a few calls were made to an area code in Montreal.

During their return flight home, Jake had briefly shared with Lou what he and Cunningham had been busy working on during the previous two days. It wasn't long before the three men had a chance to go over some of the defense preparations accomplished while Lou was away.

"Lou," Cunningham began, "I really believe the next attack will include light off-road vehicles. I think it's going to be a quick in-and-out attack, most likely ATVs or off-road bikes."

"You really think that?"

"Yeah, once a dirt bike clears the heavy underbrush, they could easily maneuver in and around the lodge and cottages to do some real damage."

In preparation, Jake and Cunningham had spent the better part of a day felling dozens of trees back in the woods to create a natural barrier that would hamper any off-road vehicle attempting to come at them through the woods at a high rate of speed.

Lou was fine with what they'd accomplished and the three of them began designing how they would deploy the ordinances that Andre had asked be flown up.

Late in the afternoon, a floatplane arrived with Fred O'Neil, the additional Mountie Andre had requested. Fred had always been high on Andre's list of potentials. He had been on leave, but when he filled his deer tag on the opening day of deer season, he returned to duty early to save vacation time. Like Cunningham, he, too, had served in the Canadian Special Operations Regiment before joining the Mounties.

Cunningham was pleased to find he'd be sharing a cottage with O'Neil. The two men were good friends and had worked together on numerous investigations, including stakeouts. Long talks during those times had enabled them understand and appreciate each other.

The day after O'Neil arrived, Duffy was released to Lou and the five of them went about deploying ordinances along the old logging road but staying within the boundaries of Havre de Poisson's property line. Lou decided to leave the gate open, hoping it might be an invitation for someone to use the road. Additional surveillance cameras were set up in the woods, the drone detection equipment was positioned, and trip wires were attached to detonators.

Once they finished setting everything out, Jake walked over to the wooded area directly behind the cottages where the underbrush had been cleared and installed yet another deadly line of defense. Using piano gauge wire, he stretched lengths of wire between a number of trees at just about neck level for anyone sitting on a dirt bike or an ATV. *Let's see what happens,* he thought. *It sure might surprise someone.*

At dinner Lou announced, "After breakfast tomorrow, I

want everyone to get a little more training using the defensive arsenal we now have at our disposal. A couple of drones will also be flying in during early afternoon. I'd like everyone back in the lodge at 1400 hours to receive training on the anti-drone and RF sensor feeds as well as the technique for destroying any incoming drones."

Lou had planted claymore mines along the shoreline east and west of the lodge and added, "After the mock drone attack, I'll detonate a claymore so everyone will be familiar with the sound."

The following morning, everyone took turns firing the rocket launchers at targets Jake had placed on a raft anchored out in the middle of the lake. Range on the launchers had been scaled back, so if a rocket missed its target, it would fall into the lake well before reaching the opposite shore.

Later, Lou had everyone practice firing automatic carbines at the range he had constructed a few years earlier for his guests to "sight in" their rifles during deer season. The biggest challenge everyone seemed to have was keeping the weapon *down* when firing on full-automatic. Since the weapon was light, it tended to rise up during a short burst. They all needed practice. The team went through a number of targets until Lou was satisfied they would be able to control their weapons.

"I still prefer a shotgun," Angelo said as they walked back to the lodge.

That evening Lou held class on how the defense plan would operate and where everyone would deploy when they came under attack. He had decided that foxholes would be an integral part of his overall defense plan. After mapping out where the foxholes would be strategically placed, he planned to fire up the old frontend loader stored in the sawmill and do a little digging.

"All right, listen up!" Lou said. "Jake and I will position

ourselves in separate foxholes to the left side of the logging road. Cunningham, you and O'Neil will defend from the right side in separate foxholes. Duffy, Dorsey, and Andre you'll position yourselves in fox holes surrounding the lodge area."

"So, four at the road and three at the lodge?" Duffy asked.

"Yes. Kate, once again I want you to monitor the screen shots from inside the lodge and keep everyone appraised of what you're seeing from the cameras. For your safety, I've added a trap door to the floor in the lodge. Should the lodge come under heavy fire, you are to immediately take your carbine, drop down into the crawl space below the lodge and move into a foxhole. I want everyone else to deploy into the root cellar."

Fletcher's shoulder injury was still healing and he was unable to fire any of the weapons during the earlier practice. Neither he nor Angelo were pleased to hear they would deploy along with Alessandra to the root cellar.

The following morning, Andre was able to reach his friend Bob Newton who was only too pleased to help Andre and shared as much as he knew about E. Baker Trucking. True to form, Bob also let Andre know he would make himself available to do more, if needed.

"Thanks, Bob. There's always a possibility for some 'off the books' work," Andre said. "I may be sending a couple of people up to Quebec City soon. I'll give you a call."

Part 4

Chapter 29

To date, Baker had received twelve cargo containers sent specifically to his attention. The containers were all picked up from Quebec's Old Port, supposedly headed to the secure compound at Baker's yard, where they would be inspected "at a later date." But in fact, the containers never arrived at Baker's regular yard since he had decided early on that moving these questionable goods into his yard was far too risky. So, instead, they went directly to the hangar Baker leased at the airport.

Once the containers were at the hangar, Baker logged onto the inspector's system, and recorded the containers as having been inspected . . . to close the legal loop.

There was no signage on the hangar indicating that E. Baker Trucking had leased the building. The only thing Baker had done since leasing the hangar was to change the locks and install a security system that he monitored remotely from his smartphone. The hangar doors were locked after each shipment was delivered, and there had never been evidence of anyone trying to tamper with the locks.

Recently, Baker had contemplated whether he might need to lease the adjacent vacant hangar but had taken no action to date. Up to this point, the logistics and the paperwork had been simple; all he needed to do was to receive and secure a few containers and enter them into the system as having been cleared by customs.

Then a few days ago, sometime before dawn, Baker received a text message from Imperial Trading: *"Our agent in Canada will be contacting you,"* the message read.

Within a day, Baker received another text message that he was to unload a few pallets from a specific container and deliver them to a warehouse in Montreal. The message was merely signed, "Dobbs." It was the first time Baker had been asked to do anything other than pick up and warehouse the containers.

Dobbs was known throughout the black market as a resource who could acquire just about anything, for a price. He was the "fence" who moved whatever funneled into Canada for Imperial Trading, and the focal point for goods flowing out of Canada to Portmagee in Ireland. He was primarily located in Montreal and frequently traveled around the provinces on behalf of Imperial Trading and his other clientele.

That same day, Baker received a second text from Dobbs: *"Arriving at Jean Lesage International Airport tomorrow at 0700, have a driver meet me. I wish to tour your holding facility."*

Baker reviewed the logbook he maintained one more time and was confident that everything was in order.

Dobbs was a man of average height who maintained a trim physique and was always impeccably dressed. His mannerisms were consistent with someone who had long enjoyed the luxuries that life had to offer. He walked with a cane, not because he needed one, but because it concealed the blade of an epee fencing sword that was housed inside its shaft. Dobbs had studied fencing from the time he was a young boy and although he no longer competed, he was still considered to be a very capable adversary in the world of fencing.

When Dobbs' plane landed, he immediately headed to the limo area. He stopped when he saw a man holding a sign with black lettering indicating "E. Baker Trucking." He beckoned the man over and handed him the luggage he had been carrying."Lead the way, please," he said and was shown to a black, non-descript vehicle. When the driver arrived at the hangar, Baker was standing at an open service door. Dobbs tapped the driver's seat with his cane. "Wait here," he said.

As Dobbs approached the hanger, Baker extended his hand. "Mr. Dobbs? Emile Baker." Dobbs ignored the offered hand but slightly tipped his hat before walking past Baker into the hanger.

After a visual scan of the interior, Dobbs was satisfied that the location was suitable and began querying Baker. "How do you manage to move the containers without the inspector's knowledge?"

"Basically, it's due to the level of trust the Port Authority has with me; we have an arrangement that allows me to move incoming containers over to my yard where they are then inspected." Dobbs was impressed with the scheme but understood that it all hinged on the relationship that Baker personally had with the Port Authority.

Dobbs, then, had Baker open several containers and he compared his list of what *should* be in the containers with what actually *was* inside. After the third container showed no discrepancies, he was satisfied.

"I'm curious, Baker, is the hangar next door available?"

"I believe it is," Baker said, then paused before saying, "Actually, I'm certain that it is."

"Splendid, lease it. I have a need for it. Shortly a container will be arriving that I'll want to be stored in that hangar. Text me later today that you've leased it."

"Consider it done. Anything else?"

"Yes. I'd like you to arrange to have a banner that says: 'Dobbs Aviation' placed over the doorway, and if there's anything inside that hangar, get rid of it."

"Okay."

"Incidentally, if there is anything in that other hangar not in working order, and I repeat, *anything at all,* get it fixed."

"Okay."

"It has been a pleasure meeting you, Baker. I'm sure that we will be in touch more often, now that we've met."

Dobbs abruptly turned, walked out the door, got in the car, and told the driver, "Chateau Frontenac, please." While enroute, Dobbs sent a text to Tinker that he had secured a location for 'Q' to reconfigure twelve dirt bikes and to pick up the ordinance that would be shipped over with them.

When Dobbs checked into the Frontenac, the desk clerk said, "There are two gentlemen waiting for you in the lounge."

"Hold this until I return," Dobbs said and placed his luggage on the counter. Bypassing the lounge, he headed straight to the maître d' and slipped him a generous incentive. "I'll be returning momentarily and would like a discreet table that is a distance away from everyone else." He then walked to meet the two gentlemen.

The men were, in fact, the senior vice president-general manager, and vice president of service, at the holding company that owned every BMW dealership in the provinces of Quebec, New Brunswick and the rest of the Maritime Provinces. Frustrated with a lack of response from Germany, the two businessmen were reluctantly exploring if a temporary solution to the parts shortage might be the black market. They had repeatedly been told that Dobbs was the one individual they needed to speak with. Dobbs had invited them to a lunchtime appointment today.

Once seated, the two men felt awkward and unsure on how to proceed. But Dobbs spoke first. "I understand you gentlemen have a need. What is it that you seek to acquire?" His respectful tone broke the ice, and the managers began sharing the pressure they were under from both their investors and a growing number of unhappy customers.

Dobbs listened with interest and took notes on specific items that seemed to be most in demand. At the end of the meeting, he said, "Gentlemen, I'll need a few days to check with my sources, but I assure you that I will get back to you promptly."

Now armed with literally a "shopping list," Dobbs returned to his room and powered up his laptop. He quickly identified which containers in the hangar had the majority of parts in which the two men were most interested.

He had no difficulty obtaining a bootleg copy of BMW's current parts catalog, including the standard dealer's cost. Dobbs had also been instructed that the initial strategy was to make prices attractive enough that they would want to play. The second part of the strategy was to keep them hungry by not providing everything they asked for at first but to stretch out deliveries and continually jack up prices.

The afternoon following their initial meeting, Dobbs sent an email to both vice presidents listing the authentic BMW parts that he knew were available, and what the cost would be for each one.

The vice president-general manager was pleased they had found a solution, but was not happy that payment was required in advance via wire transfer. But he had no other option than to go along with Dobbs' requirements. The deal went through.

Once Dobbs received payment, he told Baker which

pallets from which containers needed to be loaded onto a truck and delivered to a warehouse that the dealerships maintained. The system was now in play.

Every other week, Dobbs sent both vice presidents an email letting them know what additional parts he had been able to locate and inquired if there was any interest on their end. Periodically, Dobbs was asked to locate a specific part, which was always "difficult to locate" and outrageously expensive.

Dobbs was thoroughly enjoying the cat and mouse game. Over time, the dealership was paying close to triple the price listed in the BMW dealer's catalog, plus shipping. Business was good.

Chapter

30

Meanwhile, back at Havre de Poisson, Dorsey had been totally occupied chasing down the links between Teal and Lajoie. Duffy has been busy pulling information together from the internet on E. Baker Trucking, and now had a comprehensive profile on the company. Andre's former colleague, Bob Newton, also had added value by providing a few additional details on E. Baker Trucking.

The deal that Baker had with Quebec Port Authority was unlike any Duffy could find with other Canadian ports of entry. On the surface, the arrangement seemed to be working and the issue with storage constraints that had plagued the Old Port in Quebec for years was now non-existent.

Andre also used his influence for Duffy to gain access to the Port Authority's quarterly audit reports on E. Baker Trucking, including audit work papers and a file listing the containers in Baker's yard at the time of the last audit for comparison.

Consistently, quarter after quarter, Baker's offsite inspection facility had passed the audits with flying colors.

There were never any discrepancies that weren't easily explained with a minor footnote.

However, one deviation from the norm that Duffy noticed in audit worksheets was the fact that a few shipments coming from Portmagee, Ireland, were being sent directly to the attention of E. Baker Trucking with a final destination of "Hold Until Called For." This was unusual, as the cost of shipping across the Atlantic was costly and transportation to a final destination usually occurred immediately after arrival. Anything that deviated from the norm was always a red flag for Duffy.

During lunch, Kate sat with Duffy and shared some news. "There's a growing number of cargo containers destined for Canada that INTERPOL says they've lost track of."

"How many containers?"

"I'll go back and look, a dozen I think. One instance involves six containers of BMW parts; everyone's scrambling to try and find those containers."

"Six is half the number of containers I'm seeing with instructions 'Hold Until Called For" at Baker's lot," he said with interest.

"I'll send you a file containing all the data INTERPOL has on those six missing containers, just so you have it," she said as they finished lunch.

It didn't take Duffy long to run a file-to-file comparison. He noticed there was a match on the exact weight listed for each of the six lost containers sent from BMW against a container that had been received and "cleared" at E. Baker Trucking.

Duffy smiled and thought to himself, *"Now, what are the chances of this being just a coincidence on all six?"* The two files showed all containers had shipped from the Port of Hamburg, Germany. But there the similarities ended; no other data matched. Final destination points were different; the cargo control numbers were different; the identifying numbers on the containers, and the place of origination, were different.

Duffy decided to make a call to the chief inspector at the Port Authority in Quebec.

"Chief, this is Constable William McDuffie-Ferguson, I have you on a recorded line. I need your help. I'm trying to *discretely* verify if six containers that were received and cleared for release at the E. Baker Trucking compound are still in the yard. Is that something you could verify . . . *quietly*?"

There was a pause on the other end of the line. Then the chief said, "This is a little unusual, but I don't see why not."

"Thank you, Chief. Secondly, if the containers are gone, I'd like to know when they left the yard and what any final destinations were."

Toward the end of the day, the lead inspector stationed over at the yard at E. Baker Trucking made a call to the chief. "Chief, we've looked a couple of times throughout the yard. Those six containers aren't here; they must have left."

"Check with Baker's dispatchers tomorrow," the chief said. "I'd like to see the record of when those containers left the yard."

"Will do."

Early the following morning, the chief received another call from the lead inspector at the storage compound. "Chief, Baker's people can't find any record of those six containers *ever* leaving the yard."

The chief's immediate concern was that he might have a control problem and decided to make a call directly to Emile Baker, himself."Emile, we're trying to run something down," the chief said in his most nonchalant voice. "I need to ask that you cease any and all movement of containers going in and out of your yard for the next twenty-four hours."

"Okay," Emile said, trying not to get excited. "Does this mean for just the containers that haven't been inspected and released?"

"No, it means for *all* containers," the chief said. "Nothing is to move in or out of your yard for the next twenty-four hours."

"Is there a problem I need to be aware of?"

"No, this is just one of our periodic impromptu spot audits."

"Hmm," Emile said. "First time you've ever done one."

"I think we'll be fine once my inspectors do a complete physical inventory and get their paperwork in order. I'll send a couple of extra men over to expedite the work and get you moving again."

Two additional inspectors were sent over to assist in yet another physical inventory of all containers at Baker's storage compound yard.

Baker allowed all his drivers and yard workers to use a sick day to stay out of the way. No one complained since no one lost any pay.

When the audit was complete, the lead inspector made a call.

"Chief, we just finished the physical. You're not gonna like what I have to report."

"Go ahead."

"We now have *twelve* cargo containers picked up by E. Baker Trucking that are unaccounted for."

"Now it's twelve?"

"Chief, that's the number we came up with."

"You must have missed something."

"Believe me, that's what I thought, too. But Chief, we've gone over this more than a few times. Baker picked them up, they were all cleared, but the containers with the numbers we're checking for are just not in the yard, and Baker has no record of them leaving."

"All right, I'll take it from here. The problem must be somewhere in Baker's shipping records. You can resume normal operations and send the extra men back to the port."

The chief had long been a strong advocate for E. Baker Trucking; if this was anything more than a filing error, his professional credibility could be tarnished. He put in a call to Emile Baker. "Emile, you can resume normal operations."

"Thanks, Chief."

"Oh, one more thing, our auditors would like to come over and have access to all your outbound shipping records for the last three months."

"No problem; they can use the conference room. I'll have it cleaned up."

"Thank you. I believe they'll be over this afternoon."

"We'll be here."

The chief called two inspectors into his office and asked them to go over to E. Baker Trucking and find the bills of lading for six missing containers that Duffy was questioning. Then the chief called Duffy. "Constable, we're working on your request, but it looks like we're going to need a little more time."

"How much?"

"Oh, it shouldn't take more than a day."

"Thanks for the heads up."

Duffy shook his head, dismissing the delay as merely typical bureaucratic behavior. But he shared with Kate what he'd been talking to the chief inspector about. When Kate heard that the individual weights of all six missing containers at Baker's yard were an exact match with the weights of the six missing BMW containers shipped from the German port, she immediately let INTERPOL know what they were working on.

When the port inspectors concluded a thorough review of Baker's shipping records, they found no records of the six containers ever leaving Baker's yard. That's when the chief inspector immediately summoned Emile over to his office.

When Emile arrived, the chief was straightforward. "Emile, these six containers showed up as unaccounted for in the audit. Can you explain that?"

Emile put on a show of embarrassment. "Chief, I apologize. We've had some turnover in the shipping department this past quarter. I'm certain the problem is just a matter of misfiling or a data error. Give me a day and I'll personally go through the records and come back to you with the answer regarding just where those six containers went."

At that point, the chief let Emile know there was specific interest in those six containers. "I'll give you another day, Emile, as long as you clear everything up."

As he left the chief's office, Baker immediately suspected the six containers in question had to be among the containers he had stored over at the airport lot. On the ride back to his yard, Baker was kicking himself for thinking that "out of sight" would also be "out of mind." He had made a mistake and somebody was interested in those six containers. *Probably some damn insurance underwriter trying to get off the hook for paying a claim,* he thought.

Later that evening, Baker returned to the office and created "bills of lading" for the six "missing" containers. The documents would show that all six containers had been loaded onto a barge the day after they arrived and sent to Toronto. Baker recalled reading about a small transport company in Toronto that was unable to recover after a fire had destroyed its main office. They had since declared bankruptcy, so he listed them as the carrier.

The following morning, Baker called the chief. "Chief, I found the bills of lading for those six containers. Like I had suspected, they were misfiled. I found them in the prior year's folder and will fax copies over to you shortly."

Once the chief received and reviewed the documents, he called Duffy to report. "E. Baker Trucking has just sent me copies of six bills of lading showing that the six containers traveled down to Toronto. He said the documents were misfiled.

"Really."

"Yes, that's what he said. Now, where the containers went from *there* will be difficult to determine. Unfortunately, the carrier that was used to transport them has subsequently closed its doors after a fire destroyed their main building; they've since filed for bankruptcy. It appears they hadn't migrated to using e-logs yet, and all their records were lost in a fire. So, this may be the end of the trail for you on where those containers went," the chief said.

Duffy remained silent a moment before replying.

"Thanks chief, I appreciate the follow-through. Have someone fax me over a copy of those bills of lading, would you? I'll close out the file."

The delay in getting answers from the Port Authority, and the fact that the containers were now untraceable beyond Quebec City, immediately caused Duffy's antennas to go up. Duffy had no intention of closing out his file.

Misfiled, my ass, he thought. *I was born at night, Baker, but it wasn't last night.*

The following evening, Baker returned to the shipping department to further cover his tracks. He created more bills of lading showing that the other containers over at the airport hangar had been "shipped to a warehouse in Montreal." One that he knew was under receivership and whose records at that location would, similarly, be pretty much non-existent.

A day later, Baker received a text from Dobbs that he had an immediate and urgent need for a cargo container coming into the Port of Quebec to be transported over to the Dobbs Aviation hangar. The communication went on to say the container would be marked "Hold at E. Baker Trucking" and it, too, needed to bypass any and all inspections by customs.

Dobbs sent a separate text that he would "overnight" the padlock he wanted placed on the hangar door once the container was in the hangar. In a follow-up text, Dobbs also alerted Baker that some associates of his would be arriving to use the hangar for a couple of days in the near future.

Emile Baker was accustomed to being in charge and was beginning to get more than a little annoyed with Dobbs ordering him around. That's when he decided at some point, he would inquire as to how much of a balance he had left on his debt with the Englishmen.

Meanwhile, the more Duffy thought about the response he had received from the chief inspector at the Port Authority, the more he smelled a rat somewhere. He reached out to the Quebec ministry of transportation and requested a copy of the files containing all bills of lading filed by E. Baker Trucking in the past four months. Within hours, Duffy received a copy of the four individual data files.

No bill of lading with numbers matching any of the six containers in question appeared on any of the monthly batch files created and submitted by E. Baker Trucking at month's end. The numbering scheme on the six forms was also different from the series that Baker's shipping department had been using at that point in time.

Now the question on Duffy's mind was whether the containers ever traveled to Toronto, or were they somewhere else?

When Andre heard about the runaround given to Duffy as he tried to trace the six containers, he also became curious. So, he placed a call to Bob Newton, but the call went to voicemail. So Andre left a message: "Bob, this is Andre, see if you can find out if there's another storage yard that Baker is using, then get back to me."

Meanwhile, outside the lodge for the second day in a row, chain saws could be heard off in the distance coming from the direction of land where the lumber company held logging rights. There hadn't been any active logging done there in years, mainly because the trees hadn't matured to a harvestable size yet.

Lou decided to take a hike through the woods just to see what was going on. When he reached the area where the trees were being cut, it was obvious from what he saw that these guys were *not* lumberjacks, and that the trees being harvested were not being treated the way they should if the intent was to haul them off to a sawmill.

Lou circled around for a look at the vehicles parked on the old logging road. Lumberjacks didn't ride around in fancy SUV's. He took pictures of the license plates with his cell phone, and headed back to camp.

Later, he shared his concerns with Andre, who became just as suspicious as Lou was about the situation. Andre decided to call his assistant at headquarters.

"Jonathan, find out which lumber company has the lease on the property abutting Havre de Poisson. Ask them if any logging is being done in the area, will you? Then get back to me."

"Certainly."

Headquarters got back to Andre within fifteen minutes. Andre put his phone on speaker so Lou could hear. "Sergeant, the logging company has no one in the area and no plans to harvest timber in that area for at least another ten years."

"Thanks. Transfer me over to the Kedgwick barracks."

"Sorry, Sarge, we're having trouble with the phones, I'm only able to do that if you call in."

"No matter, thanks."

Andre next put a call into the Kedgwick barracks, himself. Shortly after, a couple of Mounties who were in the area, drove up the logging road and arrested the wannabe loggers for unlawful malicious destruction of property.

Lou had already determined this was a decoy movement somehow intended to weaken their ability to defend the base camp. He called Jake, Cunningham, and O'Neil together hoping that between the four of them they'd be able to make some sense out of the illegal logging.

"I've never heard any logger use a chain saw like that before," O'Neil agreed saying, "It sounded more like a couple of dirt bikes than chain saws."

No sooner had he said it when they all realized that was *exactly* what it was intended to sound like.

Lou sat back in his chair. "I had it all wrong. You had it right, Cunningham. They're coming at us on dirt bikes. That's a whole different animal. We'll need to deploy a little differently and get a few more passive defenses in place."

Before long, the four of them had outlined a new defense scheme that downplayed emphasis on the road and focused more on securing the overall perimeter.

The following morning, everyone received an additional assignment. Each one was to listen for the sound of high-pitched motors approaching from a distance. They were also told to keep their vests and weapons within reach at all times.

Lou reinforced exactly where everyone was to deploy. O'Neil was now to deploy near the lodge with Duffy, Dorsey, and Andre.

As an added precaution, Andre requested that surveillance drones periodically fly over the area where

Route 385 and the old logging road intersected. But it was the quiet and the waiting that added heavy tension and put everyone on edge.

Chapter

31

Within a short time, Q had no difficulty recruiting eleven "soldiers of fortune" to join him, given the compensation he was offering. Most of the men had worked with him previously. The few who hadn't were vouched for by others in the group who had a history of knowing or working with them. Flights in and out of Canada had yet to be booked. Q and his team would travel under the guise of receiving technical training on avionics from Air Canada's Ground Support Group. Employee badges would be easy to produce; however, Q was told there would be a slight delay in obtaining passports.

Rather than waste valuable time, Q rented a dozen dirt bikes and took his entire team out to a hunting preserve north of London in the Midlands. The terrain was a far cry from the wilderness surrounding Havre de Poisson, but at least they were able to practice riding around some structures for the better part of the afternoon.

Passports were finally delivered to Q the following morning, and he started calling airlines. Since Q had never traveled to Canada before, he was unaware that there were no direct commercial flights from London to Quebec City. The best itinerary he was able to find was a ten and half-hour trip, with a change of planes in Toronto.

He decided to charter a private jet, which knocked five hours off the travel time and would fly them directly into Quebec City for close to the cost of flying everyone first-class on a commercial flight. Then Q put out the word that everyone was to arrive at Biggin Hill Airport, just outside Heathrow the following morning at 0900 hours, ready to roll.

The following morning, as soon as everyone was on board, the pilot taxied out to the runway, received priority departure status, and within minutes, the jet was quickly cruising westward at an altitude of forty-one thousand feet. Before turning his attention to the team, Q sent a text to Tinker that they had left the UK and were enroute to Canada."Well, enjoy the perks of flying private, gentlemen, because our flight home will be commercial."

Hours later, when the plane landed in Quebec City, Immigration officers were dispatched and cleared everyone within minutes. Then Q and his team headed over to pick up the three black SUVs he had reserved.

When Q had finished filling out the rental agreements at the counter, he turned around just as an impeccably dressed man of average height using a cane appeared out of nowhere.

"Pardon me, would your name happen to be Q?"

"It is."

"Name's Dobbs. I have an envelope for you."

Expecting Dobbs to walk over to him, Q waited. When he didn't, Q walked over to Dobbs who reached inside his coat pocket and removed an envelope. "Inside, you'll find directions to the hangar where your equipment is located along with a key to gain entry and explicit directions to the logging road."

"Right, thanks Dobbs."

"Pleasure."

With that, Dobbs tipped the brim of his hat, turned, and left.

While caravanning to the *Chateau Le Pierre* in St. Foy, where they would all stay for the next few days, Q called ahead to advise the hotel that he would like to reserve a function room for dinner that evening. They dined well.

The next morning, Q and his team headed over to the airport and entered the hangar marked "Dobbs Aviation."

Once everyone was inside, Q said, "All right, first we inventory what's in the container to make sure that all the equipment, tools, and the ordinance that I shipped over have arrived."

The cargo container had been rigged with a special racking system which allowed the bikes to be secured and transported without risk of damage. He found all was in order.

Next, Q divided the team into work groups. "It'll take the better part of the day to organize the gear and attach mufflers to the bikes. See me if you have any questions."

Dobbs had left instructions on the container that should Q need the container transported anywhere, he was to contact E. Baker Trucking and specifically ask for Emile Baker along with mentioning his name.

The trip from Quebec City to the old logging road would take about six hours and Q had every intention of leaving the dirt bikes there once the job was complete. Finally, when ready, he made a call to E. Baker Trucking.

"Yes, is there an Emile Baker there?"

"One moment."

After a brief pause, he heard: "Go ahead."

"Emile here."

"Yes, Dobbs gave me your number. He said you could pick up a cargo container."

"I can."

"Excellent. I'd like a pick-up for 0600 tomorrow at the Dobbs Aviation hangar."

"Right, and where are we taking it?"

He provided Baker with a drop-off address that was close to the old logging road to use on the bill of lading, but the driver would merely follow Q's SUV.

When Q's team finished modifying the bikes, he repackaged the ordnance just as the sun was setting. Before they left, everything they needed was loaded back into the container and secured.

The next morning, when Q looked out his window, the fog was so heavy it could have been cut with a knife. The air was damp and had a pungent earthy smell to it. He considered whether he should delay a day, but the adrenalin that always spurred Q on in battle was already pumping through his veins.

He and his team arrived at the airport hangar at 0545; the fog was still heavy and Baker's truck was waiting.

A few minutes after 0600, a convoy of three black SUVs and a truck hauling a cargo container headed toward Q's target destination.His plan was a daytime attack; trying to maneuver dirt bikes through the woods in the dark would have been far too risky and would have hampered their ability for a quick in-and-out operation.

When they arrived at the old logging road, the fog had completely dissipated; one less obstacle to deal with. They had made excellent time. It was close to noon and he suspected that the majority of people at the Mounties' camp would be in the lodge, probably eating lunch which would make it easier to complete the mission and exit.

As soon as the container rolled off the truck, Q told the driver, "Thank you, you're free to head back."

Then Q's men walked the bikes out of the container and down the logging road to a location just beyond a bend, where they were out of sight from the highway. Their weapons and protective gear were loaded onto dollies and also walked down the road. Once the container was emptied, the doors were shut, the SUVs locked, and everyone on Q's team proceeded to where the bikes were stationed.

As Q's team strapped on their protective gear, he called out to them: "Gather round, let's go over the game plan one last time so that we're all on the same page."

When Q had everyone's attention, he spoke again. "I'll take the lead going up the road. We'll follow the road until I give the signal, then I want this half to move off to the left of the road, and everyone else to move off to the right into the woods. Any questions.?"

The team had been briefed on the game plan a number of times; there were no questions.

"Right, mount up."

In rural New Brunswick, there is absolutely nothing unusual about seeing vehicles parked off to the side of the road in the middle of nowhere. The casual observer would drive by and think nothing of it. However, to the trained eye, three identical brand-new SUV's and a cargo container would draw interest. And that is exactly what happened when a Mountie drove by on a routine patrol.

The Mountie pulled his cruiser over and walked back to take a closer look. He ran the plates on the three vehicles, opened the cargo container and said: "Empty." In the distance, he could hear the muffled sound of dirt bikes rapidly moving away from him. All three plates came back as registered to a rental agency. Given the time of day and the long drive he had ahead of him before his shift was over, he called it into the station knowing the desk sergeant on duty would take it from there.

While the Mountie was still at the scene, a drone passed overhead and in a moment, a series of aerial pictures appeared on the computer screen inside the lodge at the Mountie's camp. O'Neill was on duty and following procedures, he magnified the images. The last few frames clearly showed an RCMP vehicle, three unidentified vehicles, and a large container box off to the side of route 385 at the entrance to the old logging road.

O'Neil was no fool. He knew exactly what was about to happen, and sounded the alarm.

Chapter 32

Word passed quickly about incoming intruders. Kate hurried to the lodge to relieve O'Neil and everyone else deployed to their assigned stations. "Lt. Kate O'Grady to RMCP Headquarters," Kate called over the radio. "We're anticipating an imminent attack!" Almost immediately, Kate heard a 10-93 notification go out over the RCMP radio frequency directing all available Mounties in the area to proceed to Rt 385, mile marker 221 "without lights or sirens" to form a blockade at the logging road.

Within minutes, Lou heard what sounded like a swarm of angry yellowjackets approaching from off in the distance. As Q and his team started up the road, two of his bikers began rapidly losing RPMs and fell to the rear of the pack. Neither bike was responding to the throttle. Both riders dismounted and checked for vacuum leaks. After tightening hose clamps on their carburetors, it seemed to fix their problems. But now they were quite a distance behind their comrades in arms. Accelerating to full throttle, they tried to catch up quickly.When Q reached a point where he no longer felt safe continuing on the road, he directed his riders to split up and head into the woods.

Once among the trees, the going was far slower than Q had anticipated. Dense underbrush slowed their progress as Q's team frequently pushed their way forward through nearly impenetrable thickets. They also found themselves circling around decaying stumps and deep depressions in the forest floor left by ancient windfalls.

The terrain was totally different from the 'park-like' forest they had practiced on.

Hoping to regroup with everyone, the two riders who had fallen behind continued racing up the road, and completely missed seeing where Q had veered off the road. Moments after both bikes passed through the open wooden gate, two separate explosions occurred. Q's team was now down to ten.

Inside the lodge, Kate was able to identify multiple intruders in the woods on both sides of the road as they advanced toward the base camp. She saw they were still a good distance outside the wall of fallen trees that Jake and Cunningham had created a few days earlier. As she watched the screen, an approaching attacker accelerated his bike only to quickly dump it, to avoid being decapitated by a strip of piano wire strung between two trees.

On the far side of the road, an explosion was heard when a bike snagged a tripwire. The force of the explosion propelled bike parts in all directions including one that came upward and into the rider's neck, slicing his carotid artery. Q's team was now down to nine.

Kate broke radio silence, "Four intruders on bikes have breached the line of fallen trees and are proceeding toward the lodge at a high rate of speed. Another five bikers are deep in the woods," she said.

Those five bikers were directly opposite the defensive positions Lou, Jake, and Cunningham had taken.

Of the four bikers who had breached the fallen trees, one was quickly taken out by a length of piano wire stretched between a couple of trees as he raced toward the lodge. Q's force was now down to eight.

The three remaining bikers inside the tree barrier were now visible to O'Neil and Dorsey. O'Neil rose from his foxhole and fired off a couple quick bursts from his carbine, then sheltered down in his foxhole expecting Dorsey to fire an alternating burst of fire to cover him. But the chaotic sound of bikes, combined with the noise of weapons firing, caused Dorsey to freeze. He remained hunkered down in his foxhole and failed to give O'Neil the necessary cover.

It was Dorsey's delay that gave one rider ample time to stop and fire a rocket directly into O'Neil's foxhole. The blast caused Dorsey to hunker even further down, and curl into a fetal position. Once the bloody debris from the explosion stopped raining down on him, Dorsey opened his eyes to see a part of O'Neil's hand lying in the dirt next to his face. A wave of nausea hit him like a sledgehammer; he began retching until he finally recovered enough to poke his carbine over the rim of his foxhole and fire wildly into the air.

Andre sensed Dorsey was in trouble and moved into a different position. He sprayed a carbine burst at the bikers then heard a metallic noise as one of his shots penetrated the lead bike's oil reserve; another shot ruptured the gas line. As soon as oil began leaking out, it hit the hot manifold and ignited, causing the gas coming from the ruptured fuel line to burst into a ball of fire. On fire, the rider jumped away from his bike and began rolling around, attempting to extinguish the scorching flames engulfing his lower body. Andre emptied the remainder of his clip into his target, ending the man's agony. Q's force was now down to seven.

Under cover of a second barrage of gun fire from Andre, Duffy was able to reposition himself and saw another rider straddling his bike, preparing to launch a rocket. Duffy distracted him with a quick burst of bullets. Dorsey wasn't really in the game at this point nor offering much resistance. Andre changed clips and emptied it at the biker, taking him out just before he was able to launch the rocket. Q's force was now down to six.

Kate broke radio silence again: "All attackers have breached the fallen trees and appear to be coming in fast."

Lou was the first to see them approaching. "Here they come!" He launched a rocket in their direction to slow them down; the rocket hit the trunk of a tree, but the blast was close enough that it caused one rider to momentarily lose control. Before the rider could recover, Cunningham popped up from his fox hole and took him out with a single shot to the head. But return fire from the other attackers repeatedly struck Cunningham in the chest, and he went down.

Now moving fast, the bikers rode furiously through the trees. Even with extra mufflers, the noise from the bikes was deafening and added to the total chaos and confusion surrounding the Mounties.

The bikers managed to get behind Lou and Jake. One bike headed directly toward the lodge, spraying it with bullets. Lou pushed the button on his communicator and yelled: "Kate, take cover now! Get below the lodge."

Both Lou and Jake repositioned themselves in their foxholes, to face the lodge. The protective dirt barrier to the rear of their foxholes was several inches lower than the front, but they also had greater visibility of the building even though they were more exposed.

Then, just fifty feet from the lodge, a biker came to a stop and began preparing a rocket to fire directly at the large propane tank next to the building.

If the tank explodes, the lodge and everything in it will be gone, Lou reasoned as he and Jake both took aim and fired their carbines. Lou's shot struck the biker in the upper back, knocking him slightly forward. Jake's shot struck the rider at the waistline just below the Kevlar vest he was wearing. This second impact knocked the rider backward and off the bike just as he pulled the trigger on his rocket launcher. The rocket went high and wide right, landing harmlessly in the lake without detonating. The rider lay in a heap on the ground with a broken back, paralyzed from the waist down, alive, but out of the fight.

Staying low, Duffy scrambled like a land crab to a different foxhole hoping to gain a better line of sight. Defensive fire was now coming sporadically from Duffy, Andre, and finally, from Dorsey.

Inside the lodge, Kate dropped down through the floor and low crawled out from underneath the building. She climbed into a foxhole, now armed with her carbine.

Repeated volleys from the defenders were causing the intruders to constantly remain in motion and be vigilant of what was ahead of them as they maneuvered among the trees.

Everyone on Q's team was now aware that more than a few of their comrades had been eliminated by tripwires and decapitated by the nearly invisible piano wire strung between trees. All on edge, the bikers were no longer acting as a disciplined unit with any semblance of an organized plan of attack.

Early on, Q had dismissed the need to equip his team with radios, since he didn't think they would be necessary. Now, he had no way to communicate with anyone except through hand signals.

Q had never anticipated his men would be shooting from moving bikes. His plan was falling apart before his very eyes and his thoughts were racing.

How did they know we were coming? Was I set up? Was it Dobbs that set me up, or was it that Irishman?

The resistance his team had encountered was forcing them to constantly remain in motion. They were forced to fire weapons with one hand while controlling their bike's throttle with the other. Accuracy was proving far too challenging for Q's team and their shots were going wild. Even so, a rocket struck the cottage closest to the lake which immediately erupted in flames.

Lou put his carbine on single shot and followed the biker who fired the rocket. Knowing his adversaries were wearing body armor, Lou aimed for the biker's head and squeezed off a round; the active intruders were now down to three.

In the chaos, a bike managed to circle behind the three defenders protecting the lodge. Suddenly, out of nowhere, the bike came racing from behind the lodge at full throttle and vaulted over Dorsey's foxhole. Dorsey never saw the hand grenade drop. The explosion sent a shockwave across the area.

Kate had her carbine on single shot, rose from her foxhole and fired twice, hitting the rider in the left thigh both times as he raced off.

Trying to escape the onslaught from the defenders, the injured attacker raced down the shoreline heading away from the base camp. As he rounded the rocky point, he detonated a claymore that launched both him and his bike into the air. The attackers were now down to two active bikers.

By this time, the lodge had taken a lot of hits. Lou decided to leave his foxhole and make a zigzagging run toward the lodge to provide further protection for Kate. He didn't see the paralyzed intruder lying on the ground struggling to raise his carbine and point it at him. But Kate saw the man and fired two quick shots. The intruder's head exploded like an overripe melon.

There were only two surviving attackers at this point, and one of them was Q. He couldn't believe he'd lost ten men in such a short time attempting to take out a small group of policemen in what should have been a surprise assault. He had no plan "B" other than a humiliating tactical retreat.

Q decided to take a parting shot. He fired a rocket toward the lodge. But the rocket nicked one of the piano wires strung between the trees which arched it upward; it veered off just enough to the left that it missed the lodge and fell harmlessly into the lake. Q signaled the other biker to follow him and both men headed back through the woods toward the SUVs parked at the end of the old logging road.

From the sound of the dirt bikes, Kate could tell they were retreating. She quickly scrambled back up into the lodge through the trap door. Still visible on the monitors, she saw the intruders heading away from Havre de Poisson.

"Two armed intruders heading toward route 385," she broadcast an alert, using the RCMP's radio frequency. Mounties stationed at the end of the logging road had heard the gunfire and explosions and were prepared to stop whatever traffic was coming toward them with some pretty heavy firepower of their own.

Chapter

33

When Q figured they had retreated far enough into the woods and were beyond any claymores, he signaled to turn left onto the logging road. Once back on the road, both bikes accelerated racing full throttle toward their SUVs. Rounding the last bend, Q saw the Mounties' barricade. Without backing off on the throttle, he ducked low, apparently thinking he could break through the Mounties line. He was immediately brought down in a hail of bullets. The twelfth and final rider wisely signaled his surrender and came to a full stop.

Back at the lodge, Lou rushed in calling loudly: "Kate, are you in here?"

"I'm here," a voice called out. As soon as he reached her, she collapsed into his arms, burying her head in his chest. She was emotionally and physically drained. It took a few minutes before Kate lifted her head up, smiled, then melted again into his chest.

A call came over the RCMP radio frequency. "Two intruders stopped at the Mountie road barrier. One down, one in custody." It brought Lou and Kate back to reality and she released her hold on Lou.

"I need to warn them not to travel up the logging road." She moved quickly toward her desk.

Outside, Jake was attending to Cunningham. "You'll have some huge bruises Arnold, but that Kevlar vest saved your life."

"Yeah? I felt like someone used a jackhammer on me."

"Come on, buddy, let's go see how everyone else made out." They found Andre and Duffy inspecting the carnage near the lodge. O'Neil's body was pretty much vaporized by the rocket. Dorsey was torn apart by the grenade and had died instantly. No one else was injured.

Fletcher and Angelo emerged from the root cellar, shotguns in hand and at the ready. Alessandra followed and quickly pushed them aside as she headed toward the kitchen.

The cottage hit by a rocket was a total loss. Duffy looked at the smoldering ruin and thought, *I guess I'm glad we didn't get that cottage after all.*

At the far end of the logging road, the Mounties handcuffed the remaining intruder and took him into custody. After a brief search, they found a "burner phone" on Q, the last rider who had been killed. Andre and Duffy set out roaming the perimeter to check that all downed intruders were, in fact, dead.

Cunningham donned a mask and gloves, grabbed a rake, and began carefully picking up as many of O'Neil's body parts as he could find. What little was left was placed in a gallon Ziploc bag and stored in the walk-in freezer overnight alongside Dorsey's remains which had first been wrapped in a blanket, then in plastic.

When Andre returned to the lodge, he put a call into Fredericton. The loss of O'Neil and Dorsey was devastating for him; never in his career had he ever lost anyone assigned to his command before today. Float planes would arrive early in the morning with another load of body bags.

Realizing everyone would be coming and going in different directions for the rest of the day, Angelo began preparing a hot and cold buffet that would be available throughout the evening.

Before heading out with Jake to defuse the claymores and remove any remaining piano wires and tripwires, Lou walked over to Kate, "I'll stop by in the morning to walk you over to breakfast." He hugged her again, enjoying the feel of her body next to his, and kissed her on the side of her cheek. She smiled up at him and nodded.

Not ready to give in to exhaustion just yet, Kate decided to write her report on what had happened and send it off to INTERPOL while the details were still fresh in her mind. But her energy level was about two inches below the rug, and it didn't take long before she changed her mind and headed over to her cottage.

Once all claymores and wires were accounted for, Lou went around the camp with a frontend loader filling in the foxholes.

Fletcher volunteered to monitor the camera feeds and handle any incoming messages for the next eight hours. Andre put a call into Clarence James to fly up to help monitor the satellite feeds and incoming messages for a couple of days to give his team a rest.

The following morning, Lou stopped over at Kate's cottage and the two headed toward the lodge. Had anyone noticed, it would have been apparent that the two were no longer completely play-acting and had, indeed, become a couple.

The mood around the breakfast table was somber. Andre asked Angelo and Alessandra to join them for a moment of silent prayer for the souls of Fred O'Neil and

Matt Dorsey.

During breakfast, Andre made an announcement: "Except for assisting the Mounties that are coming up, you're all officially off-duty for the next forty-eight hours."

He also shared that he would be down in Fredericton for a couple of days.

"I'll write my report while I'm away, but I also intend to be present when they interrogate the lone prisoner. After that, I'll be meeting with U.S. customs officials to answer their questions regarding Dorsey, and I plan to spend a little time with Fred O'Neil's widow."

News of a second assault on the base camp was being kept under wraps until Internal Affairs and Andre developed a strategy on how they wanted to play "the mole." Shortly after Andre finished speaking, the sound of multiple float planes could be heard coming up the valley.

Within a few hours, the body bags had been loaded onto the planes, including one containing the remains of Matt Dorsey and another with the minimal remains of Fred O'Neil. After an initial preparation by a funeral home in Fredericton, Dorsey's body would be flown down to the States.

Later that morning, Lou finally had a chance to take a long break and he let everyone know that he was crashing until the afternoon. When he reached his cottage, Jake was already sound asleep in the spare bedroom.

That afternoon, Kate and Alessandra gathered for tea and a little "girl talk." Alessandra had noticed the developing relationship between Kate and Lou.

"You seem to be asking questions about Lou lately, Kate," she said over tea. Although Alessandra had strong feelings for Kate, Lou was her "adopted son" and like any Italian mother, she was fiercely protective. Her heart had ached as she watched Lou slowly recover after his first wife's death, and she didn't want to see him go through any more unhappiness.

"Kate, tell me, what brought you here to us?" she asked.

Inhaling deeply, Kate rested her cup of tea on her lap. "The Italians have a saying, *'In Vino Veritas,'* are you familiar with it?"

"Of course," Alessandra said, "Angelo and I come from the old country. 'In wine there is truth.'"

"Well, I'm Irish, so for me, I guess, it's not so much *wine,* but rather *tea* that makes me relax and loosen my tongue." Kate paused before saying, "Alessandra, I wasn't recruited for this assignment. I had to pull rank and call in every favor I had to get this assignment."

"What made coming here that important to you Kate?"

"It wasn't the location. For me, it could have been *any*where; it was the length of the assignment that attracted me. Ever since Liam was killed in that hit and run, I've struggled to find 'me' again. I thought that if I could just go away for a period of time, it would help."

"Have you begun to find yourself, Kate?"

Kate was slow to answer. "Sometimes I think I have, but then I'm not sure, and I hold back."

"Angelo and I are reminded every day how important it is to be able to let go of things, no matter how big they seem. We have a sign over the entrance to our cottage: *'Lascia e Problemi a La Porta'*.

"'Leave your troubles at the door,'" Kate translated. "That's your secret?"

"Well, it's certainly one of them," Alessandra laughed. "Kate, I'm going to change the subject. It's going to be a beautiful fall day tomorrow. A perfect day for you to relax and have a picnic with a special friend."

Kate paused and smiled. "He *is* a special friend,

Alessandra. Will you help me fix the basket for him?"

"No dear, let me *prepare* the basket for you this time . . . I know what he likes."

Chapter 34

It was 0900 Greenwich Meantime in the UK; the three principals of Imperial Trading were gathered in Solicitor More's study. They had expected Tinker to have heard from Q by now with a story of success. Tinker was asked to contact Lajoie for news of the assault.

But Lajoie's cousin hadn't heard anything unusual, and news channels weren't reporting anything out of the ordinary.

Solicitor More stopped pacing and turned. "I'm bloody concerned an assault has failed again and a coverup is in play."

"Richard, I can assure you that even if that were the case, we have nothing to fear," Hastings said. "Max made sure that Q was always beyond arm's length from us. Why he even sent Q a generous cash advance through Dobbs, there is no trail coming back to us."

More looked at him, then dismissed what Hastings had just said. "Regardless, I'm calling Dobbs; he may have some word."

The time was 0400 hours in Montreal and Dobbs didn't answer. More slammed his phone down. "We need to eradicate these Mounties before they completely unravel everything. I say we send in the Arab."

"Richard, listen to me," Hastings fired back. "We are *not* sending the Arab in or anyone else, for that matter. Now pull yourself together! These assaults on the Mounties are bloody damn *expensive.* All we need do is remain calm; this will all blow over."

Shortly after the sun peaked over Carleton Mountain, Lou stopped by Kate's cottage to walk her over to breakfast.

Before they reached the lodge, Kate touched his arm to stop him.

"What's your day look like today, Lou?"

"Haven't really given it all that much thought yet. Nothing really."

"Good," she smiled at him. "There's a very low-key picnic going on over at that favorite rocky point of yours today. I'd like you to be my escort."

"Yeah . . . sure. I hadn't heard about it. What time does it start?"

"Be ready for noon. I'll meet you at your cottage. We can go over together."

That being said, they entered the lodge.

Duffy was the only other early riser and was sitting in the lodge drinking coffee while Angelo was busy in the kitchen.

"Well, you certainly look like you're deep in thought this morning, Duffy," Kate said as she and Lou took seats at the table.

"You know, Kate, there's something really obvious that I'm missing about E. Baker Trucking. It's right there in front of my face, but I just can't see it!"

"Give it a rest Duffy," Lou said, joining the conversation. "Take the day off. Go for a walk with Fletcher. Clear your mind after yesterday. Just be back in time for the picnic."

Kate kicked Lou under the table and he changed the subject. "Ya' know Duffy, there's some excellent fishing halfway down toward the other end of the lake this time of year. There's a sharp drop-off about thirty feet offshore. The lunkers wait out there for the fingerlings to venture off the ledge. Even when the sun is directly overhead, they'll come right up from the depths to feed.," Lou smiled at him encouragingly. "That's where I take a lot of anglers when the fishing is slow. If you want, I can put a boat in the water and set you up with some live bait. I know Angelo would *love* to cook some fresh fish tonight."

"I don't know Lou . . . maybe . . . the solitude might do me good. I'll think about it."

When Duffy left, Lou looked at Kate. "Why the kick in the shins?"

"The picnic is by *invitation only*."

When Kate finished her breakfast, she stood up, tousled Lou's hair, and smiled. "See you at noon."

As Kate was going out the door, Duffy was coming back in. "You know, Lou, I *will* take you up on that boat."

"No problem, Duffy. Give me a half-hour and I'll have everything ready and waiting for you down at the dock."

Fletcher had been monitoring screens most of the night. A few messages had come in from INTERPOL for Kate, nothing marked urgent, so he left them sitting in her inbox. INTERPOL had finished combing through phone records of Sean Tinker and had found quite a few incoming and outgoing international calls. One phone had a New Brunswick area code, another had one in Quebec. In the messages, Kate was being asked to chase down the owners of the Canadian numbers; MI6 would run down the number outside London that Tinker seemed to be calling frequently.

Kate knocked on the door to Lou's cottage at noontime exactly with a picnic basket in hand. Lou opened the door, fresh out of the shower and dressed in his normal casual attire. He noticed Kate was wearing a more feminine top than usual and her hair was styled differently, too. It looked a little nicer than usual.

"All set?" she asked.

"I am. No need to be the last ones to show up." He took the basket of food from her hands to carry, and made small talk as they walked in the direction of Rocky Point. Upon arriving, Lou was surprised to see that no one else was there and nothing had been set up. He looked at Kate quizzically and raised an eyebrow."Are you sure you have the right time?"

She smiled. "I told you the picnic was by invitation *only. I* invited *you."* He smiled back. "Here, help me spread out this quilt," she said.

Throughout the picnic, Lou kept saying, "Kate, I don't know how you did it, but you packed just about *every* single one of my favorite foods." Their budding relationship moved to another level that afternoon as they relaxed over a bottle of wine and talked about life.

Later that day, Andre returned from Fredericton.

That evening, thanks to Duffy's skill with the fishing rod, everyone dined on fresh filet of trout, poached in white wine and elegantly served with a lightly seasoned tarragon sauce.

During the meal, Andre shared as much as he could about his last two days.

"The interrogation didn't yield much, but perhaps

INTERPOL will learn more," he said. "Fingerprints were taken off the others, and like before, they were all citizens of the UK. The intruder killed by the Mounties at the far end of the logging road had a burner phone on him. A complete file of his calls and text messages will be made available shortly."

Then Andre suddenly lowered his voice and became more reserved. "I went over to O'Neil's house and paid my respects to Fred's widow. She depended on him for everything, you know. I've assigned a clerk to help her fill out paperwork for his pension. I also spoke with Matt Dorsey's superiors and his parents. Dorsey's funeral service will be the day after tomorrow. Headquarters is sending an honor guard. I'm going to attend Dorsey's services, too. If any of you want to join me, you're welcome to do so."

"Andre, was Mrs. Girard happy to see you?" Jake asked.

"Ha, that she was! But she was in pretty good spirits anyway. She finally got that damn BMW of hers back from the shop, the one that she just *had* to have. She's been without it for weeks waiting on some parts."

For some reason, Kate locked that remark away in her mind, then, before retiring for the evening, she sent a text to INTERPOL asking if BMW had made another shipment of parts to Canada.

After dinner, everyone else went their separate ways except for Jake and Angelo. The two men decided to watch the movie *Skyfall* for the umpteenth time.

Chapter 35

When Andre briefly returned to Fredericton, he fell right back into his usual morning routine of stopping off at the local Tim Horton's on his way to work. On the second day, as he was coming out of Horton's, coffee in hand, Charles Teal was pulling into the parking lot. Teal immediately called Lajoie to let him know that Andre was back in town. Maybe he could finally get some answers on the expenses that Andre was incurring.

The principals of Imperial Trading were all sitting in Hasting's study when word arrived that Andre Girard was walking around big as life.

In between lighting his pipe, Hastings said, "It would appear that these Mounties have a rather impenetrable fortress."

"Or maybe that we've sent people from the wrong regiment there twice now."

"Third time's always the charm," remarked Herbert Maxwell somewhat lightly for the occasion.

"Max, there won't *be* any third time," Hastings replied.

"This whole thing will blow over, and if it doesn't, the three of us have a plan B. Tinker will be the fall guy, should it come to that."

"You really believe they'll stop with Tinker?" Richard said with a look of disbelief.

"I do. He's a big enough fish for whoever is pushing this. The three of us will just fade into the shadows."

Herbert Maxwell took a sip of his brandy. "The rub of it is that Tinker's been such a loyal chap; it would be a bloody shame for him to end up in the Tower of London."

Hearing this, Solicitor More turned around after fixing himself another martini. "Not to be cheeky, but I hear the food is actually quite good there."

"Tinker will never reach the Tower of London."

"Pray tell, Lord Hastings, have you made more suitable accommodations for him?"

"No."

"What then?"

Hastings paused to put his pipe down before answering. "Gentlemen, Tinker is our bloody Achilles heel."

Back at Havre de Poisson, everyone was busy. Lou and Jake had demolished the burned-out cottage and were carting the debris away. Andre's team was fully engaged inside the lodge trying to put the remaining pieces of the puzzle together.

Kate was running down phone numbers that INTERPOL had forwarded to her. One was a match to a phone belonging to Felix Lajoie. The other number had a 514 - area code and wasn't showing up on any of the phone records she had. She figured that Duffy might have an idea, but he was on his phone at the moment.

Kate went back to her inbox and read a message from INTERPOL stating that BMW had not made a second shipment of parts to Canada. She noticed Fletcher heading over to the kitchen for a coffee and followed him.

"Fletcher, I have a question for you."

"Shoot."

"If I'm running an auto repair shop, and I don't have a part that I need, how could I get it?"

"Well, there are a number of ways, Kate. First, you check with the auto part store and ask if they have it, or if they can get it. If they can't, you could order the part from the manufacturer which would take a while. Or you could call around to other shops to see if they have the part. Last resort, you call the graveyards."

"The graveyards?"

"Yeah, salvage companies. It's quite common to cannibalize parts off of wrecks the insurance companies have totaled. We're all driving around on used parts anyway. Why do you ask?"

"I'm just curious how the BMW dealership got the part that Andre's wife's car needed."

"So, call around. See if *you* can find that part."

When Kate returned to her work area, Duffy was still on the phone; she sent him a text: *"c me when u r free."*"After learning from Andre that the part was a water pump for a model 540, Kate made a couple of calls to the auto supply stores. No luck, they were completely out of BMW parts. The auto salvage yards all told her there'd been a huge demand for BMW parts and they were cleaned out of water pumps weeks ago. Next, Kate placed a call to the Service Manager at the largest BMW dealership in eastern Canada. She identified herself as an employee of a BMW dealership in Ottawa and was placed on hold. When the service manager finally came to the line, she explained: "I'm in desperate need of a water pump for a 540, do you have one that I can have?"

"Young lady, if we did, I'd put it in one of the cars that I have here waiting for one."

Kate played coy, *"Please,* this is for an *especially* important customer, one of our biggest. I will lose my job if I can't locate this part. Please . . . you have to help me. Do you have any idea where I can find one?"

There was a long pause on the line, then the service manager said, "No promises, but I might be able to locate one for you. It'll be expensive. Are you okay with that?"

"Oh, you just *totally* saved my job! How long will it take?" she said sweetly.

"I'll have to speak with my source. Call back in a couple of days."

When the call ended, Kate said to no one in particular: "Call back in a couple of days, he has a source! I wonder who the fence is?" She made a request for the phone records for the number she had just called.

Duffy was now off the phone.

"Duffy, do you have any 514 area code numbers that are suspicious?"

"514, huh, that's Montreal. I'll send you the file I just received on calls going in and out of E. Baker Trucking, you might find something. I need to go see Andre now."

When Duffy sat down with Andre, the first words out of his mouth were: "Sarge, I think Emile Baker is up to his friggin' neck in all of this. If we can crack this guy, we'll blow this whole case wide open."

Andre took a sip of his coffee. "Tell me whatcha got?"

"Well, we know he's tight with Lajoie right? Lajoie is the guy who says what moves out of Grand Manan right? We know Baker picks up the majority of what is being dropped off at the docks on Passamaquoddy Bay, right? For almost a week, six containers that were supposed to be in Baker's yard couldn't be accounted for, then suddenly, bills of lading mysteriously turn up showing they went down the St. Lawrence by barge weeks earlier to a location that *conveniently* has no records. The bills of lading are completely out of sequence with the series of numbers E. Baker Trucking was using at that time. He has a sweetheart deal with the Port Authority like nobody else. He's gotta be hiding those containers somewhere in another storage location."

"I had Bob Newton look into that. He says Baker only has one yard."

"Andre, we know what's going on in Grand Manan. If we can nail Baker, this whole thing is gonna unravel. I wanna run a sting on this guy. My gut tells me he's hiding something."

"What kind of sting?"

"I wanna put a GPS tracking device in an empty cargo container that's sitting on the docks at the Old Port, with a bill of lading that says, 'Hold at E. Baker Trucking until called for.' I just wanna see where it goes!"

After talking it over more, Andre gave Duffy the green light but wanted to be part of any conversation they would need to have with the chief inspector at the Old Port in Quebec.

Duffy returned to his work area and dialed up the chief at the port. When the chief's assistant put him through, Duffy said, "Hello chief, Constable Duffy here. I'm going to put you on hold for a moment while I link in the sergeant major."

Once Andre was on the line, Duffy said, "Chief, I need to let you know that we're on a recorded line, we're calling because we need your help in an undercover investigation."

"Gentlemen, you have my undivided attention."

Duffy explained what he wanted to do. The chief had a lot of "skin in the game" having personally backed the special deal with Baker. If anything was going on that his audits weren't catching, and if he didn't cooperate with Duffy, he'd be at risk professionally. Without hesitation, he agreed to handle Duffy's request personally. As soon as the call ended, Duffy had a GPS tracking device sent overnight to the chief's personal attention.

Meanwhile, Internal Affairs in Fredericton started a rumor that Andre hadn't been able to find any solid evidence of smuggling and that headquarters was shutting down his investigation. When Teal heard this, he immediately relayed the news to Lajoie, who passed it along to Evens and Tinker.

Just as Andre was about to grab another cup of coffee, Bob Newton called. "Andre, I just wanted to call and thank you for the opportunity to get back in the game, even if it was just on the edge of what is happening." They chatted a short while and Andre shared that he didn't have anything else for his friend at the moment but suggested that he stay tuned.

Earlier in the day, Jake had flown Fletcher Martin over to the hospital for a checkup. Martin was cleared for moderate duty as long as there was no heavy lifting. Andre met with Fletcher as soon as he returned to the lodge. "Fletcher, I'd like you to take over the work that Dorsey was doing, which was connecting Teal to Lajoie and documenting evidence against Teal. We just found out that he's the mole."

"Ha! So it *was* Teal, was it?" Fletcher said. "I never cared for him...he was an odd one."

In the meantime, Kate did a file search on the 514 number against the file Duffy had on Emile Baker and E. Baker Trucking. There was no match between the 514 number and any of the trucking company phones; however, there was a match with a cell phone that belonged to Emile Baker. The personal connection to Baker added a twist Kate wasn't expecting. She ran the 514 number and saw it was a cell phone with National Telephone as the provider.

National advised her that it was a business phone registered to Dobbs LLC, Purveyor of Fine Goods. Kate sent a note off to INTERPOL that the area code 705 phone belonged to one Felix Lajoie, a known suspect connected to Grand Manan. The owner of the 514 number was presently unknown but had a connection to Emile Baker, currently a person of interest. The pieces of the puzzle were beginning to come together.

Late in the day, a file with phone records from the BMW dealership came over. Kate quickly set up criteria for a search against the 514 number for Dobbs LLC. She hit "run" and headed over to her cottage to change before dinner.

On her way, she saw Andre heading down to a float plane carrying a suitcase.

Probably heading to Dorsey's funeral services, she thought. *Maybe I should go, too.* But then, decided against it.

Later, Lou stopped by Kate's cottage to pick her up on his way to dinner. When they entered the lodge, Kate said. "Lou, save me a seat, will you? I want to check out a program I left running."

Once she reached her work area, she looked at the report and saw that Dobbs' 514 number was a match with the BMW dealership phone records.

Kate found Duffy as fast as she possibly could.

"Duffy, that 514 area code number that I was tracking is a *match* with Baker and a BMW dealership. I think we may have just found the fence!" The telephone connection immediately catapulted Emile Baker from being a "person of interest" to a prime suspect in Duffy's mind.

During dinner, Lou noticed Kate staring off into the distance with a faraway look on her face. "What is it, Kate? Have an Atlantic salmon on your mind that's putting up a good fight?"

"Oh, I'm sorry, Lou. No, that's not it at all. It's just that *now* I realize I *should* have gone with Andre to attend Matt Dorsey's funeral."

"Really? Why is that?"

"Lou, it's Dorsey's stupid obsession with baseball trivia that's going to break this whole damn thing wide open for us."

"Okay, I'll bite: How?"

"It was that damn comment he made to me offhandedly one day: 'from Tinker to Evers to Chance.' I dismissed the whole thing as total rubbish. But Duffy overheard us talking about it, and on a whim, decided to google the word 'chance.' Lou, that's what led us to E. Baker Trucking." Kate pursed her lips and inhaled deeply. "I feel like such a total wretch for having undervalued Dorsey every single day! Now, I wish I had gone on that plane with Andre."

"Well, the only plane we have is gone, Kate."

"I know."

"Look, why don't we say a prayer for him around the time of his funeral tomorrow."

"I'd like to do that."

The following day, Lou and Kate walked over to the charred remains of the cottage that had burned to the ground, and stood next to the water's edge. They said a few prayers for Matt Dorsey's soul, and for Fred O'Neil, too.

As they turned to go back, Kate stopped him."Lou, will you be rebuilding that cottage?"

"Definitely. Everyone who has ever stayed there always wanted to rebook it because of the view."

"I've walked over here many times Lou, just to sit on the front steps and clear my thoughts. Of all the cottages, it had the grandest view down the lake. Will it be the same style cottage?"

"Honestly, I'm not exactly sure. A few guests have said they'd come up with their families in the summer if the cottages weren't so small. Maybe I'll rebuild that one bigger, like I did for Angelo and Alessandra, just to see how it works out."

"Well, if you're thinking of families coming here," Kate said, "maybe you'd best be thinking about something other than outhouses."

As they walked back toward the lodge, Lou took her hand in his. It felt good to connect with a woman . . . again.

"So, Kate, if you were to design something . . . for a family . . . what would the cottage look like?"

"Well, the old one had a grand view of the lake, but I'd angle it just a little more to the west so it could face all the way down the lake and the sunset. And of course, you'd want a large, screened porch in front, to take full advantage of the breeze that comes off the water."

"Actually, I was thinking more about what the *inside* should look like."

"Well, if you're thinking of having families here, maybe you had better start thinking now about what a wife would want, especially if they're here for a week with little ones . . . and it's rainy."

"Yeah," Lou said, 'that's exactly what I was thinking about."

Chapter 36

Within a day, the Chief Inspector at the Old Port sent Duffy a text that the GPS tracking device had been placed inside a sealed container with a bill of lading made exactly the way Duffy had requested. Also that E. Baker Trucking had been notified about needing to make a special pickup.

Duffy immediately logged into the Global Navigation Satellite System and was able to see the beeping device located on the docks at the Old Port. He created a split-screen so he could monitor the container. Within six hours, the container was moving.

Elsewhere, Kate was settling into her work area where she found a text from the BMW Service Manager. *It simply said: "have your part." That was fast,* she thought, then arranged for a Mountie in plainclothes to pick up the part from the dealership. Once the Mountie had the part, he sent a text to Kate with the skew number on the package and the serial number that was stamped on the part.

She sent the info to INTERPOL who worked with BMW and was able to verify that the part, indeed, had been inside one of the missing BMW containers. Kate was about to share the info with Duffy when he suddenly jumped up from his chair, pointing at his monitor, and shouting, "I *knew* it! Baker, you sly dog, you *do* have another location!"

"Duffy, what are you going on about?" she asked.

"Kate, I have an empty container sitting at the damn airport!"

"And?"

"And, it's not supposed to be there! I just busted Baker!"

With all the new puzzle pieces coming together, the challenge began shifting toward collecting evidence in a manner that would stand up in court.

Later that afternoon, Andre returned from the funeral; Duffy and Kate brought him up to speed on the latest developments. He decided it was time to send someone up to Quebec to get firsthand intel on Baker.

Just before dinner, Andre met with Lou and Kate, and they committed to traveling to Quebec City together. "My only request is that you two go easy on the expenses," Andre begged. "I'll let Bob Newton know you're coming up to get a closer look at E. Baker Trucking."

The following morning, Jake flew Lou and Kate over to Kedgwick where they rented an SUV and drove to Quebec City.

As Lou pulled into the entrance of the Chateau Frontenac, Kate looked at him."Oh Lou, we can't stay *here;* Andre will go crazy with the cost. He said to go easy on expenses, remember?"

"Yeah, well, he once told me it was much easier to ask

for forgiveness than to ask for permission."

"He actually said that?"

"Yeah."

"I'll keep that in mind," she said and pulled on the door handle. "All right, you take care of the valet; I'll take care of things at the front desk. Meet me in the lobby, okay?"

Minutes later, Lou arrived at the reservation desk and Kate motioned him over to the elevators. When they stepped into the enclosure, Kate nonchalantly said, "Fourteen, please." Reaching the fourteenth floor, a bellhop greeted them, carried their luggage to the suite, opened the door, and placed it all inside. Kate handed him a generous tip.

"Thanks, we can take it from here."

"Nice digs," Lou said. "What's *my* room number?"

Smiling coyly, Kate said, "Lou, the rooms here are just *incredibly* expensive. I knew how much you wanted to stay here, so I thought, 'What the hell, if we *share* a room, we'll actually be *saving* Andre a little money.'"

She stepped closer to Lou and put her hand gently on his chest. Then, looking up into his eyes, she added, "I hope you'll forgive me for not asking *permission* first." She tilted her chin upward, very close to his mouth. He looked down at her invitation and, unable to help himself, kissed her lightly.

"Then, I'm forgiven?"

Momentarily speechless, Lou looked at her for a long minute, looked at her lips . . . so inviting. "You're forgiven."

"Oh, good. And will there be more of . . . *that*?"

"You sure are full of surprises, Kate," he managed to say. He was beginning to feel things he hadn't in a long time.

"Yes . . . and I have a few more . . . surprises," she said softly looking up into his eyes.

Lou now realized that Kate had been in a playful mood all during their drive over to Quebec. He had also noticed a sexual tension slowly developing between them;

he just hadn't been sure, but now he was. No one could miss her intentions.

As he stood there, she rose onto her tiptoes and kissed him long, yet lightly, teasingly, getting to know the feel of his mouth; not pressing too hard, just playfully, until he began to respond. Gently, he pulled her closer, and for the next few moments, they left the world behind, becoming comfortable with their new intimacy.

Then gently, Kate pushed herself away from Lou's embrace. "You know, maybe we should call down to make dinner reservations before it gets to be too late."

"I'll take care of that right now," he said, a little reluctant to interrupt the moment. He released her from his arms, thinking: *Maybe she's reconsidered.* Walking over to the desk, he pressed the concierge button on the phone and was immediately connected.

"Concierge desk. How may I assist you, Mr. O'Grady?"

Laughing to himself at being called Mr. O'Grady, Lou said, "I'd like to make a dinner reservation for two in the main dining room for seven-thirty this evening."

"Party of two. Seven-thirty. Main dining room. You're all set, Mr. O'Grady. Will there be anything else?"

"No, that's it. Thanks."

Turning around, he briefly caught a glimpse of Kate's beautiful, smooth nakedness as she slipped between the sheets, covering all but her smile, and her beautiful chestnut brown hair.

Lou wasted no time undressing and joining her under the covers.

The next short while was exciting as they gently took time exploring the contours of each other's body while their desires heightened; tongues probed playfully, then more urgently, as their needs rose higher until they penetrated each other's mouths in earnest. Finally, the passion that had been building became unstoppable, and they made love for nearly an hour until both were completely satisfied.

The next morning, entering the dining room for breakfast, Lou held up two fingers and they were seated at a table next to a floor-to-ceiling window with a phenomenal panoramic view of the Saint Lawrence Seaway. As they began discussing plans for the day, Lou received a text from Andre: *"Newton wants 2 meet. Text him."*

"Kate, Andre wants us to meet with Newton."

"When?"

"He didn't say, the earlier the better I suppose. I'll text him to see when he's available."

As soon as Lou sent a text to Newton, he replied back, *"I'm free now."*

"He's free now, Kate. Let's find out what he has to say." Lou punched in: *"Meet us in 45 minutes - lobby Frontenac."* and hit the send key.

"What's the connection again between Newton and Andre?" Kate asked.

"The two of them joined the Mounties at the same time and were good friends. Newton went out on disability and ended up having to take an early retirement. It sounds like they've stayed connected."

Following breakfast, Lou and Kate found the lobby quite busy with tour people checking out, and others waiting to speak with the concierge. When Newton arrived, he immediately headed over to where Lou and Kate were waiting for him in a lounge area.

"Good morning, I'm Bob Newton."

He saw a somewhat surprised look on their faces at being recognized. "Andre sent me a text with your photos so I'd know what you both looked like," then he hesitated, looking around at all the people. "Let's move away from all this traffic. There's an alcove across the way where we can talk privately."

As soon as they sat down, Newton said, "I assume Andre has told you all about me?"

"Only that the two of you worked together years ago," Lou said. "Mr. Newton, you know why we're here. What can you do to help?"

"It's Bob. Please, call me Bob," he said. "Well, I can do any number of things for you, anything you want, within reason. I've lived up here for close to nine years now; I can certainly show you around. I've also done stakeouts and I've been a decoy; you name it, and I'm in."

"Actually, showing us around so that we get our bearings, would save us a lot of time," Kate said.

"Done! I'll pull my car around. Meet me at the bottom of the steps in fifteen minutes." As abruptly as Newton arrived, he was gone again.Lou looked at Kate. "I don't know what I was expecting, but it certainly wasn't that."

"Me, neither. Let's go get our jackets and meet him at the bottom of the stairs."

When they returned to the suite, Kate began strapping on her shoulder holster as Lou asked, "Glocks?"

Kate smiled. "Yup. Just like that old Amex credit card commercial said: "Don't leave home without it."

Chapter 37

Bob Newton was waiting at the foot of the stairs when they arrived. Lou and Kate jumped into the back seat of his black SUV. "Where to, folks?"

"Let's start out at the port and follow a truck over to Baker's yard."

Newton was nonstop chatter describing all the points of interest as they headed over to the dock area. They didn't have long to wait before one of Baker's trucks exited the gate. Following at a discrete distance, they soon arrived at the gate to Baker's yard.

"Not much to see here," Newton said. "That fenced area inside is where the containers are being held that were not officially released by customs at the port. A few of the port's inspectors have been reassigned over here now, which has made a huge difference in their ability to keep the docks clear."

"We're familiar with the arrangement Baker has with the port authority," Lou said. "Andre told us that you did some surveillance work on Baker. What else can you tell us about E. Baker Trucking?"

"Well, there's not much else to tell. Andre had me follow their trucks for several days when they left the port a while back; everything looked normal to me."

Kate gave Lou a hand signal that she wanted to change the conversation. "Is this the only location Baker brings the containers to?"

"Absolutely. Everything comes here. His whole operation has always been here. A few years ago, he expanded the yard, of course, but everything is located right here," Newton said. "He doesn't live very far away either. I guess he likes the short commute. Heck, he could even go home for lunch."

After sitting another twenty minutes while watching trucks come and go, Lou finally said, "Well, this certainly has been helpful, Bob, but I think we've seen enough. You can take us back to the Frontenac, now."

"Okay. On the way back, I'll take you by the Plains of Abraham, a very picturesque area in Battlefield Park where there's a statue honoring Joan of Arc."

"Bob, don't go out of your way . . . just bring us back to the Frontenac."

"Oh, it's on the way, actually," he insisted. "Let me know if there's anything else I can do for you while you're here. I've got plenty of time to help."

Arriving back at the Frontenac, Lou thanked Newton again for his help. "Oh, one last thing. We'll be flying back when we leave. How far is it to the airport from here?"

"Not far, about seventeen kilometers. It shouldn't take you even a half hour from here."

As they walked up the front steps, Kate spoke in a low tone of voice. "So, how did you enjoy the nonstop tour guide lecture?"

"Yeah, that was interesting, huh? My take? Andre is just trying to humor an old friend."

"Sound about right," she agreed. "Where to now?"

"Didn't you say you wanted to check out the airport? Maybe we'll get lucky and see one of Baker's trucks there."

When the valet brought their car around, Lou and Kate headed over to the freight area at the airport. The gate was open, and they were not challenged. If they had been, either Kate's INTERPOL credentials, or Lou's RCMP credentials, would have satisfied any guard.

It was a warm day and most of the hangar doors were wide open. The first few hangars housed a variety of aircraft. As they proceeded down the line, they had to weave their way around trucks of all shapes and sizes surrounding both the FedEx and the UPS hangars.

In the distance, there were a couple of older hangars that appeared to be vacant. As they continued on, the couple passed the remains of several foundations where it was obvious that hangars had previously stood. There was no name over the door of the next hangar and it looked like it wasn't being used, however, a shiny SUV was parked off to its side.

As they drove past and on to the last hangar, Kate read the name over the door and shouted: "Stop! 'Dobbs Aviation,' Lou. I just identified a phone number belonging to a Dobbs LLC from someone texting Baker."

"Kate, that hangar looks abandoned."

"Looks can be deceiving. Let's go have a look in the windows." Lou pulled to the side of the road, and they walked over to the hangar. The windows were filthy, but skylights offered just enough illumination for them to see what looked like packing material strewn about; otherwise, the hangar was completely empty.

"Can I help you folks?" a voice from behind asked,

Kate spun around, then smiled. "Oh, hello! We're looking for Dobbs Aviation. We were told to go see Dobbs

Aviation if we wanted to take a flight around the city. Do you know what time they open?"

"I think you were misinformed, ma'am. Dobbs doesn't have any planes here. There are some flight schools on the opposite side of the terminal that I believe offer scenic flights around the city." The man with a stocky build nodded across the airstrip.

"It's such a beautiful day, we were hoping to go up," she continued. "Is that your hangar? Do *you* have a plane in your hangar? We'll pay you the going rate, if you'll take us up?"

"Sorry, ma'am. I'm in the transportation business, yes, but we stay on the ground." With that, he politely tipped the front of his baseball cap and excused himself.

As soon as they were back in their car, Lou smiled at her. "Kate, I think you have more than just a touch of 'the blarney' in you."

"Well, if my dad was alive, he would have told you to be careful because I have a blend of both 'the malarkey' and 'the blarney.' He said it was truly a gift. My mother always said 'the malarkey' came from my father's side." It made Lou laugh.

"Incidentally," she continued, "did you notice the Baker Trucking logo on his hat?"

"Kate, I think we just met Mr. Emile Baker, himself."

"Really?"

"Yeah, I do. Check our GPS coordinates and see how far we are from the GPS device in that dummy container Duffy set up."

Kate searched for the app on her phone while she talked. "So, what's with this guy referring to me as 'ma'am?' Seriously, I've never been called 'ma'am' before in my whole life!"

Laughing, Lou said, "Kate, it's a sign of respect over here for *older* women."

"*Older* women? Older *women*? Did I just hear you say '*older women*' to me? Please tell me that I didn't just hear you say, 'older women,' okay?"

Lou reflected on the emphasized words Kate had used before he responded.

"Well, I was just explaining the term, that's all. Obviously, it doesn't apply to *you*. You won't ever hear *me* use it."

"Good, because I can assure you that if I ever hear you say it, you'll be calling me, '*Lieutenant* O'Grady,' if you get my drift."

Suddenly Kate froze and was serious.

"Lou, we're at ground zero with Duffy's container. It's right here where we are!"

"It must be in that other hangar," Lou said. "Baker's running too big of an operation for him to be over here unless he absolutely needs to be here. Let's go find a spot outside the gate and wait."

Within five minutes after they backed into a spot outside the gate, a truck with Baker's company logo on the door drove through the gate carrying a large shipping container. Shortly after, the same truck left without any container, followed by Baker in his SUV.

"Lou, let's go back and look in the windows of that other hangar."

"Not now, let's do it after dark. I don't want to risk having Baker come back because he forgot something and find us snooping around again."

"Okay, I'm hungry anyway, let's go have something to eat." During lunch, Kate said, "I wonder how often Baker's trucks visit that hangar?"

"For short money, we could find out if we put Bob Newton on a stakeout until we come back after dark," Lou said jokingly.

"That's actually a good idea," she said. "Anyway, he's begging to get back in the game. Let's do it! He'll feel like he's being included in something."

Lou sent Newton a text asking him to call. Newton must have been dusting the phone since he called back immediately.

"Bob, I've got a little work for you; are you available for the next five or six hours to do a stakeout?"

"Absolutely! Just tell me where, when and what you want me to do!"

"I'd like you to park outside the freight gate over at the airport and keep a record of every truck that goes in and out of the area where the freight hangars are. Can you do that?"

"Yup, I'll go over there right now. Thanks for thinking of me."

"Good. We'll relieve you sometime after dark, but not too late."

"Roger that, Lou. I'm rolling. Over and out."

Laughing at the old expressions Newton was using, Kate said, "Oh, my God, he's such a dinosaur! Why didn't you tell him we were only interested in knowing if any Baker trucks went in or out?"

"I'm not sure," Lou said. "Hey, at least this way he'll have something to report."

They returned to the Frontenac and provided Andre with an update on what they'd uncovered so far before they dined on chateaubriand in the main restaurant.

When the sun set, Lou called Newton.

"Bob we're on our way over."

"Roger that. I'll flash my headlights twice when I see you turn in; there's a parking spot right next to me."

When Lou and Kate arrived, the three of them stood outside their cars. Newton handed Lou a lengthy handwritten list of vehicles that had come and gone since he arrived, none of which were Baker trucks.

Kate had already decided she would stay with Newton

while Lou checked out the hangar. Lou moved down the row of old buildings, melting in and out of the shadows. When he reached the unmarked hangar in question, he used a small halogen flashlight to look through the windows and counted the number of cargo containers inside.

He smiled at the irony of counting a 'baker's dozen' inside. Then, setting his cell phone on 'no flash,' took a few pictures of the interior before heading back to where he had left Kate and Newton, again staying in the shadows.

Shortly after Lou had headed toward the hangar, Newton said, "Excuse me, Kate, I need to get something out of my car."

She shrugged her shoulders and continued watching Lou as he moved among the shadows from hangar to hangar. Later, the only thing she remembered was a faint noise coming from the vicinity of Newton's vehicle. Without warning, someone came up from behind her and covered her face with a handkerchief soaked in chloroform. She tried shaking her head free, but her knees buckled just before she passed out cold.

Once her limp body was lowered to the ground, Bob Newton removed her weapon, the holster strap, and its waist belt, and carefully laid her across the back seat of his car. He secured her hands behind her back with a plastic zip tie before climbing into the driver's seat and driving away from the airport, leaving Lou behind.

Chapter

38

When Lou finally worked his way back to the gate, he was surprised that Newton's car was gone. The fact that Kate was missing, too, made him feel ice cold.

Our SUV is still there, so she must have gone off with Bob, he reasoned. When he opened the door to their SUV and saw Kate's purse still on the seat, he knew trouble had found them.

Kate wouldn't have left without taking her pocketbook or texting me, he thought. He called Kate's cell phone and heard it ringing inside the SUV.

Then, he heard a voice from the shadows."Did we lose someone?" a voice asked.

Lou turned to see an impeccably dressed man of average height walking toward him with a cane.

His instincts went on high alert.

The mystery man advanced further until he was within six feet of Lou.

"Did we lose someone, Mr. Gault?"

"Who are you?"

"Someone you shouldn't have tried to cross, Mr. Gault."

With lightning speed, Dobbs drew the sword concealed in his cane and uttered the word "engarde" before lunging forward. Lou reacted fast and shifted to the left, but not before the tip of Dobbs' sword took a nick out of his shoulder. When Dobbs lunged forward a second time, Lou was ready and shifted to the right. Dobbs' blade struck the side of the SUV with such force that the tip of the sword snapped off.

Lou quickly took advantage of Dobbs' momentary surprise and drove his knee up into Dobbs' groin with every ounce of strength he had. Then he hammered the man with a chop to the side of Dobbs' neck that fractured his collar bone, sending him sprawling on the ground screaming in agony. The broken sword fell from Dobbs' hand.

Lou wasted no time rolling Dobbs over onto his stomach and planting a knee in his back before forcing one of Dobbs' arms up behind his back.

"Where is she?" he growled.

"She's gone Gault," Dobbs spit back. "Don't be a fool! Kill me and you'll never see her again!"

Lou took out his phone and called for backup. An RCMP patrol car stationed at the airport quickly responded. When the Mountie arrived, Lou still has his knee planted in Dobb's back. Lou flashed his badge and explained the situation. The Mountie put a set of cuffs on Dobbs and pulled him up. Lou frisked him and walked him to the rear door of the squad car.

"Duck your head," Lou said before literally shoving him into the back seat of the squad car. In Canada, no Miranda Rights needed to be read. Now, Lou's focus was on finding Kate. Two more squad cars arrived and Lou explained that his partner and a colleague were both missing.

"I've never heard of a Bob Newton," one Mountie said. "I'll call the sergeant on duty, maybe he has."

"Please, let me have the phone," Lou said. When the desk sergeant picked up, he reported: "Sarge, listen, this is Officer Lou Gault. I'm up from New Brunswick on a special investigation and need your help! I believe my partner and a retired Mountie working a stakeout have been abducted. Someone that's involved in whatever is going just tried to skewer me with a sword. I need you to put out an all-points bulletin for a light blue Ford sedan, late model, Quebec plates. I believe my partner is in that car, can you do that?"

"Consider it done. Anything else?"

In the background, Dobbs could be heard yelling that he was hurt and needed medical attention.

"Yeah, could you send an ambulance over to the airport on the far side? We're over at the entrance to the freight gate. I've taken someone into custody who thinks he needs medical attention."

Somewhere on the outskirts of Quebec City, Kate was slowly beginning to recover. As her head started to clear, she realized that she was lying on her stomach across the back seat of a moving car and that her hands were constrained behind her back. As the fog in her brain continued to dissipate, she sensed the zip tie holding her hands wasn't pulled as tightly as it could have been. Within a minute, she was able to wiggle her hands free.

Squinting her eyes a few times, she recognized the driver in the front seat was Newton. She also realized that her shoulder holster had been removed as well as her belt. As quietly as possible, she searched the back seat area with her hands hoping to find something, anything, that could even remotely be used as a weapon. The only thing she found underneath the driver's seat were wires that connected the seatbelt to the alarm.

Now, Kate twisted around on the seat and searched under the front passenger seat but there was nothing of value. Frustrated, but having no other resource, Kate slipped out of her bra, and in a flash wrapped it around Newton's neck like a garrote. Newton immediately reached up trying to get a hand under whatever it was around his neck, but Kate was applying too much pressure for him to even get a finger under it.

The car began to swerve left into oncoming traffic. Instinctively, Newton reacted and grabbed the wheel with both hands. The muscles in Kate's arms were on fire and began spasming. She was in agony. Then, knowing her arm strength wouldn't last much longer, she placed her feet against the back of Newton's seat and used the full power of her legs to maintain pressure.

The stranglehold was too much for Newton to endure and still maintain control of the car. Kate sensed that Newton was struggling to keep the car under control. "Pull over, Newton!" she yelled. Newton's inner sense of survival kicked in and he pulled over to the side of the road. However, Kate didn't let up on the pressure until she sensed Newton had passed out.

Once she released the stranglehold, she leaned over the front seat, frisked Newton, and relieved him of his sidearm before shoving the car into park. After a quick scan of the front seat, she noticed her Glock beside Newton and grabbed it.

Kate got out of the car, opened the driver's side door, and stood back six feet. Newton was much older than Kate, but was a big man. She knew he could easily overpower her if she wasn't careful. When Newton began to come around, Kate chambered a round in her Glock, shifted into a Chapman Stance and leveled the weapon at Newton.

"Okay, both hands up, fingers interlocked on your head. Now turn your legs toward me and put both feet on the ground." He did as she instructed.

"Now, nice, and easy, slide forward and kneel on the ground."

Suddenly, Newton lunged at Kate, but she was ready and gave the driver's side door a powerful kick, knocking Newton off balance and forcing him sit back into the car. Then, she fired a warning shot into the dirt at Newton's feet."On the ground, face first, hands behind your back."

Showing absolutely no mercy, Kate delivered a blow to the back of Newton's head with the handle of the Glock, knocking him completely out. Fishing through his coat pockets, she found another zip tie and used it to secure Newton's wrists behind his back. It was several minutes before he showed signs of consciousness.

"Get up and walk to the back of the car," she ordered when Newton had fully- recovered. He had more than a little difficulty trying to stand up with his hands tied behind his back. But when Newton reached the back of the car, he saw the trunk was wide open.

"Get in."

Newton balked and Kate fired another round at his feet. "I said *get in*!"

After a couple of awkward tries, Newton managed to get into the trunk and Kate slammed the trunk closed before climbing into the driver's seat.

At this point, she had no idea where they were, but fortunately, Newton's cell phone was sitting in a holder mounted to the dash. She powered it up only to find it was password protected. Opening the glove compartment, hoping to find a map, instead, she found a second cell phone. This one was fully-charged and wasn't password protected.

But now she had another problem. While she had

stored Lou's number in her phone, she hadn't memorized it and had no idea what it was. So, she pulled up the airport website and clicked on directions.

Once the ambulance arrived at the freight gate, Dobbs was secured to a stretcher and on his way to the hospital under guard. Lou was talking with a fourth Mountie who had responded to his call for backup when Newton's car suddenly came roaring around the corner and screeched to a stop in a cloud of dust just before the gate. Lou's Glock was instantly out and ready.

"It's me!" she called out, relieved to see Lou standing there. She turned the headlights off and opened the door. Once out of the car, she slammed the door, and said, "Well, this little car has got some guts to it, but it pulls to the left wicked when you brake, and there's an annoying thumping noise coming from the trunk."

Lou holstered his weapon and ran over to her. "Are you all right? I didn't know how to get to you!" Turning to the Mounties, Lou announced: "Fellas, this is my partner, Lieutenant O'Grady."

One of the officers tipped his hat. "Pleased to meet you, ma'am."

Kate smiled at his words. Then, turning to her partner, she said. "I'm all right now, Lou, Newton surprised me is all. What happened to you? Your shoulder is all bloody."

"Did you just say *Newton*?"

"Yeah, can you believe that little weasel came up from behind me and knocked me out with a drug. I'm still a little foggy."

"Where is he?"

"In the trunk," she said, then turned to a Mountie. "Officer, will you come help us? I have some baggage I need taken down to the station house."

She popped open the trunk as the three of them looked into the rear of the car at Bob Newton."I was going to have him sit in the back seat, but I then I thought, maybe he gets car sick riding in the back seat." She paused before saying, "So, I told him to get his ass in the friggin trunk."

"Kate, you're a piece of work!" Lou laughed.

A couple of hours later, Dobbs was released from the hospital and taken to the station where both he and Newton were fingerprinted, booked, and held without bail. Records of their arrests were temporarily "misplaced" making it necessary to remain in lock up until such time as the RCMP decided otherwise.

Following the departure of police cars, Lou and Kate cleared the area and gave Andre a call to fill him in on the day's adventures. He couldn't believe Bob Newton had been working for the other team and apologized profusely to Lou and Kate. They all agreed to talk again first thing in the morning.

By the time the couple arrived back at the Frontenac, their adrenalin was still running high from the night's activity, so they headed directly into the lounge.

"Kate, you never did tell me how you managed to subdue Newton?"

"Well," she said, "an *older woman* is never without one strategic weapon . . . I took my bra off and wrapped it around the bastard's neck, then strangled him until he pulled over."

Lou practically spit his drink out laughing.

"What's worse," she continued, "that was my *favorite* bra, too. Now, I don't even remember where I left it. But, on the flip side, my 'girls' had a chance to get out earlier than usual tonight and get some fresh air."

A while later, they were still laughing as they headed up to their suite arm in arm.

Chapter 39

The following morning, Andre called Kate early to let her know he wanted to talk with her when Lou was present, so the three of them could figure out Baker's involvement.

"Right, give me forty-five minutes to get ready," she said. "I'll ring you back."

When she ended the call, Lou was propped up on one elbow. "Does it really take you forty-five minutes to get ready in the morning?"

"Of course not," Kate said smiling. "I just thought a little extra time would be nice in case . . . something came up." He laughed, then kissed her again.

"I like how you think."

Forty-five minutes later, when Andre answered Kate's call, she winked at Lou as she said, "Andre! Lou and I are together now and I have you on speaker."

"Great! Good morning to you both. Our guys in

Quebec worked through the night and downloaded the history on Dobbs' cell and both of Newton's phones. Duffy is working on it now. It seems that Newton and Dobbs have been communicating with one another for over a year. It also looks like Dobbs began contacting Baker only recently. I'm thinking we might be able to turn Baker into a Crown Witness. What are your thoughts on that?"

"We hadn't thought about it actually but it's certainly worth a try. He's not aware we have Dobbs and Newton in custody yet, is he, Andre?

"No."

"Once he understands the whole thing is falling apart, he might easily be turned if he thinks it's to his advantage," Kate said.

"Lou, what are your thoughts?" Andre asked.

"It's worth a try," Lou answered. "If he doesn't go for it, we'll just put the cuffs on him. What kind of a deal can we offer him, Andre?"

"All we can promise is that we'll let the crown attorneys know he has fully cooperated with us from the very beginning, and that would be in his favor."

"What do we want in return?" Kate asked.

"The names of everyone else that he knows, or even suspects, is involved in this."

"Anything else, Andre?"

"Yes, two things: We've run the numbers on the cell phone found on that one Brit who was killed trying to escape after that last attack on us. Records show he made a few calls to Dobbs, and one to Baker. So, be aware, Baker is definitely involved in all of this.

"Secondly," Andre continued, "you'll be on Baker's home turf today, so, don't forget the first rule of law enforcement. You both were just damn lucky last night."

After a slight pause, Kate said, "Okay, Andre, I'll bite.

What *is* the first rule of law enforcement?"

"Make sure that when your shift is over, you go home alive!" With that, Andre hung up.

Kate turned to Lou with a quizzical look on her face.

"Ten bucks says Andre watched "The Untouchables" last night with Angelo and Jake," Lou said. During breakfast, Lou and Kate worked out the mechanics of how they'd play "good cop/bad cop" with Baker. Before leaving the Frontenac, Lou made a call to the local RCMP station and arranged for a patrol car to be parked just out of view by Baker's yard.

No one challenged them as they drove through the gate at Baker's compound. Before exiting their SUV, they checked their Glocks and walked into the office where Kate flashed her credentials.

"I'm Lieutenant O'Grady, this is Officer Gault, RCMP; we're here to see Mr. Emile Baker. Is he on the premises?"

"Why, yes he is, ma'am; he's in his office down the hall . . . last door on the right."Kate bristled at the word "ma'am," but immediately proceeded down the hall and entered Baker's office without knocking. Holding up her credentials as she walked in, she saw Baker seated at his desk. Walking in right behind her, Lou flashed his own RCMP credentials.

"Mr. Baker, I'm Lieutenant O'Grady, this is Lou Gault, RCMP. Sir, we are here to take you into custody."

The color immediately drained from Baker's face as if his worst nightmare had come true.

"Mr. Baker, you can cooperate and make this easy, or it can be extremely unpleasant," Lou said. "It's your call, sir, and please, keep your hands where we can see them at all times."

As Kate turned around to shut Baker's office door, Baker immediately reached into an open desk drawer while Lou drew his Glock. "Freeze!"

Baker threw his hands into the air. "Whoa, whoa, I'm just going for a pack of cigarettes. May I?" A large ashtray on Baker's desk was filled with butts and, based on where it was situated, Lou guessed that Baker was righthanded.

"Go ahead, but only use your left hand, very slowly, and keep that right hand up high."

Baker pulled out a pack of cigarettes from the drawer, lit one, and took a deep drag.

"Mr. Baker, last evening we arrested Mr. Dobbs," Kate said. "You've been identified as an accomplice of his. We also know you're connected to a Mr. Felix Lajoie. We know a great deal about you, Mr. Baker, and we know about the containers in the hangar.

"If you work with us, it'll go much easier for you," Lou said. "Not everyone has to go to jail. Some first-time offenders end up with only probation which is a lot easier than jail time, sir."

"I knew this was going to happen. Damn it! I shouldn't have done it," Baker said.

"Done what, Mr. Baker?"

"Taken their damn money."

"Whose money, Mr. Baker?"

"From those damn English bastards."

"Why did they give you money?"

"Because I lost my ass in Vegas."

"And they gave you money?"

"Yeah, so, I would stay in the game. Then I lost that, and I was in even deeper. I knew what they wanted me to do was wrong, but I had no choice. The bastards set me up!"

"Kate, that's enough for me," Lou said. "Let's just cuff him and take him in."

Kate stayed in the role of good cop saying, "No, not yet." Then she turned to Baker. "Mr. Baker, we suspected that you were being used. If you help us bring the others to justice, we'll help you in every way that we can. Quid pro Quo. Is that a deal?"

Lou countered with, "Come on, Kate, this guy's up to his neck in this; he knew what he was doing." Lou holstered his Glock. "Let's just put the cuffs on and take him in".

"No, Lou, let's give Mr. Baker a chance to think about what I'm offering him." Now Kate looked straight at Emile Baker. "Mr. Baker, if you choose to cooperate with us *right now,* it will go a lot better for you. You have nothing to lose and everything to gain." She waited for half a minute. "Would you like to cooperate with us, Mr. Baker?"

Baker slammed his fists on the arms of his chair. "Damn, I knew this would frigging happen! I never wanted this. I just knew this would happen, and now it has."

"Last chance, Mr. Baker. Will you cooperate with us?"

"'Chance,' ha, that's funny. They used to call *me* 'Chance.'"

"Mr. Baker . . . ?"

"Yes, *damn* it! Yes, I'll cooperate."

"Good choice, Mr. Baker, we're going to put the cuffs on you now and take you into custody. The cuffs are only for your safety as well as for ours."

As Emile Baker passed his secretary's desk, he looked at the woman. "Monique, call Simone and let her know that I've been arrested, and that I need to speak with our attorney."

Lou called for the backup cruiser to come into the yard and transport Baker to the station house. When they left Baker Trucking, Lou and Kate made a swing by the airport just to satisfy themselves that the two hangars had been officially cordoned off as a crime scene, and that a cruiser was stationed there. They found everything in order.

Once Andre heard that Baker had been brought in and

was willing to cooperate, he called Ottawa and arranged to have the Mounties' most capable interrogation team flown in.

Baker honored his word and shared as much information about the three Englishmen and Dobbs as he could remember.

Once Fletcher had a transcript of Baker's deposition, he was on the phone with the Hotel Bellagio, trying to peel back the onion on the identities of the Englishmen. On the other side of the pond, MI6 was working on identifying Sean Tinker's connections.

When Lou and Kate returned to the Frontenac, Kate headed over to the front desk while Lou headed up to the room to retrieve their luggage. As they got in their SUV, Kate asked him, "You mentioned something about flying back to Kedgwick, Lou?"

"Let's just take our time and enjoy a leisurely drive back down to Kedgwick," he said. "Jake can pick us up in the morning."

"I'd like that."

Word of the Baker and Dobbs bust traveled fast within INTERPOL. Throughout the drive down to Kedgwick, Kate was bombarded with text messages requesting additional information. For most of the ride there was little conversation between the two of them as Kate concentrated on texting her colleagues back.

Finally, totally exasperated, Kate let out a long sigh. "Will you people just give it a bloody rest!" after which she turned her phone off.

Then, she turned to Lou. "You know, the bill from the Frontenac was really expensive."

"I'm not surprised, you had us on the concierge floor."

"What's he going to say?"

"What *can* he say?"

"He's going to ask why we stayed there."

"If he ever does, which I doubt he will, I'll just tell him that we thought it would be far more believable if we stayed in character the whole time that we were away."

Kate laughed. "You seem to have a little touch of the blarney yourself."

"Someday, I'll share a few Abenaki legends with you," Lou said. "The Irish aren't the only one with creatures like the leprechauns."

After a pause, she turned and looked at him. "Lou, I want you to know that I've never done anything like this with anyone else before in my whole life. Somehow, I just knew I didn't want it to be playacting anymore."

"Kate, I feel the same way. Hell, it crossed my mind to call Andre and tell him that we just needed a few more days when we were down on Grand Manan."

"You never even hinted about that to me."

"I know."

"I wasn't ready then," she said.

"I know."

That evening, they raised a glass of wine over dinner.

"Here's to you, Kate."

"No, here's to *us*, Lou."

"You know Kate, you never did tell me what you thought the inside of a cottage should look like if a woman where to design it."

Shaking her head, she said. "Give me your napkin . . . I'll draw you a picture."

The following morning, Jake was waiting at the airport and within the hour, they were circling Lake 980 preparing to land.

In the days that followed, the Port Authority in Quebec rescinded the unique deal that had been in place with E. Baker Trucking. Once all the containers in the secure area at Baker's compound were cleared, all the inspectors who had been regularly assigned to the yard were returned to duty at the port.

The chief inspector eventually presented a plan to the Ministry of Transportation that basically replicated what Baker had been doing to alleviate the back up at the port, only the offsite location would be leased and run by the Port Authority, itself.

Emile Baker's attorney sent a breach of contract letter to the Port Authority, however, the contract was written in such a way that it gave the Port Authority the right to terminate the contract at any time with or without cause.

Baker's lawyer argued that keeping him in confinement until he went on trial was too harsh a punishment, especially given the fact that he was cooperating with authorities and was not a flight risk. The crown attorney agreed, and Baker was released on bail, with an ankle bracelet. He was allowed to travel daily from his home to his office at E. Baker Trucking and back, and to church on Sundays.

Pending the outcome of any future trial, the Port Authority agreed to allow E. Baker Trucking to continue delivering containers to the port and picking up containers that had been released by their inspectors.

The Hotel Bellagio finally returned Fletcher's inquires and let him know that on the dates in question, a number of International travelers had registered at the hotel. Among them were five gentlemen from the UK including a Mr. Charles Dickens, a Mr. Sherlock Holmes, a Mr. Winston Churchill, a Mr. Isaac Newton, and a Mr. Oliver Cromwell. They had all produced valid forms of identification and each had provided sufficient funds up front that waived the need for a credit card when registering. They had all paid cash when checking out. Fletcher sent a "thank you" note for getting back to him.

Chapter

40

Andre lingered over coffee with Lou. "I'm confident I have enough evidence to file charges against Evers, Lajoie, Dobbs, Baker, and Newton," he said but then hesitated.

"And?"

"And Internal Affairs will arrest Charles Teal when we no longer need a conduit for passing misinformation along to Lajoie."

"When will that be?"

"We're waiting on INTERPOL."

"What's the hold-up?"

"Them. They haven't figured out who the head of this snake is yet."

"Are they close?"

"Good question. In the next twenty-four hours, I need to formally charge Baker, Dobbs, and Newton. I'll find a way to do it discretely, so nothing leaks to the press. My INTERPOL counterpart is pretty closed-mouthed on what's happening across the pond."

Elsewhere, Baker's lawyer guided him through his interrogation with the understanding that he had chosen to be a Crown Witness. True to his word, Baker continued to give them every possible piece of information that he could recall.

Dobbs quickly "lawyered up" and his interrogation yielded nothing.

Newton sang like a canary during his interrogation in the hopes of receiving a more favorable sentence and saving his pension. Thanks to Newton, the warehouse location that Dobbs was using in Montreal became known. Dobbs had used Newton merely as an errand boy and kept him at arm's length as much as possible. Therefore, Newton had little else to share beyond the first names of a few individuals who operated on the black market.

Duffy has requested phone records for Dobbs and Newton's cell phones and the records for the Dobbs LLC landline.

Over at the lodge, a conversation was just beginning. "Cunningham, can I see you?"

"Sure, what's up Sarge?"

"Just come over when you have a chance."

Cunningham walked over, hoping that he wasn't going to be grilled about who the hell kept going into Andre's cottage and short sheeting his bed.

Once he sat down, Andre began talking.

"Arnold, if Dobbs suddenly fails to respond to people in a timely basis, it will be noticed. I want you to come up with a cryptic text and send it to anyone reaching out to him that he'll get back to them."

"Got it."

"Okay, that's all I wanted to talk about."

Once the Mounties inspected the containers that Baker had in the hangar, it was clear that six belonged to BMW. The challenge was whether they could finally release the containers to ease the parts shortage for the dealerships without tipping their hand that Baker had been busted.

"Sarge, why don't we send a couple of containers with BMW parts back to the port and have the Port Authority announce they've just identified two containers without proper documentation, which were opened, and found to contain BMW parts?"

"Run the idea by the Crown Attorney Cunningham. He may want to keep all the evidence intact. But if he's okay with it, coordinate with the Port Authority, and give INTERPOL a heads-up."

Across the pond, Chief Inspector René Allard, who was on loan to INTERPOL from France's Directorate-General for External Security, let it be known that he wanted more evidence before he felt comfortable taking any action at Portmagee, Ireland, which would bring charges against Sean Tinker. He still had everyone focused inside the belly of the beast; no one was even tasked with trying to determine who the ring leaders were just yet.

Andre was anxious to get a look inside Dobbs' Montreal warehouse and any records that might be there. Phone calls made to the number listed for Dobbs, LLC, were going directly to an answering service that merely said Dobbs would get back to them. Andre asked Montreal's building inspector to send him a copy of the building's recorded floor plan.

Kate's work was becoming far more focused on running down requests from MI6 and INTERPOL in an effort to help them peel back the onion on Sean Tinker than supporting Andre.

Duffy finally received the full file for Dobbs' and Newton's cell phones and made them available to everyone. It was agreed that Kate would focus on any International calls, while Cunningham and Duffy focused on any calls within Canada.

Initial analysis showed Dobbs had made frequent calls to Felix Lajoie, which implicated Dobbs as the most likely individual directing Lajoie on what needed to be shipped from Grand Manan. But like Lajoie, Dobbs was just a middleman; the question still remained, who or what drove Dobbs to direct the movement of goods?

The first search routine that Kate ran showed no European numbers on Newton's phone; however, Dobbs had quite a few hits against European numbers.

After a day of programming sorting routines, Kate had a comprehensive picture of the International phone calls made to Dobbs, and those that Dobbs had made during the past four months. Three phone numbers stood out as having weekly activities. The one number with the most activity showed both incoming and outgoing texts. One of the other two numbers was only used by Dobbs to send text messages to someone. The remaining number only had incoming text messages.

Once Kate double-checked her results, she forwarded a copy of her work to her contacts at INTERPOL.

Meanwhile, Cunningham was looking at the average time that it took Dobbs to respond to phone or text messages.

"Sarge, the trend that's coming together is that Dobbs consistently replied within a day."

"Okay, then here's what I'd like you to do: Set up an automatic reply that he's traveling and will get back to them; then, keep a record of the phones that are contacting him."

"What about Newton? Won't his wife be curious when

he doesn't come home?"

"Already taken care of. I called her last night to let her know that Bob was in good hands and will be down at the station overnight debriefing people on the work he's been doing."

"Nice play on words."

"Yeah, although I never figured him for being involved in any of this."

Kate expanded the initial report she had created and was now merging the content of the text messages sent to Dobbs from the three International numbers in chronological order. This program would take a few hours to run since the files were huge, after which she would need to create subfiles to compile the data before she could produce a report.

Within an hour, INTERPOL sent a message to Kate that they had matched the number sending texts both *to* and *from* Dobbs to a phone belonging to Sean Tinker. Another matched a restricted number and would take time to determine the owner. The third number wasn't a match with any record on Tinker's file.

At lunch, Kate shared her approach with Duffy and he quickly realized the value of the program she had created. He asked Kate to send him the algorithms. It was just before dinner time when he finished modifying the program to fit his own needs. The file he was working on was humongous and would take all night and into the next day to process.

Kate's own report had finished running by the time she arrived at the lodge for breakfast.

Messages between Tinker and Dobbs appeared to have tones of 'peer-to-peer' in them. Texts sent to the number appearing on Tinker's records seemed to be more formal; there was a slight indication that Dobbs might have been addressing a superior. Otherwise, texts coming from the number that didn't have a match with Tinker's file were very succinct, nor did they seem to be providing explicit instructions and were comprised primarily of a series of numbers.

She made a note to check if any of the numbers the messages contained coincided with the containers found in the hangar that Baker had been using over at the airport.

The clock was ticking, and Andre was getting "antsy" about obtaining more information on Dobbs' operation and his warehouse. If he asked Kate to make another trip to Montreal with Lou it would slow the investigative process down. So, Andre decided on another tact.

"Lou and Jake, I'd like to have a word with you both after breakfast," Andre said.

Jake leaned over and whispered to Lou, "Ten bucks says I'm getting my old job back."

"Don't count on it, Cuz."

When Andre finished breakfast, he nodded to both men. "Come, let's take a walk."

Once they were outside, Andre said, "I'm going to miss this place when this is all over and done with."

"You're welcome back anytime Andre," Lou said. "You know that."

"Next year, I'll have more time."

Andre sat down on the bench next to the boathouse and waited for Lou and Jake to grab a seat. He casually looked out over the peaceful water.

"Lou, I would have asked you and Kate to do this, but I can't take her off the work she's doing now. Jake, I need *you* to play the role of Kate and go over to Montreal with Lou to do a little reconnaissance work at Dobbs' warehouse."

"Andre, I can't play Kate; every dress I own is at the cleaners. I don't have a single thing to wear!"

Andre stared at him.

Lou smiled. "Andre, we're in. When do you want us to go?"

"The sooner the better."

Jake sighed heavily. "Okay, but I need time . . . my nails are a mess!"

Andre lost his patience. "That's fine, Jake! Now, let's get serious."

Jake wiped his hand down his face, and shook his head. "Okay, I'm serious."

Andre cleared his throat. "We haven't been able to determine if anyone might be at Dobb's warehouse, but I'll provide you with a floorplan and search warrant so you're authorized to access the building and are able to take anything of interest. I'm going to insist that you enter the building with a Montreal Metro police officer though. I want to make sure that anything you remove will hold up in court as being legally obtained evidence."

Early the next morning, the two cousins flew down to Fredericton's airport. Andre had arranged for a Mountie to meet them at the gate with a search warrant before they boarded a flight to Montreal.

Once landed, Lou punched the warehouse address into an app on his cell phone and they headed out in a rental car. The building was located on the opposite side of the city in an area that urban renewal would likely never reach. It was well past noon when they arrived at the location. The street had a barren look to it; even the few trees on the street had seen better days, as they now showed roots that uplifted sections of crumbling cement sidewalks.

Typical of every partially abandoned industrial area, the buildings had that neglected, run-down look. A few had faded For Sale signs posted while others had No Trespassing signs.

"Jake, I don't think Dobbs could have picked a better location for what he's been up to," Lou said."Yeah, the whole street kind of looks like it's been abandoned. The sidewalks are a real mess. I'm glad I'm in flats and not trying to wear Kate's designer heels."

Lou didn't respond, but just took a deep breath and shook his head.

There were no vehicles parked anywhere near the building Dobbs has been using. If someone had been there and gone out for lunch, they would certainly have returned by now.

"Place looks empty, Lou."

"Looks that way. I'll pull the car over and call Metro."

Within a reasonable amount of time, a squad car arrived. They briefed the officer on their intentions and showed him the search warrant. All three proceeded to the door.

Jake rapped on the wooden frame a few times, waited a minute, then picked the lock with little effort; they entered the building. Inside, the temperature was cold; it was obvious that no one had been there for quite a while. Further inside the warehouse, there wasn't much either beyond an empty overseas cargo container, a few pallets stacked against the wall near the freight door, and layers of dust that had built up over several years.

"Jake, let's check out the office on the far side."

The door wasn't locked and inside, the office had a typical look - two fluorescent lights hanging from the ceiling with glass walls from the waist up. There was also an old wooden roll top desk, a chair that had seen better days, and a row of file cabinets.

"That roll top has probably been here from the beginning," Lou said. "I'll check out the file cabinets, Jake, you check out the desk."

Jake was intrigued with all the small cubby holes and tiny drawers in the top section of the desk. He sat down and explored each one. Pulling open the top right-side drawer, he found a few blank bills of lading; the rest of the drawers were empty.

Then Jake said, "Well, lookie what we have here, Lou, a little red envelope with the name 'First Bank of Montreal' on it."

"Smart money says the key inside belongs to a safety deposit box."

"Find anything in those files?"

"Nothing of value to us."

They did, however, let the Metro officer know they were confiscating the key before they left the building.

"Lou, wanna make a guess on which First Bank of Montreal branch has a box that this key fits?"

"Jake, let's save ourselves some time and just head over to the bank's main office."

On the drive over, Lou called Andre. "Andre, we've found a key to a safety deposit box. We're headed over to the bank now; we'll need a warrant."

"Which bank?"

"First Bank of Montreal."

"I'll have a warrant faxed over to the bank's main office within a half-hour ."

When Lou and Jake arrived at the main office, they showed credentials to the receptionist and asked to speak with the bank president. After a few phone calls, they were led into the office of Maurice Quimby.

Quimby's office smelled like a cross between decades of cigar smoke, and a cheap plug-in air freshener.

They introduced themselves. "There's a warrant being faxed over giving us access to a safety deposit box here," Lou said. "We're just not sure which branch the box is located at."

"May I see the key, please?" As soon as Lou took the envelope with key out of his pocket, Quimby smiled. "That's a home office key," he said. "That box is located downstairs."

"You're certain of that?"

"We use a different color envelope for every location," he said. "Red is our home office."

Quimby called his secretary in and when she arrived, gave instructions: "Miss Audrey, a warrant should be arriving soon by fax for a Constable Gault. Please bring it here when it arrives."

While waiting, Lou assured Quimby this was nothing that involved the bank; however, he would need a copy of access records for the security box. Within moments, Quimby's secretary returned with the warrant authorizing access to the contents in the box.

"Thank you, Miss Audrey. Now, please show these two officers to the safety deposit desk and see to it they get a copy of the box access records."

At the safety deposit desk, Quimby's secretary explained the situation to the attendant, Lou presented the warrant, and they were led into the vault area where they had no difficulty locating the box. They were then taken to a private viewing room.

Among the contents was a ledger with entries as recent as a week ago, a checkbook, and bank statements, a stack of business cards with a rubber band wrapped around them, and a leather address book with names, addresses, and phone numbers. There was also a handwritten sheet with people's names and a list of goods they apparently dealt with. Lou read the box access card. "Looks like the only person who ever signed the card was Dobbs."

"Not a bad haul, huh, Lou?" Jake said.

"Andre will be pleased with this, 'Kate.'"

"Ah, excuse me," Jake said. "Did I just hear you call me, 'Kate?'"

"Did I?" Lou smirked.

"I can't freaking believe it! You just called me 'Kate'!"

"Come on, let's go see if we can get a flight back to Fredericton tonight."

"I can't believe you called me, 'Kate.'"

Lou just smiled.

There was a late flight to Fredericton, so they headed directly over to the airport before grabbing something to eat. Jake put a call into Andre while they were in the car and brought him up to speed on what had transpired.

"Thanks, Jake," Andre said. "I'll call down to Fredericton and have someone make hotel reservations for you two near the airport for tonight when you land."

While waiting to board the plane, Lou gave the real 'Kate' a call.

"Hey, Kate, has Andre said anything to you about our expenses in Quebec?"

"No, why?"

"Well, he must have seen the bill from the Frontenac because he's putting Jake and me up in an Econo-lodge tonight."

"He hasn't said anything to me."

"He probably won't, even if he's pissed. He can be so non-confrontational at times."

The night flight from Montreal landed without incident. The next morning, after a quick breakfast, Jake did a pre-check on the Otter and they flew back to Havre de Poisson.

Andre greeted them at the dock.

As they walked up to the lodge, Andre said, "I'd like you to debrief everyone during lunch on what you saw at the warehouse and what was in the safety deposit box."

After lunch, Kate caught Lou's eye and signaled that

she'd meet him outside. Following a few more questions and answers from the group, Lou excused himself.

Kate was standing down by the lake near the cottage that had had been destroyed. He could instantly tell that something was bothering her.

"What's wrong, Kate?"

"Lou, I have to go back."

"Okay, I'll see you at dinner, then."

"No, you don't understand. I have to go back . . . *home*."

"Why, what's up?"

"I've been recalled. The chief inspector of the INTERPOL group I'm attached to has called me back. I haven't told anyone yet."

"Did he say why?"

"He would never say 'why.' I told him I had maybe three days more of work here before I could leave; that I couldn't go until it was finished."

Lou silently assessed his feelings. He didn't want her to leave."Will you be coming back?"

"It looks like he wants me back full time. He was against my coming here in the first place. I had to go over his head to get the nod for this assignment."

"Could Andre talk with him?"

"It wouldn't make a difference; he's pompous, he never bends." Kate paused and looked at him. "Lou, coming here has been the absolute *best* thing that has happened to me in the last two years. I don't want it to end . . . *you* are the best thing that has happened to me, but now I have to leave. My job, my whole life, is across the damned friggin pond."

"You could always try to join the Mounties. Andre would put a good word in for you."

She smiled at his attempt to figure something out.

"If it were only that simple. Lou, I don't *want* to go back, but I *have* to go back. I agreed to return when requested.

Now, I have to let Andre know, but I wanted to tell *you* first."

They looked at each other without saying a word. She touched his arm, and he drew her close. They kissed long and tenderly. Then, Kate turned and headed back to the lodge; Lou just watched her go while still trying to digest her words and what it would mean to him.

Andre was surprised that the chief inspector, his peer on the case, didn't have the courtesy to give him a heads-up on his plans to recall Kate.

Before dinner that night, Andre went to the kitchen to speak with Angelo. "Chef, Kate is being recalled. I'd like to have a special dinner the evening before she leaves and I'd like you and Alessandra to plan on dining with us."

The chef nodded. *"Non c'è problema.* I will make it nice for the *la bella donna."*

For the next three mornings, Lou walked Kate to breakfast and they spent time together well into the evenings. During the day, Kate was fully immersed in finishing up loose ends so she could transition her work over to Cunningham and Duffy.

Lou was out in the forest every day with Jake marking the trees he planned to cut down and haul back to the sawmill to rebuild the cottage.

Alessandra and Kate began taking a little more time together over tea. The two had become each other's confidants and were now savoring the time they had left.

On the afternoon of the third day, Alessandra lit the fire box underneath the hot water boiler in the bath house earlier than usual, so there'd be ample hot water in the tanks for everyone to clean up.

Dinner that evening was filled with laughter as stories of the crazy pranks that Duffy and Jake tried to pull on everyone were shared.

Andre was glad to hear he wasn't the only one who had been "short-sheeted" in the past. It was difficult to distinguish tears of joy from sorrowful ones in Kate's eyes. At the end of the meal that evening, two presentations were made to Kate. The first was a garrote that Duffy had made for her using piano wire, and that Lou had curled and mounted on a polished wooden shield with the words 'conqueror' on a small plaque underneath. The second was a meritorious service award for her contributions to the team, presented by Andre.

As Lou walked Kate over to her cottage later that night, she said, "Lou, I never did answer you when you asked if I would be coming back."

"Well, are you?"

"I'll be back for Andre's retirement party. Will you be my escort?"

As they entered Kate's cottage, any doubts that Kate might have had as to whether or not Lou would be her escort, were completely erased.

In the morning, Kate left for Dublin.

Chapter 41

The contents found in Dobbs' safety deposit box shifted the focus of Andre's team to now shutting down distribution channels established by Dobbs within Canada.

Duffy was running names and phone numbers listed on the handwritten sheet Dobbs had stored in the security box against the Canadian Criminal Records database.

Fletcher was comparing names on checks that had been deposited into Dobbs' account against business cards on the handwritten sheet.

Cunningham was comparing deposits made to Dobbs' bank account against the names in the ledger; he was also requesting numerous bank account records.

The names of people Dobbs had used to move goods into the black market and names of individuals who had reached out to him for goods were now becoming clear. But the reality was that many of these minor players would never be brought to justice unless authorities could prove a parole violation or the fact that stolen goods had been actually found in their possession.

For the major players, however, it was a totally different situation. Andre had begun collaborating daily with various Crown prosecutors who would present cases before the magistrates during preliminary trials.

The case against Constable Orson Evers was already airtight, as was the case against Felix Lajoie. Internal affairs had prepared a disciplinary dismissal for Charles Teal after which he would be immediately arrested to stand trial alongside Felix Lajoie as an accomplice.

A separate trial would be held for any locals who had worked the docks at Grand Manan. The cases against Dobbs and Bob Newton were still being assembled, as was the case against Emile Baker. These men were also main players, and the attorneys had yet a lot of work to do.

Andre was more than a little frustrated knowing that he was ready to take down Grand Manan, but was being forced to wait for MI6 and INTERPOL. Surprising to him was the fact that they didn't feel there was enough evidence to take Sean Tinker into custody and shut down the operation in Portmagee, just yet.

However, he *did* realize that once they took Tinker into custody, his arrest would send the leaders of the ring underground. So, Tinker's take down remained on hold until MI6 and INTERPOL could identify "the head of the snake." Once that happened, the timing of raids and arrests on both sides of the Atlantic would be coordinated down to the minute. Andre understood that he had to be patient.

In central New Brunswick, it had been an unseasonably mild fall. With Jake's help, Lou made significant headway in building a completely new cottage to replace the one that had been irreparably damaged. The foundation and outer walls were up within a week; rafters for the roof had been completed yesterday, and in another two days the roof would be enclosed.

Construction had moved along quickly, due in part to the excess lumber that the Abenaki guides had cut and stored under the sawmill's shed during the summertime. Newly harvested logs would be delivered shortly and, once dried, they would be used to build the porch.

Every day at noon, Alessandra walked down to the construction site with a picnic lunch so neither Jake nor Lou wasted time walking back and forth to the lodge for lunch.

Every other day at four, Lou put his tools away and headed over to his cottage to make a phone call to Kate. Nothing was going to stop him from connecting with Kate, not even an ocean between them.

And so the days passed.

Chapter 42

It didn't take Kate long to fully integrate with her INTERPOL colleagues once she returned to Dublin. The team was focused on gathering evidence against Sean Tinker, but it surprised her to find that it didn't seem to be anyone's priority to find "the head of the snake."

The only direction she received from Chief Inspector René Allard was to get settled and see how she could help the team. What surprised her, even more, was the fact there didn't seem to be any reason for her sudden and immediate recall back to Ireland.

She decided to continue using the analytical search programs that she had developed while in Canada. Once she loaded the programs, she ran them against Sean Tinker's phone records.

The first report generated was in descending order by volume and location, including names of who owned the phones. She also ran a report by date with text messages.

The "by volume" report was viewable as a "scattergram" which she overlaid onto a map of Europe. The report could be generated using different date parameters and specific geographies. A colleague who had been trying to trace the six lost BMW cargo containers was highly impressed with the reports Kate was creating. "Could you run a report showing the call and text activity to Tinker from phones located in Germany around the time BMW would have been preparing a shipment to Canada?"

"Absolutely."

Kate quickly keyed in the parameters and hit "run." When the program finished, it showed that Tinker had received several texts from a number belonging to BMW and from a number belonging to the Port Authority in Hamburg, Germany.

Always inquisitive, Kate decided to run those numbers against the restricted number and another unknown number she had seen on Dobbs' phone. The program came back with several matches for each phone and the so-called "restricted phone." Then she ran the restricted number and the unknown number on Dobbs' cell phone against Tinker's phone records. There were literally *hundreds* of matches.

"Whoa," Kate said, "Can't deny they were talking to one another."

From there, it was relatively easy to find out who BMW and the German Port Authority were using as phone carriers. Kate was about to call and request records for both numbers when her colleague returned to the office."The chief is available now and would like to hear more about what we've just learned."

"Now?"

"Yes, he told me to get you."

After Kate and her colleague briefed Chief Inspector René Allard, he put out his hand, gesturing that he wanted to see the report Kate had generated. As Kate's colleague handed Allard the report, she stressed, "It's *critical* we find out who the owner is of the phone that is restricted, as well as the unknown number."

Her colleague added, "And I need the phone records for the BMW and German Port Authority phones, both are crucial to my investigation."

Chief Inspector Allard leaned back in his chair, looked up at the ceiling, and placed both hands behind his head. After a few moments, he spoke. "I can see where this is going. I will inquire about obtaining the phone records that you are requesting."

As they left the meeting, Kate looked at her colleague. "Aren't you able to request the files from the phone providers yourself?"

"No. That's something only the chief inspector is allowed to do!"

Kate was amused at the bureaucratic separation of duties and autocratic leadership style that was still so prevalent within INTERPOL, and just shook her head. But after a full day went by without word from the chief inspector regarding the phone numbers, Kate walked over to her colleague's work area,

"Have you heard anything about the phone files?"

"Oh, the inspector has been called to a meeting in Brussels. We won't hear anything now until he returns."

"You're kidding, right?"

"No, this is standard protocol . . . we just need to be patient."

Walking back to her desk, Kate couldn't help but think: *Allard is so old school, no wonder his team is behind Andre's. Even the higher-ups in the Irish Defense Force are more responsive than he is.*

Patience might well be a virtue, but it certainly wasn't one of Kate's attributes. She decided to go around the chief and take matters into her own hands. The first six digits indicated the phone numbers were in the UK. She began by calling down a list of top phone providers in the UK. The network provider for both phones turned out to be Vodaphone.

Kate was surprised to learn that the phone number she had previously been told was "restricted" was oddly enough a "house cell phone" located in the Palace of Westminster for exclusive use by members of the House of Lords.

The second phone was a private cell line belonging to a London-based solicitor by the name of Richard More. Kate called Vodaphone, identified herself, and asked for an electronic file of the phone records for the two numbers spanning the past six months.

"Records for the solicitor's phone shall be sent over within the hour," the Vodaphone representative said. "However, we will need permission from the Prime Minister's office before we can release the records for the phone located in the common area of House of Lords chamber.

"Is that a problem?"

"It hasn't been a problem, just a delay."

Kate was surprised at how easy it was to obtain the files for these two phones, her intuition told her to remain quiet about going around Chief Inspector Allard for the time being.

While waiting for Allard's return from Brussels, Kate decided to run the two numbers against both Dobbs' and Tinker's phone records using a modified version of a program she had created to display the content of all text messages sent or received by Dobbs or Tinker involving either the solicitor's phone or the phone at the House of Lords.

The report showed that text messages were sent *to* the solicitor's phone, but no texts were received *from* that number. All sent messages to the solicitor's phone were vague, and usually confirming that some unknown action had just been taken. On the surface, the messages could merely be something one sent to one's lawyer; however, it struck her as being highly improbable that Dobbs, a Canadian citizen, would be using the same English solicitor that Tinker would for legal work.

One thing Kate began noticing was that the texts going back and forth from the phone assigned to the House of Lords were far more directional. Every text sent from that phone always included a series of numbers followed with the word "move." While texts sent *to* the number were generally short, conveying that something had been achieved or accomplished.

Well, well, she thought, *someone is taking direction from someone else, it seems.*

Andre, and everyone involved with Operation Delta-Tango were on hold waiting on Allard and his team to identify the ring leaders, so both sides of the Atlantic could move forward in unison. Oddly, Allard still wasn't putting any pressure on his people to work overtime or weekends to expedite things, so no one did.

Kate had been living out of a suitcase long enough that she was looking forward to spending a few nights at home in Abbeyfeale, so she headed out of the office midday on Friday to get an early start on the weekend. Not long after Kate left her office for the day, the file for the phone belonging to the solicitor arrived in her inbox along with a message that the release of the second phone's records had just been approved by the prime minister's office and would be forwarded "momentarily."

Later that evening, while she was waiting for Lou's call, Kate again reflected on how polar opposite the leadership styles were between Andre and René Allard. When anyone made a request of Andre, he immediately pulled whatever strings needed to be pulled. Allard, on the other hand, just didn't seem to have any sense of urgency.

His team is uninspired and even cowers under his dominance, Kate thought, laughing to herself. *I wonder if he has compromising pictures that he's hanging over their heads.*When Lou called, her mood instantly brightened. He shared what he and Jake had been doing with the cottage. "We should have it finished by early spring."

"Have you designed the inside, yet?"

"Not yet, why?"

"If you're serious about creating an interior that any woman would go for, there's a wee cottage in Abbeyfeale that you should take a look at."

"Did I just hear an invitation?"

"You know you don't need an invitation."

"Yeah, I do know that."

"They'll be an honest Irish breakfast waiting for you, whenever you come."

Throughout the weekend, Kate kept coming back to the question of *why* was it so difficult for the chief inspector to obtain the phone records as he had been asked to do. Monday morning, the normal drive going into Dublin took longer than usual due to thick ground fog that had settled in during the night. Kate ended up arriving later than she had planned. As she walked toward the lift in the parking garage, she saw Chief Inspector Allard ahead of her waiting.

"Good morning, Chief Inspector, I hope you had a pleasant weekend."

"Yes, I did thank you," he said without smiling. "Incidentally, I'll look into acquiring those phone records for you this morning." Kate was about to ask what possibly could have been the delay when the lift arrived. Since there were others already in the lift, the conversation between them ceased. Reaching their floor, they each headed off in opposite directions to their separate work areas.

Just as Kate was powering up her system, the food trolly arrived at her workstation, and she selected her usual morning cup of tea. Amenities in the Dublin office were quite nice, and the atmosphere was very relaxed. *Actually, too relaxed,* Kate thought, *but the chief inspector runs the show here.*

When she finally turned around to her screen, she was pleased to see that both phone files she had requested had arrived. She quickly launched various sorting programs against the files which were quite large. It would take a while before she could generate any reports.

While waiting, she called a colleague assigned to a London MI6 unit that did quite a lot of work with the British Parliament. After the usual banter that always happens when two friends reconnect, Kate asked, "What do you know about a common area in the House of Lords chambers?"

"They're mostly a thing of the past now, Kate. All but one of the common areas were eliminated during the last renovation. The only holdover is a room that once served as a "telephone room" for the Lord's exclusive use when they were in session."

"Interesting."

"Yeah, now that everyone has cell phones, the landlines were all taken out, but the private booths were retained," he said laughing. "However, there is actually one fully charged cell phone that is kept there for the exclusive use by any of the lords in the event their own personal cell phone runs out of juice. Rank does have its privileges!" Kate thanked him for taking the time to talk, and they agreed to get together for lunch at the end of the month in London.

Just as she hung up, the chief inspector's aide stopped by her cubicle. "Hello, Kate, your line was busy, so I decided to pop by. The chief wants you to know that he's still trying to obtain the phone records you requested. We must be patient at such times. Well, cheerio!"

Either the chief is totally inept, or something else is going on, she thought. Then, she pulled up the internal phone directory for the building and scrolled down until she reached the chief inspector's number. She just stared at the number for a complete minute before finally writing it down on a yellow sticky tab.

Her instincts told her to run the chief's number against the two files she had received, but the files were so large that it seemed more practical to do it overnight.

Kate then made a few more calls to the phone carriers and received a commitment to receive phone records for the numbers at BMW and the Hamburg port authority. When those files came in, she initiated a routine search to compare a check against René Allard's direct line.

By midafternoon, the report had finally completed its run and was sitting in Kate's inbox. She took a deep breath and opened the report.

Chapter 43

Once she realized what the phone report indicated, Kate placed a call to INTERPOL's Head of Criminal Investigation and requested an urgent confidential meeting. "His schedule is fully committed currently," his aide said, "But, there is a window of opportunity to speak with him privately at the end of the day, if you'd like to wait."

"I'll take it, thanks."

She picked up her laptop and went down to the cafeteria just to create additional physical space between herself and Chief Inspector Allard. Close to the end of the workday, she returned to her office, transferred copies of the reports she had created onto a thumb drive, and went upstairs to the head of the criminal investigation's office to wait for the opportunity to share her findings.

Kate had no idea what to expect from the meeting. She hadn't had a lot of previous experience with INTERPOL since she was on loan from The Irish Defense

Force and protocols were quite different between the two organizations.

After close to an hour's wait, the aide finally told her that she could go in. The head of criminal investigation was a tall man who stood up when Kate entered, then motioned for her to join him as he moved toward a couple of leather chairs. Once both were seated, he immediately put her at ease."Kathryn, I've just had an opportunity to read your file. You've made quite an impression with the Canadians. We're quite fortunate that the Irish Defense Force was willing to loan us someone with your talents."

Impressed that he'd at least done a little homework on her, and had found some degree of credibility, she relaxed a little. "Sir, I have uncovered something that is quite disturbing, and I need your guidance."

"Proceed."

Kate shared the troubling fact that her chief inspector seemed to be connected in some way to the very criminals they were trying to bring down, complicated by the fact that he was now stonewalling their attempts to gain access to critical information.

"I feel no alternative but to go around him," she said. Then, briefly shared the damning information her report had generated.

The head of criminal investigations took a deep breath and called in his aide.

"Please clear my calendar for tomorrow morning and inform the Deputy Chief of Investigations and the Head of Security that I'd like them to meet with me at 0800."

Then, turning to Kate, he smiled. "Kathryn, you have nothing to fear. I'd like you to also join us tomorrow morning. Between the four of us, we'll get this straightened out."

She left the office feeling she had just been thrown a lifeline.

That evening Kate shared details of her meeting with Lou.

"Kate, if he's involved, there's no telling what he might do."

"I don't believe I'm at risk, Lou, but it certainly feels like I've gone way out on a limb."

"There's not a lot going on over here this time of year Would you feel safer if I flew over?"

"Thanks, Lou, you know I'd *love* to see you, but I'm all right."

"Are you sure?"Laughing, Kate said, "Yes, I'll be fine. Hey, worst-case scenario, I'll use that garrote you guys gave me . . . if I have to."

"Don't even go there," Lou said.

The next morning, Kate provided an overview of the reports she had generated the previous day. The Deputy Chief of Investigations was enraged with what he had heard. The Head of Security listened carefully and calculated whether they had enough incriminating evidence to arrest Chief Inspector Allard immediately.

At the end of the meeting, the Head of Security was very sincere. "Lieutenant, thank you for coming forward with this. I believe we can take it from here and suggest you go back to your work area and continue on as if nothing has occurred. Should we need anything further, we'll be in touch."

A red flag went up for Kate and she pushed back. "Gentlemen, with all due respect, I am *not* at all comfortable with doing that. I sit with my back facing the opening of my cubicle. All of you sit in offices a couple of floors above me. What happens if René Allard somehow finds out that I went around him? I have phone records proving his involvement, and I've been up here meeting with you. What if he finds out?"

"I don't believe you're at any risk, Lieutenant," the Head of Security interrupted her, "however if it would make you feel safer working remotely until Chief Inspector Allard has been taken into custody, then by all means please do that."

"Thank you. I believe that will help make me feel more comfortable."

"Let me ease your concerns, Lieutenant O'Grady," he continued, "René Allard will be called away from this building by tomorrow on false pretenses. He will be taken into custody and immediately placed in a holding cell. The charges that will be brought against him will prohibit any chance of bail. At no time will you ever be at risk."

"As bloody embarrassing as it is to find out that one of our own is complicit in this," the deputy chief of investigations added, "at least now we know why this investigation has gone so poorly. Lieutenant, I'm familiar with what you've accomplished working with the Canadians on this investigation. I'd like you to step in as acting leader for the team once Allard has been taken into custody."

When Kate left the meeting, she gathered everything she needed from her office to work remotely from home for the next few days and headed directly to her car.

Meanwhile, the Head of Security arranged to have the cell phone in the House of Lords chamber temporarily disabled and re-routed to a "burner" phone he had in his office. He also arranged for any text messages sent from that "burner" phone to appear to be coming from the cell phone at the House of Lords Chamber. When arranged, he sent a text requesting Chief Inspector Allard to come to the lobby of The House of Lords the following day at exactly noon.

When Allard received and read the text, he was impressed the higher-ups actually wanted to meet with him. He instructed his aide to book him on a flight to London first thing in the morning.

The following day at exactly noon, René Allard entered the lobby of the House of Lords and was confronted by three MI6 agents. Caught completely off guard, Allard was enraged; however, his show of indignity had little effect, and he was taken into custody without difficulty.

The evidence now clearly indicated that someone in The House of Lords was involved in the ring. Faced with personal disgrace and imprisonment, René Allard quickly declared that he wished to become a Crown Witness.

On the off chance that Emile Baker might be able to identify a member of the House of Lords, Kate decided to send a file containing the head shots of every one of the lords over to Andre so Baker could do a photo lineup. The following day, word came back that Baker had identified Lord Clark Hastings as one of the three men with whom he had met in Las Vegas.

With René Allard out of the picture, and Kate acting as team leader, things began moving along at a much faster pace. To foster unity and coordination, the team now met daily for a working lunch. There was no formal agenda; everyone merely shared where they were making progress and what challenges they were pursuing.

Toward the end of the first lunch, Kate asked one of her colleagues to dive into social media to see if there were any connections between Lord Hastings and a solicitor by the name of Richard More.

Baker's deposition revealed there were three men with whom he had met in Vegas. Now knowing that one was a member of Britain's House of Lords, they needed to identify the other two.

Among the pieces of information that continued to flow between Canada, MI6, and INTERPOL was the fact that quite a few deposits into Dobbs' bank account came via a wire transfer from an account at the Central Bank of London. Kate assigned one of her team members to follow the money trail and find out who owned the account and how the account was being funded.

She issued a priority request for the personal phone records of Solicitor Richard More and Lord Clark Hastings, as well as for any phones at their home addresses. The files arrived in a matter of hours and Kate assigned another team member to run a program to identify any common numbers being called or calling them during the past six months.

Within another few hours, two phone numbers surfaced that were common to both Hastings and Richard More. One number belonged to Sean Tinker, the other was a new number. Without being asked, the team member who ran the report was already running down information on the ownership of that phone. The social media search revealed that Lord Hastings and Solicitor More had attended the same prep school and undergraduate college and had served together in Military Logistics. They also lived near one another, belonged to the same country club, the same yacht club, and the same social clubs.

The unknown phone number appearing in the files for Hastings and More came back as belonging to a Herbert Maxwell, executive vice-president of the Royalty Bank and Trust Company. The bank was highly regarded among Britain's social elite and one of the oldest banking institutions in London.

Kate then asked a team member to see how closely Maxwell's background paralleled those of Hastings and More. She then obtained photos of Maxwell and More from the UK Driver and Vehicle Licensing Agency and called Andre.

"Andre, I'm emailing you two photographs. Please see if Emile Baker can identify either of them in a photo lineup."

"We'll get back to you a quick as we can, Kate."

"Thanks, Andre, I believe we're closing the loop at last." *It feels good to say that,* she thought.

"Good, we're waiting on you."

Chapter 44

Back in Canada, the demand for BMW parts again became a major issue now that Dobbs had been arrested. To appease the enormous pressure being placed on the dealerships from their customers, the Crown prosecutors agreed to release three of the original six missing containers to the BMW parts warehouse in eastern Canada.

Word quickly circulated throughout BMW headquarters that half of the missing parts destined for Canada had been located and delivered to the warehouse.

Imperial Trading's BMW accomplice sent a text to Richard More in the UK inquiring about the sudden release of parts.

"Should the next shipment to Canada be diverted?"

"Y do U ask?" More immediately replied.

"U just released half of the last shipment."

When Solicitor More received the second text, he was surprised that he had been left out of the loop and sent a heated text to Maxwell and Hastings.

"?? When did U decide 2 release BMW parts??"

When Hastings saw the text, he immediately called an

emergency meeting at Maxwell's office. As the men gathered, it became obvious that everyone felt the other had left them out of the loop. All were surprised about the release of BMW parts.

Multiple attempts to reach Dobbs merely resulted in replies that he'd "respond shortly."

"Well, chaps," Maxwell said, convinced the game was up. "I believe it's the proper time that we fold the tent and take action to protect ourselves."

Solicitor More was in total agreement, but Lord Hastings was not.

"Gentlemen, relax! We have more than enough of a buffer on this. We're perfectly safe. We just need to remain calm and stay on the sidelines for a while; the wind will eventually change, and everything will blow over."

At the very moment that the principals of Imperial Trading were meeting, Kate's team identified who the BMW phone number was assigned to and who had exclusive use of the phone at the Port Authority in Hamburg.

To help Kate move the case along, the Head of Investigations had assigned a senior investigator on his personal staff to assist her, now that she'd taken on full team leadership responsibilities.

The following morning, Kate and the senior investigator met to review the status of the investigation. They agreed there was enough evidence to arrest Sean Tinker and shut down Portmagee. Many of the dock workers would be taken into custody as accomplices.

Phone and text records were sufficient evidence against the chief inspector at the Port of Hamburg along with the BMW executive to charge them as conspirators.

They also had a positive ID on one of the ring leaders and were pursuing verification on two prime suspects.

"Kate, you're close to shutting this thing down," the

senior investigator offered. "Let me draft a coordinated takedown plan that will ensure Canada, the UK, and the intelligence units in Germany and Ireland will all have the same playbook, so once you give the word that you've greenlighted the takedown, everyone will act in unison."

"Excellent," she said. "Please do that."

During lunch, the team member who had been following the money trail spoke.

"Wire transfers to Dobbs at the Central Bank of London were consistently made from a personal account at the Royalty Bank and Trust Company."

Kate had only been half-listening, but when the Royalty Bank and Trust name was mentioned, her attention was riveted. "Isn't that the same bank where Herbert Maxwell works?"

"It is."

That same afternoon, Andre called Kate with results of the photo lineup.

"Kate, Baker has just identified Richard More and Herbert Maxwell as the other two individuals he met while in Vegas!"

"Thanks, Andre, you are the best."

Kate was confident that the identities of those at the top of the ring were now known and placed a call to the senior investigator assigned to help her. Unfortunately, the senior investigator had already left for the day, however, he sent a working draft of the takedown plan out to Andre, the coordinators for MI6, Germany, and Ireland for their review, and of course, to Kate.

Rather than leave a voice message, Kate sent the senior investigator an email: *"I now have sufficient evidence to accurately ID the remaining two individuals at the top of the ring. We need to strike while the iron is hot."*

Early the next morning, when the senior investigator

read Kate's email, he quickly responded with a poorly written cryptic reply: "acknowledging your 'go' message." Without realizing it, he also inadvertently copied everyone he had earlier sent the draft of the takedown plan.

Unfortunately, Germany interpreted the second email as notification that the plan had just been "green lighted" and was now in play.

News of the arrests at BMW Headquarters and at the Port of Hamburg spread quickly and received headline coverage on CNN International.

One of the duties of Solicitor More's secretary was to monitor news feeds and to alert him immediately should any of his clients ever be mentioned. When she saw the news, More's secretary interrupted the call he was on and passed the information about BMW along to him.

Over a half hour passed after CNN International first broadcast the news of the arrests at BMW and the Port at Hamburg before word reached Kate that Germany had jumped the gun. Within minutes Kate notified Andre, MI6, and Ireland about Germany now in play and that she was officially 'green lighting' the takedown for everyone.

MI6 agents based in London were immediately dispatched to the individual offices of More, Hastings, and Maxwell with warrants for their arrests.

A team of officers from Ireland's National Protective Services flew into Portmagee by helicopter and Sean Tinker was taken into custody, along with the local constable and the harbor master. The trio were flown to London and placed in holding cells; Tinker would be held without bail. Tinker's senior employees, all of whom would have been complicit in the smuggling, were all taken down to the local jail. Officers taped off the warehouse and the dock area and remained posted there.

In Canada, two RCMP Airbus H145 helicopters were dispatched to the island of Grand Manan. Constable Orson Evers, his stevedore, and the warehouse manager were all arrested and flown back to Fredericton, where they were held without bail. The warehouse was secured and guards posted around the clock.

A coastal patrol boat was dispatched to Campobello Island and Felix Lajoie was taken into custody, then flown to Fredericton where he was also held without bail.

Charles Teal was taken into custody at Fredericton's RMCP headquarters, put into a holding cell, and held without bail. Warrants were issued for the individuals who had fenced for Dobbs' that were on parole and local police were responsible for rounding them all up.

In London, when MI6 agents arrived at the office of Richard More, they were told that he had already gone for the day. The same scenario played out at the offices of Lord Hastings and Herbert Maxwell. MI6 agents were quickly dispatched to their private residences in Surry. But at that exact moment, a Gulfstream G650 lifted off the main runway at the regional airport just outside Surry and was airborne in minutes.

Once in the air, Hastings sent a coded text authorizing a hit on Sean Tinker.

Chapter 45

Several years before, while sailing along the eastern coast of the Adriatic, Herbert Maxwell had become aware of an olive tree plantation in Montenegro that was about to go on the market. The listing agent wasn't quite prepared to show the estate but accommodated Maxwell's request to view the property.

For entirely different reasons, Maxwell and his wife Evelyn were extremely impressed with the estate that was known locally as Bella Luna.

The property sat on a hill and had a commanding view of the Adriatic to the west and Lake Skadar to the east. A large olive grove encompassed the lower portion of the property. The majority of the olive trees were well over a hundred years old and yielded an abundant crop, the first press was always considered one of the finest produced in the region.

The hillside facing the Adriatic was crisscrossed with rows of grasevina grapevines which produced a light, crisp white wine local to the region. The architectural design of the main house rivaled many of the exquisite chateaus dotting the shores of Italy's Lake Como and Lake Garda. The property encompassed approximately four hectares and had a mill for pressing olives for making wine, a wine cellar, a building for making cheese, and various small barns and compounds where livestock were kept. There was even a modest house a short distance from the chateau where the estate manager lived.

Evelyn Maxwell fell in love with everything about the estate. Maxwell was impressed with the estate too. The fact that Montenegro did not a participate in the United Nation's extradition treaty made it even more attractive to him.

The listing agent was shocked when Maxwell offered to buy the estate on the spot without even attempting to negotiate the asking price. The agent wondered how much money he may have left on the table. Arrangements were made for the current estate manager to remain in place, and he was told to carry on as if no change in ownership had even occurred.

News spread quickly throughout the village that the annual harvesting of the olives and the grapes, the making of wine, the olive oil, and the cheese at the Bella Luna estate would continue without interruption.

Solicitor More handled all the legalities for Maxwell during the purchase of the estate, and the name of an innocuous trust was entered into the town records as the new owner of Bella Luna.

As soon as title transferred, Hastings and More, along with their wives, joined the Maxwells for a long weekend in Montenegro. It was a memorable time.

Although the common areas of the chateau were quite spacious, the sleeping quarters were rather small. Electrical fixtures and plumbing in the baths and kitchen area were original and in need of being modernized. Several architects were flown down to view the estate, and soon the property was transformed into a luxury villa providing all three couples with more spacious accommodations and far more privacy than could be imagined.

Shortly after acquiring the property, the principals of Imperial Trading begin to discuss the advantages that the estate in Montenegro presented should they ever needed to make a hasty exit from London and escape to a safe haven.

The estate itself was quite self-sufficient and actually generated a rather nice income on its own. In addition to an extremely well-stocked wine cellar, a cache of gold coins soon began to accumulate in a vault hidden in the basement of the chateau.

It was to this destination that the Gulfstream G650 now headed.

Chapter 46

Back in Dublin, Kate was feeling confident as she read the reports as every piece of the black market ring was going down like a row of dominos. However, she was still waiting for a report that the three ring leaders had been brought into custody. When the MI6 agents arrived at the private residences of Hastings, More, and Maxwell, their wives were horrified and in total disbelief about what they were hearing. They had been kept completely in the dark about the nefarious activities in which their husbands had been involved.

When it was finally reported that the three ring leaders were nowhere to be found, a wide net was cast around the greater London area. Personal secretaries and all three wives of the ring leaders were brought in for questioning. MI6 agents were dispatched to both Heathrow and Gatwick airports and the twelve major train stations in and around London.

The wives swore they had no idea where their husbands had gone.

After Lady Beatrice Yardley Hastings recovered from her initial shock, she was infuriated that they had been brought into a police station like "commoners," and made it known to all present that they'd be hearing from her solicitor shortly.

The secretaries couldn't offer much information on the whereabouts of their bosses. Richard More's secretary stated that shortly after she informed the solicitor of the arrests at BMW headquarters, he made a couple of quick phone calls and abruptly left the office without saying a word. The other two secretaries agreed that after a call came in from Solicitor More, their bosses also abruptly left their offices without saying anything to them.

Each member of Imperial Trading knew that should they ever need to make a quick exit; their wives would not be accompanying them. Hastings had successfully argued that point, although he had no intention of ever *completely* abandoning his wife or family. The reality was that the precious time it would take to include them in any escape would severely jeopardize their very own ability to escape.

Eventually, all had agreed that if they were ever forced to invoke "Plan B" and flee to Montenegro on the coast of the Adriatic Sea, they would do so without their wives. Once things settled down, arrangements for their wives and families to join them at Bella Luna would be made.

Elsewhere, the aide to the head of Criminal Investigations placed a call to Kate, letting her know that she was being summoned to a meeting already in progress. When she arrived upstairs, she was immediately told to go into his office.

Inside the room, the atmosphere was tense; the Head of Security and the Deputy Chief of Investigations were already seated.

"Please, have a seat, Kathryn. We've received word

that the takedown has been bungled. What happened?"

"I take full responsibility for what has happened, sir," she said.

"I won't allow that," the Deputy Chief of Investigations interrupted her. "The mess of the matter occurred when *Germany* misinterpreted a communication sent out by the very person I had assigned to help you. Kathryn, this is not an interrogation or a critique of your efforts. We just need to know what has transpired so we can help put it back on its proper course."

"Thank you," she said and walked them through what exactly happened, stopping only to clarify or expand whenever questions were asked.

As a result of the meeting, bank accounts of the three suspects still at large were frozen. Additionally, an all-points bulletin for the capture of the three men was entered into INTERPOL's database, which would be widely distributed across all of Europe. The three wives were put under surveillance and their phones monitored. Kate was asked to stay on as acting lead for the team and was acknowledged for the superior contributions she had made since she began leading the effort.

When Kate returned to her work area, she placed a call to Andre to keep him in the loop regarding all next steps. For the moment, her role shifted to transitional tasks, which she referred to as "mop-up" work, while they waited for information on where the three fugitives were hiding.

MI6 was not aware that all attempts to capture the fugitives inside the UK had been useless or that the fugitives had already fled the country.

Later that evening when Kate spoke with Lou, he heard the frustration in her voice as she said, "I just want this whole ordeal to be over!"

Those are pretty much the same words I heard Andre say earlier today, Lou thought.

The following day, MI6 discovered that a jet had taken off from the regional airport outside Surry with a flight plan filed for Montenegro.

Kate and her team immediately began to investigate the incident. The plane was a privately-owned Gulfstream G650 stored at the airport's common hangar. Kate made a call to the regional airport manager."Hello, this is Kate O'Grady, I'm with INTERPOL and I'm requesting a copy of the flight plan for the plane that left for Montenegro yesterday," she said. "I also need to know the owner of the plane and the names of the pilots and crew.""Ma'am, I'll need a few minutes to gather that information."

Kate winced again at the use of the salutation "ma'am," but let it go.

The information she received was that the pilots were both full-time professionals who routinely hired themselves out to fly private aircraft on demand. Both had flown fighter jets for the Royal Air Force and neither had any criminal records. After going over the flight plan, Kate reached out to the two men who were found at their respective homes and were asked if they would cooperate with the London MI6 office for a virtual interview. Both pilots agreed and were amenable to answering any questions, as they had no intention of placing their Transport Pilot Licenses at risk.

Each man stated separately that there were three passengers on board the flight to Montenegro the day in question, and that they had flown the same route for them several times a year.

"Usually, their wives were onboard," one pilot attested, "but this time they were not."

"Oddly, there was no luggage that needed to be stowed." the second pilot noted, Because the plane was privately owned by a trust, once the passengers disembarked, the pilots refueled, and flew the plane directly back to Surry.

Both pilots identified Richard More, Clark Hastings, and Herbert Maxwell in separate photo line-ups as the passengers who had been onboard.

Kate passed word along to Andre and her higher ups that it had been confirmed that the three ring leaders had fled to Montenegro.

Later that night when Kate and Lou spoke, Lou asked, "Why Montenegro?"

"Simple. Montenegro doesn't extradite anyone. At some point, when we've pinpointed exactly where they are holding up, we'll send in a small covert team, extract them, and bring them out."

"Does Andre know about that?"

"Yes, he and I had that conversation earlier today. In fact, he said that Canada would *definitely* participate in any covert op. What's sad is that it sounds like Andre has been told that his retirement is on hold until this whole mess is finished."

"I don't doubt that," Lou said. "He hasn't said anything, but I don't see him remaining here at Havre de Poisson much longer."

The following morning, Lou pulled Andre aside after breakfast. "Andre, are your boots nailed to the floor until this case is closed?"

"That's pretty much what I've been told."

"You know you're welcome to stay here as long as you like, but I'm guessing the fun of sitting on those chilly outhouse seats every morning is beginning to get old."

"You've got that right. Lou, there's no excuse for us to remain offsite now that we've got everybody on our side of the pond in custody. I figured I'd tell my team today to pack up because we're going back to Fredericton."

"Kate said that Canada will have a representative in the covert team that goes in to retrieve the three who flew to Montenegro. Is that right?"

"Yes."

"I want it understood right now that you're talking to the guy who will be Canada's participant in any covert op that goes down in Montenegro. Agreed?"

"Agreed."

Chapter 47

Special agents representing INTERPOL were immediately dispatched to Montenegro where they discreetly reached out to various sources about the presence of three English-speaking male visitors. It took only days before they began to hear rumors that "the Brits," as they were referred to, had returned to the estate known as Bella Luna.

Even with grainy satellite photos, it was easy to identify Herbert Maxwell, Richard More, and Clark Hastings lounging around the pool in the courtyard behind the chateau Bella Luna.

MI6 and Canada handpicked a team of three commandos to parachute in and surgically remove the targets from their hideout. Britain chose a sergeant in the Royal Marines who had participated in several extraction hostage rescue missions in the Middle East.

Ireland chose a master sergeant in the Irish Defense Force known as "Sarge," who had distinguished himself several times during covert operations in the Middle East. He was a trained paratrooper and veteran of numerous night jumps.

Lou Gault, representing Canada, rounded out the three-man extradition team.

Once it was verified by multiple sources that the targets were at the Bella Luna estate, MI6 was able to obtain a blueprint of the chateau's interior from the architectural firm that had remodeled it a few years earlier. A replica of the chateau was quickly constructed from its prints for the team to use for planning and practice.The extraction date was fluid until phone surveillance picked up chatter that the wives and children were planning to head to the airport in Surry the following morning for a flight to Montenegro. Once the message was heard, "Operation Chateau" was greenlit. The extradition team boarded a C-37A and flew to a military base in Italy directly across the Adriatic from Montenegro.

On the morning the wives and children arrived at the airport, they were told their plane had failed a preflight inspection due to a mechanical problem and was grounded until a part could be flown in. Within the next twenty-four hours, the wives would have no reason to travel to Montenegro, nor would they be allowed to leave the country.

When the extradition team landed in Italy, they waited until dusk before boarding a Twin Otter. When the plane took off, it quickly rose to an altitude of 13,000 feet and crossed the Adriatic in two and a half hours.

From Italy, an AW 101 Merlin helicopter took off twenty minutes after the Twin Otter reached its flying altitude. The chopper would remain two miles offshore from Montenegro until called in to extract the team and their captives.

Weather was clear with no crosswind; conditions were perfect for a low-altitude night jump. As the Otter approached the drop zone, it descended to 3,000 feet; when the green jump light illuminated, all three passengers exited the plane through the rear door without incident.

The men steered their chutes to the left and all three landed in a clearing just below the olive grove with ease. They stowed their chutes and prepared to move forward. The extraction would be executed exactly the way they had practiced with the model chateau.

Then, as planned, the British commando began circling around behind the chateau and would enter the building from the rear. Lou and Sarge waited at the front of the chateau in the shadows. The Brit would send them a signal when he was in place.

It was close to 2200 hours and lights inside the chateau were still on, indicating the targets had not yet retired for the evening. However, there was no way to determine exactly *where* within the chateau the men were staying.

The Brit took longer than planned to reach the back entryway, but finally signaled he was ready and moving in ten seconds. Lou and Sarge counted to ten before racing across the lawn and bursting through the front door.

Hastings and Maxwell were caught in the front foyer just as they were about to head up to the second floor. Maxwell turned and attempted to make a run for it but fell to the floor withering in agony when Sarge's taser struck him in the middle of his back.

The commotion drew Richard More out from the downstairs study where the Brit quickly subdued him from behind with his taser, then zip-tied his hands behind his back.

Meanwhile, Lou's taser stuck on his belt, giving

Hastings just enough time to reach the top of the stairs and turn down a hallway. Lou raced upstairs, two steps at a time, only to find the hallway empty.

Hastings had just enough time to duck into one of the four closed rooms. Taser in hand, Lou now opened the first door;

it was a service closet. The opposite door was a linen closet. The second door on the left was locked. Lou was about to kick it in when he noticed the door across the hall was ajar.

Easing the door open with his foot, he slid in and pressed up against the wall next to the door, as he scanned the interior of the dark room. Just enough light was coming in from an open window to allow him to see the curtains moving ever so slightly in the night air. He reached the window in time to see Hastings running across the yard toward a shed.

In a flash, Lou was through the window, dropping down onto the ground, and racing toward the shed where Hastings had run.

Now, taser in hand, Lou ripped open the shed door and fired his taser point blank catching Hastings by surprise. The man withered in agony from fifty thousand volts of electricity delivered to his body.

Before Lou zip-tied Hastings's hands, he let up on the trigger and then pressed it again, delivering another jolt. "That one's for O'Neil." Hastings screamed out in pain. Lou pressed the trigger again, saying, "And this one's for Dorsey!" Hastings again screamed out in pain.

Lou radioed that he had Hastings under control. Richard More and Herbert Maxwell were being held in the foyer. As they called in the AW101 Merlin, the commandos did a quick search of the chateau and gathered three laptops and three cell phones. Tossing the electronics into a grab bag, all three targets were brought out to the courtyard just as the AW101 Merlin was setting down outside on the lawn.

The targets were strapped into the chopper and the pilot was given the "all clear" sign, for lift off. Then the co-pilot radioed ahead that Operation Chateau had completed its mission and was returning to base with its cargo.

Interpol agents were waiting to take charge of the

three fugitive noblemen, once highly respected members of British society and now criminals, as soon as they landed in Italy.

As soon as they touched down, the three commandos headed over to the NCO quarters to clean up and toss down a couple of brewskis before hitting the sack.

After breakfast the next morning, the three warriors boarded a military Gulfstream and were flown back to Lakenheath Air Base just outside London. Once Lou and his comrades finished their debriefs on the operation with MI6 and INTERPOL, they were free to leave the base.

Lou hitched a ride on a transport heading to Dublin where Kate awaited him. When he arrived, they headed off to Abbyfeale to unwind for a couple of days and enjoy each other's company.

The following morning, Lou experienced Kate's culinary talents for the very first time. "Kate, this breakfast would absolutely put any chef to shame, including Angelo!"

"Well, 'tis a proper Irish breakfast, that's for sure," she said. "You won't be having an English breakfast in *this* cottage!"

"And what, pray tell, is the difference between an Irish breakfast and an English breakfast?"

"Ha! Well, the English don't drain the grease from the pan. There's many that will say an English breakfast is the only meal you'll need all day, because it keeps coming back on you."

"Sounds like the Irish haven't quite let go of their disdain for the British yet."

"Oh, 'the troubles' are behind us now. But Ireland is a land of many superstitions and deep traditions, Lou. Times have changed, the people have changed, but our heritage and our traditions haven't," she said. "It's difficult for some to let go."

"What about you, Kate, have you been able let go?"

"If you had asked me that a few months ago, I would have said that 'no, I hadn't.'" Then she changed the subject. "So, tell me, what do you think of this wee cottage?"

He looked around. "I like it. It's similar to a sketch I once saw drawn on a napkin."

She tousled his hair. "Put your walking shoes on and I'll take you over to the river Feale. On the way back, maybe we'll go for a pint at the pub . . . you'll meet a few of my cousins there."

Lou learned quickly that in Ireland the phrase 'go for a pint' was plural and seldom, if ever meant just one drink.

The next day, Lou and Tim O'Grady, a cousin of Kate's, spent the entire morning trying to catch one of the few Atlantic salmon that were still in the river Feale. Kate's cousin managed to get a hook into one on his fifth cast, but the fish threw the hook. Shouting a string of expletives almost impossible to envision anyone ever being able to put together, Kate's cousin took an oath and challenged the fish to try *that* again. Lou shook his head wondering if all the Irish talked to fish.

A few casts later, Lou's line went taut; the hit was so powerful the rod was almost pulled out of his hands before it bent in half. The reel screeched like a banshee as the line raced out. Lou could feel the strength of the huge fish on the line and was amazed at both the length of the run and the fight the fish was putting up. He battled the fish for well over thirty minutes and found himself respecting the courageous life that was fighting to survive on the other end of the line.

During the struggle, Lou unknowingly began talking

out loud to the fish. Kate's cousin was standing nearby and added his own two cents of encouragement to the colorful conversation. After more than a dozen powerful runs, both up and down river, the fish finally began to play out. When Lou managed finally to bring the fish close to shore, Tim stepped into the river and scooped it up with a net.

"Lou, this one's a keeper, and a grand fish that it is! A couple more weeks from now, and the ones that are still in the river won't be fit to eat. Kate does a fine job with the cooker, ya know. You'll be having a feast to remember tonight, that's for sure."

When Lou arrived back at Kate's cottage, he proudly presented his catch. "Woman of the house, I've brought you supper!"

"Ha! You've brought me some *work* is what you've done. Tell me, now, did ya talk to that one when he was on the line?"

"Well, I hadn't planned on it, but yes, I did, actually. Your cousin even said that I spoke so eloquently, the poor fish had no choice but to give up the fight before he was talked to death."

Kate just looked at Lou and smiled.

A day later, Kate drove Lou to the airport. He had been away from Havre de Poisson for more than a couple of weeks now and was anxious to return home so that Angelo and Alessandra weren't left alone too long. But he admitted to himself that it was becoming more difficult to go their separate ways.

Chapter 48

On Friday, December 15th, Jake had a short-day delivering mail. It was late when he flew into Havre de Poisson to pick up Lou for the trip down to Fredericton for Andre Girard's retirement party. Kate O'Grady had flown into Fredericton late that same afternoon and when she stepped off the plane, she walked right into Lou's arms.

To no one's surprise, the retirement party was an extremely well-attended, formal sit-down affair that included a "roast" of Andre followed by the presentation of a commendation for his leadership role in the investigation that ultimately took down the International smuggling ring. The formal portion of the event concluded with the archaic tradition of presenting the honored guest with an expensive gold watch.

Duffy volunteered to act as emcee during the roast which gave him an opportunity to talk about the pranks that were pulled on Andre at Havre de Poisson while introducing each speaker. Kate was the last person Duffy invited up to the microphone to "roast" Andre. When she finished and started to return to her seat amid a roomful of laugher, Duffy asked her to wait a moment. To Kate's surprise, the commanding officer of the New Brunswick RCMP came forward and presented her with a plaque designating her as an Honorary Member of the Royal Canadian Mounted Police. Completely taken by surprise, Kate was humbled by the award.Throughout the rest of the evening, whenever Lou and Kate returned to their table after a dance, Kate seemed to leave Lou and walked over to the head table to talk with Andre's superiors. At one point Jake leaned over to Lou. "The way Kate's working the room, Lou, you'd never know she came here as your date for the evening."

"Ha, I know, right?" Lou said, "At least she's having a good time talking with all the top brass. You know, the only thing constant in life, Jake, is change. Ya' can never say 'never!' Look at me: I vowed I'd never fight another man's fight again, but I did. And I never thought I'd find anyone else I could care about, again . . . But I did that, too."

Suddenly Kate hurried back to the table. "Lou, they're playing the song "Moonglow!" I *love* that song . . . come dance with me . . . *please*!" Smiling, Lou rose to his feet and joined her on the dance floor.

The following day, Kate flew back across the pond. She was a key witness for the Crown in the trial of René Allard. Opening arguments in the case had begun the day Kate flew over to New Brunswick. The only way she had been allowed to travel was by committing to returning to London within forty-eight hours. And she always kept her promises.

Part 5

Chapter 49

The Canadian winter had finally arrived at Havre de Poisson. The lake was now completely frozen over, dry crisp air had set in, and the valley was covered in a thick blanket of snow that seemed to silence everything except the wind. During the day, when the sun was out, the contrast between a cobalt blue sky and the pure white snow constantly blowing off the peak of Carleton Mountain was spectacular.

This was a quiet time of year in the valley; the loons went south, bears were hibernating, beavers were in their lodges, and even squirrels spent most of the day in their nests high up in the trees.

Even though days were shorter now, there was still much for Lou to do. The windows and doors that he had ordered for the new cottage had been brought in on the old logging road, along with a few other items while he was away. Jake now flew in every weekend to help Lou finish work on the new cottage and spend time with the only people that he considered to be "family."

Angelo had a lot of free time now that it was off-season. When the weather permitted, either he or Lou would put out a few ice fishing tilts early in the day, then go about their business. When a flag went up, one or the other bundled up and traipsed out to either bait the hook and reset the flag, or haul in the trout that thought it had found an easy meal.

On weekends, when Jake was there, the three men enjoyed Sundays ice fishing out on the lake.. They never went out on the ice without pulling a sled loaded with firewood. There's a unique comaraderie that occurs among men when they stand around an open fire chewing the fat while ice fishing. It's a guy thing. On nights when the temperature didn't dip too low, Angelo and Lou would often go out with lanterns and jig through the ice for smelt near the mouth of the brook.

As Christmas approached, Angelo began planning his annual Christmas Eve dinner. Lou began scouring the woods looking for just the right symmetrical balsam fir tree for the lodge. And every evening for the past few weeks, Alessandra had been stringing popcorn and making colorful bows to adorn the tree.

The day before Christmas, Jake flew in loaded with packages for everyone, along with the special ingredients Angelo had ordered. Late that afternoon, Lou placed his regular call to Kate, and briefly put the phone on speaker, so she could wish everyone a joyous Christmas Eve.

It would be unfair to refer to the Christmas Eve meal Angelo prepared as merely "dinner." It was an adaptation of the traditional Italian "Feast of the Seven Fishes." This year, the first course was a shrimp cocktail followed by grilled octopus, and then, deep-fried smelt. After everyone had devoured those appetizers and sufficiently rested, Alessandra brought out four chafing dishes and placed them on the buffet table.

This year, for the Christmas Eve meal Angelo had prepared cod baked in a light tomato sauce, poached trout served in a rich creamy herb sauce, baked stuffed calamari, and Vongole Bianco served over linguini.

After the meal, anyone who could still move, helped clean up. Whatever was left of the feast was put away for the following day. When all was finished, the men sat before the fireplace, as they did each year, enjoying cigars and brandy and listening to each other's stories before retiring for the night.

As Lou walked back to his cottage, he paused and listened to a lone wolf howling far off in the distance. *That's interesting,* he thought. *We haven't had a wolf in this valley for decades. If they're back, the coyotes won't stick around. Angelo would like that.*

On Christmas morning, Lou woke up to the shrill ringing sound of his cell phone.

"Happy Christmas, Lou," Kate's voice was cheery and bright. "The Abenaki necklace and beaded bracelet are stunning! Thank you! Have you opened *your* present yet?"

"Hi," he answered back. "Great! Ah, no, I haven't," Lou managed to reply, still half asleep, then yawned. "We were going to open our presents after breakfast," he said.

"No worries. I just wanted to call you before I went off to my cousin's house. We'll be pub-crawling today. That's what the Irish do. It sounds like I woke you," she said. "We'll talk later. Hugs! I *love* you!" With little problem, he fell back to sleep.

Later that morning, Lou opened the gift that had come from Kate. Inside the beautifully wrapped box were two presents. One was a traditional hand-knit O'Grady Clan scarf with a note pinned to it: "Here's a nice scarf to keep you warm until I see you again." The other present was a bottle of Jameson 30-year-Old Special Reserve Irish Whiskey. It, too, had a note attached to it: "In case you need something beyond a scarf to warm the cockles of your heart, this is sure to do the trick! Happy Christmas!"

Jake googled the Jameson bottle on his cell phone. When he saw the price, he thought to himself: *"Whoa, Lou, you better not spill any of that stuff . . . a shot glass of it costs more than this whole damn bottle of Canadian Club we're drinking!"*

Lou's gifts to Angelo and Jake doubled the number of DVDs already in the lodge's library. Jake hustled outside to start up the generator so they could watch "The Godfather," and then "Top Gun," while Angelo positioned chairs in front of the flat screen television.

Following the holidays, Lou completed interior work in the new cottage in just under three weeks. As soon as the building was finished, he dove right into preparations for the upcoming season. Fly rods and reels were brought up to the lodge and carefully inspected for needed repairs. Generally, the fly reels only required a little oil and new line; a few of the rods always needed a new tip and guides. Alessandra inspected the nets and skillfully made needed repairs. The outboard motors were all winterized before being put away, but when the weather warmed up, Lou would place each one in a barrel filled with water, fire them up, and make any needed adjustments to the choke. The gas lines which sat out in the sun all season, usually needed to be replaced every few years. The wooden oars always managed to get banged up and needed to be sanded down, oiled, and painted on the blade tips.

Within a week, Lou knew exactly what equipment he needed to replenish, what could be flown in, and what he would need to go into town to pick up.

By early March, the sportsmen who hadn't booked before leaving the previous year were beginning to write and call Lou to inquire about accommodations close to the time of "ice out." To the avid spring fisherman "ice out" was the best time of year to be on the water, wetting a line with light tackle. As soon as the ice left the surface of the lake, the colder water on the surface began sinking to the bottom, causing the lake water "to turn." Until the water stratified into separate temperate zones, the trophy size trout and salmon usually found in the depths were close to the surface.

Within a matter of weeks, the only vacancies Lou had remaining were basically in early August. *This coming season, even the fall period, has booked up fast,* he thought.

By the second week in April, Lou had all the guest cottages open, and Alessandra had readied them for the sportsmen who would be arriving by the end of the month.

The smelt had started to "run" in the brook, the ice was now "honeycombed" and beginning to retreat from the shoreline; all good indications that "ice out" wasn't far away.

For the approaching season, Angelo developed a new menu and presented it to Lou. "Around July, I'll change the menu again so that any sportsmen returning later in the season will have a different culinary experience," he said.

Alessandra stuck her head around the corner. "Lou, don't you believe a word of that. He changes the menu because he gets tired of cooking the same thing over and over again, week after week, like a cafeteria cook."

By the beginning of the third week in April, all the boats were in the water; the snow had melted everywhere but in the higher elevations. Full "ice-out" was about a week away and Angelo had already tested his new recipes on Lou and Jake with great success.

The following Saturday, five float planes flew into Havre de Poisson. It was always a little hectic on opening day of the season. But by dinner time, everyone was settled in and looking forward to their first evening meal.

Only one no-show was noted, a first-time guest named Dunn. No-shows were unusual since payment in full was required when people booked. Dunn's reservation had been made only a couple of weeks before as a single, also unusual. Lou had assigned Dunn to the one cottage still available, the one generally last on anyone's request list because it was furthest away from the lodge and the dock.

The following Tuesday, Lou received a text from New Brunswick Air saying they would be flying up a passenger named Dunn on the following afternoon and asking if he would need any supplies.

"This early in the season, we're pretty well set," Lou texted back, *"but thanks for the offer."*

By Wednesday noon, Lou's guests had already had three long days of fishing and most everyone had come back in early. As Lou was going about the task of refilling the gas tanks in the boats, the sound of a plane coming up the valley broke the silence. Lou shuffled a couple of boats around to make room so the plane could tie up at the end of the dock.

The lake was unusually calm, and the windsock was hanging limp, which meant the float plane would be able to make a direct landing. Lou waited at the end of the dock to secure the plane and welcome his guest to Havre de Poisson.

The first unusual thing he noticed were that the shades on the plane's windows were half drawn; it was difficult to see inside. Then, it was usual for passengers to disembark first, followed by the pilot who would unload their luggage. But that's not how it happened. The amount of luggage handed out to Lou caused him to wonder if someone else might be accompanying Dunn. After all, he didn't get a lot of single reservations.

Hmm, this pilot must be new if he's passing the luggage out to me first, Lou thought.

As he picked up several suitcases, he remembered another single guest who had come up late one year. *Maybe he's another 'hoity toity' single guest,* Lou thought. Then, as the passenger began to exit the plane, Lou heard a familiar voice.

"You're lucky you have both hands full, Mr. Gault, otherwise, I'd expect you to be practicing lesson number one!"

Lou dropped the luggage and spun around to see a smiling Kate at the doorway.

"You're here!" he said wrapping her in his arms as they kissed. Even though they'd talked every other day on the phone, Kate had never let on that she would be coming over.

"Come on, let's pick up a few of these suitcases," she said tousling his hair. "You can show me where I'll be staying." When they walked past the cottage Lou had been living in, the smile left Kate's face.

"Oh, I thought there would be room in *your* cottage, that I'd be staying with you."

"You are," he said. "I'm just not in that one anymore. I've turned that one into a cottage I rent to larger groups. Keep walking, I'll show you where I'm bunking now. By the way, what's in *this* bag, it weighs a ton."

"Oh, you must have grabbed the one with the two cast iron skillets in it. They belonged to my mother's mother."

"Well, Angelo will appreciate them, I'm sure, but I hardly think he needs any more pots and pans, Kate. What's in this other one? It feels heavier than just clothes."

"Yeah, take care with *that* one, it's got heirloom crystal in it." As they approached the cottage Lou had recently built, Kate was impressed.

"Oh Lou! You've angled it just right to capture the best view and catch the breeze coming off the lake." She nodded toward the magnificent screened porch stretching across the entire front and halfway down one side.

When she stepped inside the cottage, Kate was completely stunned. The interior was.identical to her own cottage in Abbyfeale, right down to the exact same shade of light green paint on the walls that Kate had in her kitchen back in Ireland.

"I designed the inside after a sketch that someone drew on the back of a napkin for me once," Lou said before she could say anything else.

"Oh, it's simply beautiful! And the view . . . the *view* is just *grand,* Lou! It's so much larger than your old cottage and it has closets, too! And the plumbing is all *inside!"*

"Like I said, I just went by a sketch on a napkin that someone drew for me." He put the suitcases down on the kitchen floor and took her into his arms for a longer kiss. "Hey, dinner will be starting soon," he said when they came up for air. "Maybe start unpacking your stuff, and I'll go fetch the rest of your luggage."

"Which room am I in?"

"Which room do you think?"

As he went out the door, he looked back at her. "With all the stuff you've brought, Kate, I sure hope you're planning to stay longer than just to the end of this week."

Once Lou brought the rest of Kate's luggage to the cottage, they headed over to the lodge. As soon as they entered, one guest grabbed Lou's attention and wanted to talk. The next time Lou saw Kate, she was wearing an apron and helping Alessandra serve dinner to the guests. When the meal was over, Kate pitched in and helped Alessandra clear tables and put the kitchen back in shape for the following morning.

"Kate, I totally forgot that I promised a guest who brought his son here that they could help us net some smelt tonight to replenish the bait cage. I usually have a couple of Abenaki guides do this, but they left early for a council meeting over at the village tonight. So, I'll meet you back at the cottage in about an hour."

Later that evening, when Lou and Kate were back at the cottage, Lou opened a bottle of wine and poured two glasses.

"So, how long before you have to head home, Kate?"

"Well, looking around, it certainly feels like I *am* home!" Her eyes had a twinkle he hadn't seen before.

"Kate, come on, you live and work in Ireland. Tell me, when do you need to return?"

"Go take a look inside that round box over there and tell me what you see."

"Okay, but first a toast to you and me."

"To us!"

They touched glasses and sipped a delicious red. Then, Lou set down his wine glass and went over to the chair where the box was.

"Ha, it's a Smokey the Bear hat. So, when did the Irish Defense Forces start wearing campaign hats?"

"They haven't. I've transferred to a unit that wears them." Her smile was broader now.

"Really? I thought it was just the Mounties and the Boy Scouts who wore these fool things."

"Well, you're right about that. You are now looking at 'Lieutenant Kathryn O'Grady, RCMP.' There's no travel involved; it's mostly all virtual. I'm basically a consultant on retainer. They debated whether they even needed to give me a standard issue side arm. And the best part is they agreed to carry over all my years of service with the Irish Defense Forces and count them toward my retirement and my vacation entitlements." Her words came flying out.

"Whoa, whoa, when did all *this* happen?"

"Well, do you recall during Andre's retirement party how I kept leaving you at the table?"

"Quite vividly, in fact."

"Well, Andre's superiors approached me that very night and asked if I would be interested in changing my honorary status to an active one. I told them I was extremely interested, but there was a lot that needed to be negotiated. All night long they kept suggesting ways to make it happen. I'd go back to the table, have a dance with you, think about their offer, and go back to them with an idea. I never said anything to you because the whole thing kept running into snags, and we'd end up going back to the drawing board. We only just finalized everything two weeks ago," she smiled. "Besides, I wanted to surprise you."

"Well, I'm absolutely surprised that you've become a Mountie! But I knew you were coming." She stared at him in silence.

"Oh, did you now? And *how* was it that you *knew* that I was coming?"

"You told me that you were coming."

"I did no such thing!"

"Oh, no?" he smiled back at her. "Well, I noticed that Dunn's reservation was sent from your personal email account and when I went to run the credit card, the name that came up wasn't 'Dunn' . . . it was 'Kathryn O'Grady.'"

"Hmmm, a little obvious, huh?"

"Maybe just a little," he smiled, taking her into his arms. "I didn't run your card, though, and accounting said they'd waive all charges . . . if you said 'yes' to being my wife."

Her kiss left nothing more to be said.

Epilogue

The British Crown Prosecution Services group spent months putting together the case against the principals of Imperial Trading. When Tinker realized that the Imperial Trading partners planned to sacrifice him to save themselves, he quickly turned Crown's Witness and sang like a canary.

Andre Girard and his team were called upon from time to time to work with the Canadian Crown attorneys, but for the most part, the attorneys had what they needed to bring their cases to court. Eventually, both the Canadian and British governments agreed on which crimes would be brought against the three members of Imperial Trading. Once the charges became public knowledge, the three once-highly respected members of Britain's social elite, and their wives, were shunned by the very society in which they had grown up.

Clark Hastings was suspended from the House of Lords. His permanent expulsion was only a matter of process. Once convicted, his family was stripped of the hereditary title of nobility that they had held for over three centuries as a result of his disloyalty to the Crown.

Richard More was temporarily disbarred and prohibited from practicing law anywhere in the Commonwealth. Permanent disbarment occurred once he was convicted.

Herbert Maxwell disgraced himself within the banking community and was suspended without pay from his position as Executive Vice President at the prestigious Royalty Bank and

Trust Company. Once convicted, he was terminated.

NOTE: All three men ultimately received life sentences without the possibility of parole for their nefarious actions and breach of trust. The majority of their assets were seized and moved into a court-appointed trust to handle the numerous damage claims brought against them.

Former Chief Inspector Rene Allard asked for clemency, but none was granted. Allard received the full extent of punishment allowed by British law and spent the remainder of his days in a British prison. He was dishonorably discharged from France's General Directorate and forfeited his government pension

Sean Tinker did receive clemency for turning Crown star witness and was incarcerated in a facility commonly referred to as a "country club." However, he was sentenced to the maximum number of years allowed. His assets were also placed in a court-appointed trust to satisfy any claims brought against him. Members of Tinker's family, who worked on the dock, received various probationary sentences and were prohibited from earning a living on any commercial dock for the rest of their days.

Emile Baker was granted clemency by the courts as a result of his willingness to cooperate with Canadian authorities. Baker was sentenced to five years' probation and heavily fined. Never again did his business gain the professional dominance it once held.

Dobbs, Lajoie, Evers, and **Teal** all received maximum sentences. Their assets were frozen, and court-appointed trusts were set up to handle the numerous damage claims brought against them. Additionally, Evers, Lajoie, and Teal forfeited their government pensions.

Bob Newton disgraced himself and tarnished the image of the Royal Canadian Mounted Police. His hopes of receiving leniency fell upon deaf ears. He received the maximum jail time for kidnapping an officer of the law, which far exceeded any sentence he would have received for merely being an accomplice in Dobbs' black-market shenanigans.

Minor players at Grand Manan all received lengthy probation sentences and were given a lifetime ban from working at any commercial docks.

It is believed, however, that at some point, the "fences" used in Dobbs' scheme would one day trip up, at which point their probations would be revoked.

The BMW executive and the official at Port of Hamburg were both convicted of conspiring to commit grand larceny. They too received the maximum prison terms allowed by law, terminated from their positions, and forfeited their pensions.

Fred O'Neil's widow was awarded a one-time special compensation for the loss of her husband. His retirement benefits were calculated and awarded to her as if he had been fully-vested and retired at the rank of a corporal.

Mathew Dorsey's parents were awarded a significant sum as compensation for the loss of their son. They established a scholarship in his name for promising high school athletes of limited means.

Andre Girard was given permission to officially retire once the Canadian court cases concluded, Charles Teal's belief that Andre would walk away with a huge cash windfall as a result of unused vacation and sick time proved to be prophetic.

Lieutenant Kathryn O'Grady was formally recognized by INTERPOL with a Medal of Commendation for her contributions before releasing her back to The Irish Defense Force.

Lou's cousin, Jake, was released from active status with the RCMP and returned to his role flying the mail plane.

Lou Gault was released from active status with the RCMP and awaits payment from Ottawa for the use of his lodge and reimbursement for damages sustained.

Keep reading for a preview of
Book 2 in the Lou Gault Thriller Series

War
Chief

by Dave McKeon

Chapter 1

The hunter had been watching the glen since midmorning. The day's sweltering heat didn't bother him as much as the flies that were landing on his bare shoulders and back did.

Should have worn a shirt under my overalls, he chastised himself. Usually, he stayed well to the west but had recently overhunted that area of the forest. It was also rare that he took a stand this close to a road, even a dirt road like this one, but the game trails that crisscrossed just above the bridge where he was now, looked far too promising to pass up.Shortly after he had arrived, a doe had walked up the trail, but she spooked when the wooden planks on the bridge below suddenly rumbled under the weight of a passing car. He had brought his rifle up before she bounded off, but only for practice; it wasn't camp meat that he was after today.

Slowly, he shifted his position when he saw the unmistakable profile of a large buck as it approached the edge of the glen.

It was the buck's thirst and the smell of cool water just beyond their position that was drawing him to the spring.

The animal was skittish and had paused before entering the clearing. The only reason the large buck had survived this long was that he was naturally cautious. If he sensed danger, every muscle in his body was ready to take flight. The hide covering his chest and upper front shoulders seemed to shimmer as if in nervous reflex; his ears were constantly moving in all directions, He seemed to dismiss the noise a few kids were making down by the bridge as no threat.

Now, the buck raised his head into the air. The hunter could see the animal's nostrils flare open, then shut, as it searched for the slightest scent of danger.

Once it was satisfied that it was safe to enter the glen, the beautiful animal moved forward, his neck stretching forward, almost horizontal with his back. The hunter raised his rifle, carefully aimed, and fired.

The young game warden had stopped to talk with two youngsters who were fishing off the bridge.

"How's the fishing?"

"Not so good."

"What are you using?"

"Crawlers."

"Best to keep them out of the sun; they'll stay lively longer."

The warden watched the boys fishing for a few minutes, "Do you see that dark pool further down?"

"Yeah."

"Well, leave the bail open the next time you cast; let the current take your bait down into that pool."

"Okay," one said. No sooner had the bait entered the pool than there was a swirl on the water and the line began to race off the young boy's reel.

"Whoa!"

"Set the hook."

The boy pulled back on the rod and set the hook as a nice-sized brook trout surfaced, attempting to throw the barb now caught in its mouth.

"Wow! Thanks, mister!"

"You won't find any trout close to the bridge, it's too shallow. They're waiting behind those rocks just beyond the entrance to that pool. Some wait under the bank that overhangs on the right. I'd put money down there'll be a few more fish in that pool, but remember, you have a daily limit. So, don't let me catch you with more than two trout apiece."

"How'd you know they were there?"

"I used to fish here when I was your age."

Off in the distance, a shot rang out, surprising the warden. "Gotta go boys. Did you hear that shot? Hunting season is still months away, and that was no squirrel gun." He looked back at the boys. "Remember what I told you now, keep that can of worms out of the sun."

"Yes sir!"

Just as the hunter was approaching his kill, he saw movement to his left. A wave of panic washed over him when he spied the bright yellow shoulder patch on the warden's uniform approaching the edge of the glen, and he quickly hid behind a tree.

After twenty minutes, when no one showed to claim the deer, the warden figured he had been seen and the shooter was long gone. As he reached the animal, he looked down in disbelief at the enormous hole in the deer's chest.

"What the hell was he using, a cannon?"

Inching out from the tree, the hunter once again raised his rifle and squeezed the trigger.

The shot entered the warden's upper back and took out most of his chest.

After reloading, the hunter came forward, knelt next to the deer and took out a small saw; removing the antlers, he placed them in a plastic bag, stood up, brushed off his knees, and walked away.

The game warden's name was Lloyd Bancroft. He had been a game warden for just under a year; the following Tuesday he would have celebrated his twenty-fourth birthday.

Chapter 2

The sun was setting as Lou Gault stepped out onto the screened porch running across the front of his cottage. Brilliant amber-colored clouds set against a sky rapidly changing from blue to violet gave the horizon a picture-perfect contrast. Out of habit, his eyes scanned the horizon, searching for anything that didn't seem to belong. As far as the eye could see, the land, wide lake, forest, streams, all of it belonged to him.

There was enviable independence about Gault, and it was obvious to even the most casual observer that he had found his niche in life and was good at it. The calm, self-confident demeanor he projected masked the warrior's spirit that lay hidden deep within him. His tall, wiry physique belayed the tremendous strength of his limbs. Even though he was no longer a member of Canada's elite Joint Task Force Two commando unit, he still cropped his hair close on the sides. He lived a quiet, simple life now, far away from the carnage that he saw during the Afghan war.

He didn't know, however, that his resolve to live a simple life was about to be tested once again.

Enjoyed this excerpt from

Book 2 of the Lou Gault Triller Series?

War Chief

Now available on Amazon.com

BOOKS BY DAVE MCKEON

Relentless Pursuit

War Chief

Coming Soon:

Howl of the Banshee

Sabotage

Acknowledgements

Seldom have I been as grateful to take hold of an opportunity as I was during early 2020 when we were all sequestering due to Covid-19. It was March, when in-between fine-tuning my culinary skills, I decided to depart from writing short stories and enter the rhelm of the novelist.

I am beyond thankful for the early encouragement that I received from my wife. She devoured every word of my initial chapters, before her advancing Alzheimer's robbed me of her insights and helpful critiques.

Special kudos to my early readers, especially: Barry Covin, Barbara Cheney, Tom Mullin, and Carl Johnson.

I can't adequately express my appreciation to Paula Howard, my editor and publisher, for all the work she has done to help me bring this book to the public. Paula, it's been an enjoyable journey.

About the Author

Dave McKeon is an award-winning author of short stories and creator of the Lou Gault Thriller series.

His stories reflect a diverse background of life experiences, and **an** unquenchable love affair with the outdoors.

A native New Englander, he has hunted, fished, hiked, camped, skied, and traveled in the eastern United States and throughout New Brunswick, and Quebec his entire life.

A Vietnam-era veteran, Dave has formerly held both a Top-Secret Clearance and the Department of Energy's "Q" Clearance. His stories are influenced by experiences working with the NSA, the EPA and the Department of the Navy.

To learn more about Dave McKeon,
visit www.avillagewriter.com

Made in the USA
Middletown, DE
08 January 2024